Transcendence

The Spirit Quest Series
Book 1

A. L. Waddington

Cover Design by Mad Hat Designs
Edited by Charlene Burgett

This is a work of fiction. Names, characters, places, brands, media, and incidents are either the product of the author's imagination or are used fictitiously. Any resemblance to similarly named places or to persons living or deceased is unintentional.

PAPERBACK ISBN 978-1-948143-14-1
ISBN EBOOK 978-1-948143-15-8

Library of Congress Control Number: 2019915676

For my gorgeous, adventure-loving granddaughter,
Scarlett Maesynn

Acknowledgments

I would like to thank Shari Ryan at *Mad Hat Designs* for her amazing talent with cover designs. Plus, I would also like to give a warm, heartfelt thanks to Charlene Burgett for her dedication to editing my words and understanding my ramblings. She is a true hero.

I would like to thank my daughters, Alyssa, and Mia, for their patience, for picking up the slack, and for their support. They were amazing. Most importantly, I want to thank the most incredible man in the world, my husband, Eric. You have shown me that true love does exist, it is unselfish, kind, and unconditional. I am so blessed to have found you and am forever grateful to share my life with you.

1

WEDNESDAY, JULY 17, 2019

THE PLANE BEGAN TO DESCEND slowly in the Chicago night sky. I hated flying. Not so much the act of flying itself but crashing. I am terrified of crashing. Granted, crashing into Lake Michigan isn't the same as crashing into the Andes, but still. Being horribly mangled and crushed doesn't ring good times for me.

Instead, I tried to think of other things to take my mind from where I was. I tried to recall my work schedule after our short break, but my mind was blank.

Pet peeves, I closed my eyes and thought. What are my pet peeves? People who put the toilet paper roll-on, so it rolls out from the bottom instead of over the top. People who litter. People who don't respect others. Chaos. Double standards. Cold showers — I truly hate cold showers, liars, and thieves — probably more than anything in this entire world.

Turbulence jolted the plane just enough to make me jump and grab my boyfriend, Landon Harrison's hand. He was sitting beside me with his headphones in watching *The Avengers* movie on his iPhone. He smiled over at me and squeezed my hand.

"You all right, babe?" he asked with a smile.

"Yeah," I grimaced.

Landon's eyes shifted back to his little screen. It amazed me how calm and collected he was. I was ready to come unglued, and he was more interested in the Hulk pounding Loki. I shook my head and tried to focus on the words written on the page before me. I had brought along a copy of *Doctor Sleep* by Stephen King. I had fallen in love with *The Shining* years ago and was dying to read the sequel but hadn't quite managed to even put a dent in it yet. My fear of crashing was too overwhelming.

I leaned my head against the window and watched the Chicago skyline draw closer around us. The skyscrapers towered in the night sky twinkling like fireflies across the dark blue backdrop. It looked so beautiful and serene from this distance. The city from this height resembled nothing of the sporadic outbreaks of violence advertised on the evening news.

As instructed by the captain, Landon turned off all electronic devices in preparation for landing. He tucked his phone into the side pocket of his backpack and put his seat up straight.

"For such a short flight, it feels like it takes forever," Landon complained.

"Remind me it's better than driving," I glanced over at him.

"Much better than driving." He chuckled. "Hell, we'd barely be out of New York in the time it took us to fly here."

"I know. I know." I muttered under my breath. "Still doesn't make me like it." I said with sarcasm.

"I know, my dear." Landon leaned over with a coy smile and kissed me quickly on the cheek. "But your dad appreciates you making the sacrifice for his wedding."

"Are you alright?" I felt my younger sister, Jocelyn's hand on my shoulder. She and her husband, Jackson, were seated right behind us.

"Yes, I am fine." I turned around and smiled reassuringly at her.

TRANSCENDENCE

My sister was aware of how much I hated to fly. It had taken her and Landon several days to convince me that it would be easier, faster, and cheaper than driving. Personally, I thought a road trip with the four of us would be fun, but considering we were on a time crunch, we wouldn't have been able to stop-over in New York for a couple days or any of the other tourist attractions along our way across the Midwest.

Our parents had gotten divorced two years ago, the summer after our younger brother, Ethan, had graduated high school. Our mother, Amy, had taken a position as the head of pediatrics at some hospital in Seattle, and neither Jocelyn nor I had spoken with her much since she'd transferred. She was a good mother, a little overbearing perhaps, extremely career-driven, and maybe even a bit too judgmental, but we all knew she loved us and would be there if we needed anything.

Our father, Shane, was a lot more laid back than our mother. He was the type of parent that even if he didn't always agree with the decisions his children made, he accepted them without judgment and always supported us, had our backs, and loved each of us unconditionally. So, six months ago, when we had all journeyed home for the holidays, and our dad announced that he had proposed to Patsy, a child psychologist he had been dating for the last year, the three of us couldn't have been happier for him. Patsy was so different from our mom, which I believe was her main appeal to my dad. She was like a duck, things just washed over her, and she handled anything stressful with grace, style, and, most importantly, humor.

Our mom was extremely feminine, whereas Patsy, not so much. Mom never left the house without her hair and makeup fixed to perfection or looking anything short of ladylike. Patsy was a little younger than our mother, but not much. She looked professional in her work attire, but outside of the office, she was a jeans and T-shirt kind of gal. She rarely wore makeup, and her hair spent more time pulled up in a low ponytail than down. I'm not even sure if she owned a curling iron. Patsy had more of a natural beauty about her that didn't require a great deal of effort, and her radiant, fun-loving personality gave her a personal glow. I had to admit I liked her from the start.

The wedding was three days away, and my sister and I were bridesmaids. Ethan was set to be the best man, and Patsy's son, Donnie, who was twenty, was also standing up with them. We had sent Patsy our sizes and seen photos of the dresses we were supposed to be wearing but had not even tried them on yet. Hopefully, they will fit, and we wouldn't spend tomorrow doing alterations. It was to be an outside wedding by a lake at the country club my father golfed at frequently. I was hoping the weather would hold out, but given the inconsistency of Midwest summer showers, I wasn't sure what to expect.

I gripped Landon's hand as the wheels finally touched the ground. He rolled his eyes playfully at me but patted my hand, nonetheless. I let out a deep sigh as we taxied down the runway towards the gate.

I could hear Jocelyn and Jackson discussing what they wanted to eat, and I remembered we hadn't eaten since brunch at Jackson's parents' house before we left and realized I was famished as well. His parents, Emily, and Robert were flying on Friday afternoon for the wedding. Robert was an attorney and had to be in court early on Friday morning. So, they were unable to fly with the rest of us.

Landon grabbed our carry-on bags from overhead and waited impatiently for people to start filing out of the plane. He rattled his fingers on the back of his seat in frustration. He had slight ADHD and was always on the move. He hated idle time and couldn't relax if his life depended on it. His mother had said she'd wanted to duct tape his butt to a chair as a child. He wasn't much different as an adult.

I placed my hand over his, making him stop. He looked over his shoulder at me and gave me a coy smile.

"Sorry."

"Patience," I whispered.

"My strongest suit." He slightly shook his head.

"I wish." I replied, elbowing him in the back.

Slowly we edged our way off the plane. The four of us walked side by side down the long hallway through the terminal. We'd each only brought carry-on bags in hopes of getting out of O'Hare airport in record time. Our dad was supposed to meet us outside, and Jocelyn had told me she had texted him when we landed. He had responded back with a simple 'okay,' but instead of finding him on the curb as planned, we were all surprised to see him and Patsy waiting for us as we left the secured area of the terminal.

"There's my girls," Our dad exclaimed happily as soon as he saw us.

"Daddy!" Jocelyn was the first to reach him and threw her arms around him. She was Daddy's Girl. "What are you doing here?"

"I missed my girls." He smiled and kissed her on the cheek before releasing her and hugging me.

"How was your flight?" he asked.

"Good." I kissed his scruffy cheek.

"Hello, Landon." My dad shook my boyfriend's hand before shaking my sister's husband's hand. "Jackson, it's good to see you both. Are you guys taking care of my girls?"

"Always," Landon replied with a cocky grin. He and my dad got along exceptionally well, of which I was genuinely grateful. Plus, he also got along famously with Jackson. However, that one had taken some time considering he had eloped with my sister during their senior year of high school. My dad had punched Jackson for that one, and I admit I was not too thrilled with them either, but after I knew the truth of why they did it, I was truly happy for them.

No, she wasn't pregnant. Everyone initially thought so and speculated for a long time about it, but she wasn't. That would have been easier for me to accept than the real reason. Not to mention, I never would have believed them in a million years if I had not inherited the same ability and experienced it firsthand. As insane as it sounds, my sister and I had inherited an ability called *Essence Voyager Era*, or *EVE*, from our uncles. *EVE* was the genetic gift of being able to live parallel lives on two separate planes of existence. Jackson and his entire family had also inherited the same gift, and my sister was fortunate enough to have him with her on both planes. I, unfortunately, was not so lucky.

This gift or curse or whatever it is, is quite unusual, to say the least. How many people have it? Who knows? My Uncle Nicholas has spent his entire adult life doing research on it and has barely touched the tip of the iceberg as he put it.

But what we do know is that the barrier in the consciousness between the two worlds remains intact until late adolescence or early twenties. When it starts to disintegrate, the individual with the gift begins to have visions or experience episodes from their other life. To say that this can be slightly unsettling is a mild understatement.

Personally, I thought I was going insane. And unfortunately, due to familial structures today, most individuals who reach this phase of enlightenment are diagnosed with schizophrenia if they do not have a close family member with the gift to help them through this difficult transition.

Plus, with divorce being so prevalent these days and families spread out across the country if not the globe, misdiagnosis is often made. When that occurs, and the person is placed on antipsychotic medications, it halts the barrier from full depletion, and that individual gets "stuck" in that phase. Lucky for me, I had my sister, our uncle, Jackson, and his family.

My uncle Nicholas had volumes of notes of research he has conducted throughout his life as a professor of history. He speculated that *EVE* has always existed but is mostly mistaken as prophecy or in the last half-century or so, schizophrenia. It seems that most cultures across time have had some form of prophets, from oracles to medicine men to most notably Michel de Nostradamus back in the sixteenth century and his collection of quatrains. More recent "prophets" have even capitalized on their abilities and made names and money for themselves.

True or not, my uncle's hypotheses were uncanny in their resemblance to what I experienced nightly when my soul drifted off from the twenty-first century to my other self, who wakes to a new day in the mid-nineteenth century.

My sister was set to marry Jackson in the latter half of the nineteenth century when he and his family learned that she too had the gift. That sent them all on the journey from Boston to Chicago to aid her in the transition, and during the process, she fell head over heels in love with him on this plane as well, and the two of them eloped only a couple months after meeting.

That alone tore our family apart, and our mother still has not forgiven her. However, true to their word, the couple had remained together and strong as ever for the last three-and-a-half years. My sister will graduate next May with a BS in psychology from Boston University, just like her husband and the rest of his family.

The fall semester after I learned about *EVE*, Landon and I transferred from Northwestern University to Harvard, citing that it was better for us when applying for their medical school. But the truth of it was I wanted to be closer to my sister, Jackson, and his family.

Plus, our Uncle Nicholas had successfully procured a position at Boston University, where Jocelyn was going to school. It made dealing with this most bizarre and strange gift easier being surrounded by family and loved ones who understood its blessings and its curses.

"Hello, Patsy, how are you?" Jocelyn's greeting broke my train of thought.

"Good." Patsy reached out and gave us both a brief hug. "I'm glad you're all here. Now your father can stop worrying." She laughed easily.

"Is Ethan here?" I inquired as we started towards the airport exit.

"Yes. He arrived last week. I think he's having a little too much fun at Notre Dame." Dad put his arm around me and took my carryon.

"He's supposed to enjoy himself the summer off from school. He's earned it. Besides, it's a great school for him." I knew how proud my dad was when Ethan got into school there and became part of their legendary football team after high school. He'd driven down for every home game throughout Ethan's undergraduate studies.

"Yes, it is," he agreed.

"What about Donnie?" I asked him while Jocelyn and Patsy made small talk about the wedding.

"He's out with his friends. He should be home later. He's not returning to the University of Kansas until the week before the start of the semester. We've turned the guest bedroom into his room," Dad replied.

"That's good."

Even though none of us technically lived at home any longer, I was glad none of our childhood bedrooms that still contained our stuff were offered to him.

TRANSCENDENCE

We rolled the windows down on our ride home and the warm evening breeze floated in around us. The Midwest humidity was stifling. Patsy talked a mile a minute about the rehearsal dinner, the wedding, the reception, the gowns, tuxes — the woman was on a roll of excitement. I rested my head on Landon's shoulder in the crowded back seat and let the warm night wind blow through my hair. I was exhausted, and it felt like soft kisses from my childhood across my cheeks. I missed the smells of fresh-cut grass and burning wood from a bonfire as we passed by.

My dad pulled into the long drive of our large 19th century pre-Civil War estate. The house was built in a year before the America Civil War by, as strange as it sounds, the oldest of my younger brothers, Patrick in my 19th century life. The Antebellum architecture with wide columns and wrap-around porch was majestic. It stood like a beacon behind the mature trees in the darkened sky. I let out a deep breath I had not realized I was holding.

I was home.

2

THURSDAY, JULY 21, 1859

THE OLD WOODEN PLANKS creaked as I stepped out onto the front porch. The late afternoon sun was beginning its downward descent towards the tree line off in the distance. Soft pink, purple, and gold hues glowed in the backdrop. I loved this time of day. The air was thick with humidity and the smell of my grandmother's lilac bushes. A layer of sweat clung thinly to my skin. I knew it wouldn't be long before the clouds broke, and what a relief it would be when the rain finally fell.

My grandmother, Marissa, was sitting on the swing absentmindedly swaying gently back and forth with her feet, humming a soft hymn, and working on the hem of the new dress she was sewing for me. Her long brown hair streaked with white hair was pulled up in a low bun at the nape of her neck like it was every day for as long as I could remember. Her soft, freckled hands worked the thread expertly.

For her, sewing was as simple as breathing and came just as naturally. The lines on her face were etched from years of laughter, a few tears, and the worry that came with watching your family and loved ones grow and mature.

TRANSCENDENCE

My grandmother was a gentle soul, and the only person I have ever known who was genuinely kind and without a mean bone in her entire body. She loved her family dearly and had lost the love of her life, my grandfather Nathan, almost a decade ago.

The pain of his passing wore heavy on her, and his absence in her life was felt daily. He was the cornerstone of her world and the foundation on which her life was built. He took care of everything for her, and when he passed, it had taken some careful guidance from me to help her take over the running of the household and oversee the bigger expenses and care of the household staff. I guided her through the finances and explained how my grandfather had managed things, but essentially, I took over the management of the estate.

Our estate, Terrace Falls, was an elaborate one that spread over a three hundred and sixty acres on the outlying regions of east Braintree off the Monatiquot River near the Weymouth Fore River only a short distance south from the city of Boston. It was simply my little piece of heaven on earth, and I couldn't imagine ever parting with it.

Recently, it had become more challenging with the country being torn in two over the issues in Washington regarding federal rights, states' rights, expansion, and slavery. Being in Massachusetts, we didn't have slaves on our farm. It was illegal in our state, but there was a brewing controversy across the country that was spreading like wildfire.

The home my grandfather built our estate on during the turn of the 19th century was a two-story reddish-orange brick home with black shutters and a half dozen steps leading up to the front porch, the roof of which provided the foundation for the identical second-floor balcony.

The high-style residential windows had characteristically thin muntins with eighteen-inch windowpanes. The interior woodwork was designed in cherry with interior shutters, paneled apron, wall reveals, and molding surround. The coffered ceiling in the dining room was accented by the exposed wooden beams and hardwood flooring throughout the remainder of the home, especially in the vaulted ceiling in the master bedroom. The mature trees surrounding the house provided an abundance of shade on hot summer days.

Terrace Falls was too small to be considered by most a plantation. Plantations were generally associated with the south and slavery. We had neither. We did have workers that were paid and housed on our land. The difference being they were hired and paid for the work they did for us, and they were free to leave, be fired, or live off the property.

However, none of them did. We provided a small row of cabins that families resided in, and they seemed happy with their quarters and were free to come and go as they pleased. We were fortunate that most of them had been with us for years, some for generations, and were very loyal to my grandparents and our family.

Our foreman, Casper, was indispensable. He had been handling the daily grind for my family for the last twenty-five years, and I had high hopes that his son, Duncan, would take over once he retired. Casper was gradually introducing Duncan to the trade. He was only nineteen, but a very calm and level-headed boy who I had known since the day he was born. His mother passed away when he was five, and his aunt had taken over the greater part of his upbringing.

Casper was a robust black man, slow to anger, quick to laugh, with an amazing mind for numbers. He had a reputation amongst the workers as a stern man, but one who was also fair and impartial. He maintained certain expectations of our workers and was quick to reprimand those who fell short. Every evening, six days a week, he would meet me in my grandfather's old office and go over the daily reports. We would discuss what needed to be changed, improved, dismissed, or reconfigured. I hated the thought of him ever retiring, but for the last month, he had been allowing Duncan to join our discussions to see how things worked to make our farm profitable.

As much as I had had enough of changes in my life in the last several years, things were always going to change. Such was life, and there was no stopping it.

After learning about the gift of *EVE* from my sister, Jocelyn, her husband, Jackson, his family, and our Uncle Nicholas, I spent almost half a year in a haze before I finally worked up the nerve to speak with my grandmother about it. My uncle repeatedly assured me that she had the gift as well, but I had seen no evidence to suggest it and was, therefore, extremely reluctant to approach her with it.

Once I had, I felt like the weight of the world had been lifted off my thin shoulders. She told me her *other* life was in the early 20th century, but she was born at the tail end of this one. It was all so confusing to me still, and when I attempted to riddle it out in my brain, I was only successful in giving myself a headache.

Plus, I knew there was something my grandmother was keeping from me. She was a secretive lady in some ways, and while she loved the tales, I would tell her of the world in the 21st century she told me very little of her *other* life despite my constant reassurances that I was well versed in history and knew what significant events were going on during that period.

She would discuss events, places, and news with me. I knew she lived in New York City and traveled extensively, but she would not elaborate further than that. She loved to be evasive on the subject, and I couldn't quite figure out if there was something I shouldn't know or if she was simply toying with me. Knowing her as well as I did either was possible.

Of course, that never deterred her from inquiring about my experiences in the 21st century. She absolutely loved listening to me rattle on about my life *there* and my journey through college and now medical school. She was intrigued by the advancements in technology in the seventy-some odd years between our lives and how much society had declined alongside it. She remarked more than once a week how she was happy that she was not around to witness such hate.

A bonus of *EVE* was also the business classes I had taken during my undergraduate studies had greatly enhanced our lives now, and the small business we ran with the estate had become substantial over the last few years. Casper often remarked that I had a unique talent for business, and although he never said it, I knew he was tempted to add – for a woman.

"It's a beautiful evening." I remarked, taking a seat beside her. "I hope we get some rain soon. The crops could use it."

"We will, by late this evening. I can feel it in my bones. My arthritis has been aching all day." My grandmother was a staunch believer in the correlation between her arthritic flare-ups and the barometric pressure. Strangely enough, she was never wrong.

"Good," I replied.

"I am surprised Keifer hasn't arrived home yet?" Keifer Lee Marshall was my husband. He was a physician with a small practice in the heart of Braintree. He was dying to move us to Boston and continue his work at the hospitals there, but after my grandfather passed and I basically took over the management of Terrace Falls, he had let the subject drop knowing how much this land meant to grandmother and me. But I knew eventually we would be living there.

Instead, Keifer journeyed to Boston several times a week to work at the hospital there. He became a skilled surgeon and highly respected physician despite most people's initial opinion of him because he was a Southerner from Savannah, Georgia. He worked twice as hard as every other doctor to earn the respect of his peers, patients, and community. I felt horribly guilty about it, but Keifer never complained.

Keifer and I had gotten married three years ago. He stood over six feet tall with sandy blond hair and hazel eyes. He was a good-natured man with a huge heart, but at times could be rather temperamental. He cared deeply for his patients and always did his best for them, and I loved him for it. Although at times, his devotion to them kept him away from home until late at night or being aroused out of bed in the middle of the night for some emergency or another.

"I would imagine he should be here shortly." I closed my eyes and rested my head against her shoulder.

"Are you feeling all right, my dear? You look a little peaked." She paused a moment and looked over at me with concern.

"I think I may have caught a bug of some sort, and I cannot seem to shake it. I have been nauseated for over a week now and am always tired."

"Are you late?" She inquired with a raised eyebrow and sly smile.

"Late for what?" The obvious didn't even register in my head as a possibility since I was so careful on both planes.

"Your monthly? Is it late?"

"I do not believe so," my voice trailed off as I quickly did some calculations in my head. "No…" I whispered softly in disbelief as I realized I was, in fact, almost two weeks off schedule. "I can't be," I looked up at my grandmother with tears already welling up in my eyes.

"Well, it is possible darling. You do have a husband," she lowered her voice considerably. "And a boyfriend."

"No," I repeated quietly. My body had gone numb, and I started to hyperventilate.

My grandmother put her arms around me and lovingly rubbed my back. "Breathe, darling. Breathe. This is a good thing. Keifer will be so thrilled. You know how much he wants children." She reassured me.

"Keifer, yes. Landon, no!" Tears streaked down my face as everything I had worked so hard to accomplish in my *other* life was now in jeopardy. "Landon is going to be devastated. We've only just started medical school. We cannot afford this. We can barely make rent."

"I understand, my darling, but children come in God's time, not ours." My grandmother stroked my hair away from my face.

"Please, don't preach to me now, Grandmother. You know how I feel about that." I stood up and walked over to the railing facing out across the vast lawn. "I will never understand how you can have any faith in a God as cruel as one that would make us live with this wicked unnatural gift." I hastily brushed the tears off my cheeks.

"I have to have faith that there is a purpose behind us having this amazing ability." She got up and walked up behind me. Her hand rested lightly on my shoulder. "Sidney, I know you harbor some bitterness about *EVE*, but you have to let go of your anger and try to view it as a blessing." She gently turned me around to face her. "You have an extraordinary gift, my sweet girl. You get to witness two vastly different eras and be an important part of each." My grandmother smiled, gently touching the side of my face lovingly.

"Perhaps I have too much career-driven ambition in me from Amy, but I cannot help but feel stifled *here*. And now for this to happen," I sobbed. "It is going to alter everything I have worked so hard for and strived to be in my life *there*. I do not want this baby."

"You hush now, darling, and do not let me hear you utter that ever again. Keifer would be devastated if he ever heard such nonsense pass from your lips. That man loves you dearly, and all children are a blessing."

"At least Jocelyn doesn't have to deal with this." I crossed my arms hatefully. "She was always the fortunate one, and she has the same husband in both her lives." I had never admitted before my true feelings in that regard, and my grandmother didn't even look shocked by my words. Instead, she took my hands and gently unfolded my arms and led me back over to the swing. We sat down together, and she patted one of my hands gently between hers.

"Yes, Jocelyn is very blessed to have Jackson and his family with her on both her planes, but you – you have two exceptional men who cherish you, love you deeply, and will both celebrate the arrival of this blessing. And I know you are very driven like your mother, Amy. I see it in you every day, and the further you progress in your studies *there*, the more confident you become in your life *here*."

I smiled up at her soft blue eyes.

"I know you are not completely satisfied with your life *here*." She accurately observed.

"I just wish I could find the balance that Phoebe has. She seems at peace with both planes of her life. She is in love with both Carson and Silas and has managed to thrive in the peace of her nineteenth-century life and prosper in her twenty-first-century life. I envy her so." I hastily brushed aside a tear that escaped before it could trace down my cheek.

Jackson's older sister, Phoebe, and I had become close friends since my move to Boston. She was an attorney and one of the sweetest and strongest women I had ever encountered. We bonded quickly when I was struggling with the concept of *EVE* — a gift we both shared along with the fact that the men we loved did not.

Jocelyn was fortunate. Jackson possessed the gift as he traveled with her on both planes of her existence. Robert and Emily did, as well. However, their eldest son, Alex, Phoebe, and I, were not as lucky. We all had two spouses or a boyfriend, in my case, in our separate lives.

I struggled dearly with it, and Phoebe understood what I was going through. She had been in my shoes and knew how conflicted it felt to be in love with two men more than hundred years apart and to share a life with each of them. My sister was empathic, but she couldn't fathom how it was possible and often made me feel guilty about it.

"Perhaps once I finish school, and things slow down, then I'll find that as well. But now, this screws it all up." I complained.

"Please do not think that." My grandmother offered me a weary smile. "This child was conceived in love regardless of the timing."

"Yes. Yes, it was." I sighed audibly as my grandmother wrapped her arms around me.

Tears ran down my cheeks and dampened the front of my grandmother's apron. She continued to stroke my hair as if I was a small child again who had had a nightmare. But this was much worse. Now I was living one.

3

MY EYES OPENED WITH A start. I jumped out of bed and ran to the small bathroom in my top floor loft and immediately vomited everything I had eaten the day before. When the wave finally passed, I sat down on the floor and rested my head against the cold side of it. The realization of everything that had just transpired in my *other* life came crashing down upon me like a wrecking ball. And the tears began flowing freely.

I cleaned myself up and got dressed. The alarm on my nightstand told me it was only six in the morning. Landon was still sleeping peacefully. I stopped at the foot of our bed and watched him for several minutes, feeling horrible. Little did he know his world was about to come crashing down upon him too. We had talked about this — marriage, children, our lives together. It was something we both wanted, just not yet. We had been living together for almost three years and had been extremely careful with avoiding pregnancy until after we were through our residencies and married.

But life forgot to ask me what I wanted.

I dressed quickly and snuck down the old creaking stairs that led to my third-floor hideaway. The house was eerily quiet. Everyone was still in deep slumber. I stopped in front of my sister's room, where she and Jackson were surely sound asleep. I carefully opened her door and peeked inside. The two of them were wrapped around each other, looking like the beautiful, loving couple they were. They had been through hell together, and yet somehow, they had survived. I was envious of my little sister and Jackson's love for her. He truly adored her and always put her first in every aspect of their lives.

I crept over to their bed and placed my hand on her shoulder, rubbing it gently. "Jocelyn?" I leaned in close to her. She stirred a smidgen and opened her eyes.

"Sidney?" She lifted her head slightly off the pillow and looked at me.

"Get dressed. I need you." I whispered.

Jocelyn nodded and slipped out from beneath Jackson's arm that was draped over her. She threw on an old T-shirt that had our old high school logo printed across the front and a pair of gym shorts. I grabbed her flip flops and purse, and she followed me out into the hall. I stood there patiently as she disappeared into the bathroom for a few minutes.

By the time she returned, I was nervously pacing the length of the hall.

"What's going on?" She whispered as we climbed down the front staircase of our childhood home.

"We need to run to Walgreens?" I told her as I grabbed my dad's car keys off the hook by the front door.

"Are you serious? You woke me up at the butt crack of dawn to ride with you to Walgreens?" Her voice quickly turned annoyed, and I remembered how much my little sister truly valued her sleep.

"Don't get your panties in a bunch. I'm not on some trivial errand here." We climbed into my dad's car.

In the short two-mile ride to the nearest store, I quickly gave my sister a recap of what happened in my life *there* the day before and the reality I had awoken to this morning.

Jocelyn sat there silently for several moments without saying a word. I pulled into the parking lot and parked in the closet spot near the door, waiting for her to say something. Out of nowhere, she started giggling like an idiot.

"I hardly see the humor in this," her laugher immediately annoyed me. "How is this funny to you?"

"Remember all the shit Mom gave me about getting pregnant because Jackson and I got married? Well, we've been married for three and a half years and never even had a pregnancy scare. And you have always been Mom's golden child, her perfect little angel following in her footsteps to be a doctor just like her and you have been living with your boyfriend for the last three years, and you are the one who got knocked up. Not me!" She continued laughing.

"It is not funny," I stated angrily, climbing out of the car. "If I had known you were going to react this way, I wouldn't have bothered asking you to come with me."

"I'm sorry," she stopped on the sidewalk, attempting to recompose herself. "You're right. I am sorry. It's not funny." She took a noticeable deep breath and followed me into the store.

༄

Twenty minutes later, the two of us were pacing around the kitchen, drinking coffee, and watching the clock in the microwave.

"No matter what that stick says, Sidney, it's going to be fine." Jocelyn stopped in front of me and pulled me into a hug. "We're all going to be here for you, and we will make it work. You know that." She reassured me.

"Thank you," I tried to grin, but silent tears kept rolling down my cheeks.

"You ready? It's time?" She grinned and kissed me lightly on the cheek.

"No," I stated flatly but walked towards the bathroom anyway with her close behind me.

I picked up the stick, and my heart sank to my toes. "It's blue."

"That's great," she said excitedly and wrapped her arms around me. "It's wonderful, Sidney."

"I'm glad you think so," I muttered, trying to maintain my breathing. I sat down on the toilet seat lid and covered my face with my hands. "What am I going to do?"

"Celebrate," Jocelyn knelt in front of me and placed her hands on my knees. "Look, Sid, you know I'm here for you, and so is Jackson. Plus, his family and Uncle Nicholas. We will all help you. You know that. Whether it's babysitting or whatever you need, we are all here for you and Landon. You two are not in this alone. You have a huge family that is more than thrilled to step in and help."

"But that's not fair to any of you." I complained.

"We're family. That's what we do. We help each other out, support one another through the good times and the bad. And this is wonderful news, Sidney." She assured me.

"Yeah, well, let's see if Landon thinks so." I looked up at her through my tears. Somehow, I didn't believe he was going to see this as joyous news.

"Of course, he will. It might take some time for the shock to wear off, but he will. Landon loves you, and it's not like you two aren't planning on getting married and having children. This just speeds things up a bit." She shrugged. "It happens."

"I think I'll wait until after the wedding this weekend before I tell him. I don't want to ruin things for Dad and Patsy." I brushed the tears off my cheeks.

"I understand. I promise I won't say a word." Jocelyn grinned and wrapped her arms around me again. "Can I please tell Jackson? You know I am no good at keeping secrets from him. I swear the man is a human lie detector. He can always tell when I'm keeping something from him."

"Yes. But tell him not to say anything." I knew she'd cave with him.

"He won't. You know that."

"Yes, I know I can trust him." I agreed. "You are lucky, you know that?"

"I know."

"I wish I had the same man with me in both eras of my life." I admitted.

"Whose baby do you think it is?" She hesitated a moment. "I didn't want to ask."

"Keifer's. It must be Keifer's. Landon and I have been so careful, and with Keifer, birth control is not quite so simple."

"I know what you mean." She sat down on the floor and leaned against the wall. "I am honestly shocked that Jackson and I have been so fortunate. We use condoms and rhythm method just to be careful *there*. So far, we have been extremely lucky."

"The timing is just all wrong." I brushed the tears off my face and looked up at my little sister. "If it were five or better yet, ten years from now, it would be great. But we have so many plans and dreams we've both worked so hard for, and this baby just ruins all of that."

"No, it doesn't have to. We will make it work." Jocelyn assured me. "I'm actually surprised you are not having a complete meltdown." She smiled weakly. "I was expecting you too."

"No, I did that in front of my grandmother *there*. No need to do it again." I blew my nose on some tissues and ran my fingers roughly through my hair. "What would you do if you were me?" I couldn't stop myself from asking.

"If I got pregnant?" She thought about it for a quick second. "I would be so thrilled you would hear me bragging to everyone. I want to get pregnant. I want children more than anything, especially *there*. I hate that everyone I know is having, or has already had children, and I don't. I despise the pitiful looks they give me for being childless." My sister shook her head slightly. "I hate the whispers and the speculations people make about why Jackson and I have been married so long and still have not had children. And it's not like I can explain the truth to them."

"I'm sorry, but I do understand. I've gotten the same looks, heard the same whispers and everything else since Keifer and I have been married for years and don't have children yet." I paused. "Guess they will shut up now." I chuckled sarcastically.

"True, plus, you know Keifer's going to be thrilled about this." She pointed out. "When are you going to tell him?"

"I was thinking about tomorrow evening. His sister, Eugenia, is coming to visit us for a while. She should arrive on Friday, and I would like to tell him before she arrives."

"How long is she planning on staying?"

"I have no idea. The last time she came for a brief visit, she was there for three months." I rolled my eyes. "So, she should be with us most likely through the holidays." I snorted. "It's not as if she has any other purpose than to annoy everyone in the family; fat old cow will never get married."

"You are mean," my sister laughed. "Please tell me Keifer doesn't know how you really feel about her."

"No, and I would never tell him either." I rolled my eyes. "I just do not understand how the two of them are related. They are as different as night and day. He's tall, good looking, charming — a little moody, but nothing unbearable. And that woman — Ha! She's about as two-faced as anyone I have ever met. She eats nonstop and is lazy as the day is long. It is no wonder she's twenty-five years old and never been kissed or been courted by a beau."

"I would love to see what this woman looks like." Jocelyn giggled.

"Mrs. Potato Head with fatter arms, enormous thighs, and a mustache." I couldn't help but laugh.

"Wow," She let out a low whistle.

"I'm serious," I confessed.

"Are you feeling any better?" Jocelyn put her hand back up on my knee and asked.

"Yes, tons. Thanks!" I smiled. "Come on," I stood up, taking her hands in mine and pulling her to her feet. "I need some coffee."

"You can't drink coffee, Prego." She retorted.

"You really think no one's going to suspect something if I abruptly stop drinking coffee?" I turned and gave her a coy look. "Seriously?"

"You know it isn't good for the baby." She stated with a smart-ass grin.

"It wasn't yesterday when I didn't know either, right?"

"But now you know," she pointed out.

"Monday, okay? I will give it up Monday." I reasoned.

"If you say so, Mom!" Jocelyn teased.

"Enough of that. I mean it." I gave her a stern look as we moved back into the kitchen.

I loved my little sister dearly, and in the last four years, we had grown very close. We had a somewhat rocky relationship before that since we really did not have anything in common. However, our mutual gift of *EVE* that we had both inherited from our uncles had changed any differences we had once had and brought us close together. Now we were the best of friends and relied heavily on one another. My only regret was that we did not share our second lives together.

As strange as it sounded, Jocelyn, who is two years younger than I, is my little sister in the twenty-first century, but in the nineteenth century, she is my niece and the daughter of my younger brother, Patrick.

The whole thing was difficult to explain and even harder to wrap my brain around. And as much as I loved having her in my life on this plane, I dearly missed her in my *other* since I still had to wait another year and a half until she was even born. Her mother *there*, Annabelle, had just given birth to her older brother, William.

Slowly, one by one, our family began to trickle downstairs in search of coffee and food. Our little brother, Ethan, was the last to make an appearance and looked as if he had been dragged fourteen blocks by a Mac truck when he did appear. Most likely he had been out with his buddies the night before. He had been thoroughly enjoying his break before he had to start training for the upcoming football season mid-summer.

"Good morning, sunshine." I gave him a hug as he stumbled slowly into the kitchen holding his head. "You look marvelous, darling."

"Thanks, sis," he grumbled before letting me go in search of coffee.

"Late night?" I sat down on one of the barstools and asked.

"Not really, but definitely too much tequila." He confessed.

"How can you drink that crap?"

"I can't," he smirked and disappeared behind his oversized mug.

"Hey, you're up — finally." Our dad entered the kitchen and refilled his own cup. "Lots to do today, remember?" He looked between the two of us and straight at Ethan. "You'd better chew on some aspirin, or you're gonna be hating life all day."

"I know," Ethan replied, barely looking up.

"You realize that you're going to have to kick it up a notch this fall. The partying all night is going to have to stop, Ethan." Dad told him.

"I know. I know." Ethan muttered then rolled his eyes at me.

"Okay, well, let's get ready before Patsy starts hollering at us." Our dad grinned sheepishly before existing out of the kitchen.

I disappeared back to my third-floor hideaway.

My childhood home was built shortly before the start of the American Civil War. It was a huge, old, elegant estate whitewashed with black shutters and a grand porch that was wrapped around the front and sides of the home. It had three floors with a fully finished basement that the three of us kids had used as a hang-out with our friends in high school.

Our home was originally built by my younger brother Patrick in 1859 and stayed in our family until the turn of the twentieth century when it fell into disrepair. The costs to bring the electrical and plumbing up to date were enormous, and my great grandfather was forced to sell.

Thankfully, our father Shane was able to bring it back into our family. He purchased it when our mother, Amy, was pregnant with Jocelyn. Throughout our childhood, Amy had redecorated it to a showpiece. The front parlor was her favorite room. She had restored it with antiques from the nineteenth century, grand piano, and all. It was her masterpiece and the one room our father left intact after their divorce.

The vast grounds were expertly manicured. The mature trees provided ample shade about the grounds and adorned a base of various flowers and shrubbery. The three-car garage in the back yard had, more than a century ago, served as the housing for the servants who worked for my ancestors. The barn that also served as the stables had burnt down sometime in the 1930s when it was under the ownership outside our family.

Landon was still snoring softly in my large canopy bed hidden behind the soft cornflower blue drapes. I smiled over at him, thinking about how much I didn't want to tell him about the baby. I didn't want to do anything that would alter the peaceful slumber that he had right now.

Landon was a good man. He was raised to be considerate and kind. Traits I knew would make him an amazing physician. He always put me first in every situation, regardless of how big or small.

Each morning when he rose before me, he would start the coffee and then place a hot mug just the way I liked it on my nightstand before he kissed me on the cheek, whispering my name and rubbing my shoulder telling me it was time to get up. Wherever we were, he always insisted on walking outside closest to traffic just to keep me a little safer.

It was always the little considerate things that Landon did that stood out above all other men. He was a true gentleman, in some ways so much more so than Keifer, who was supposed to be more of a gentleman fitted for the time.

I tried my best never to compare the two men. They were drastically different in so many ways, yet in others, they were very similar. Keifer was a practicing physician. Landon was well on his way. If Landon were on the same plane with Keifer, he would already be a practicing physician as well.

Both men were dirty blonds with deep hazel eyes that were green, gray, or hazel, depending on their mood. Both were over six feet tall, broad-shouldered, and muscular. But that's where their similarities ended.

Landon was much easier going than Keifer. At times Keifer could be very intense and extremely moody. There were times when I wasn't sure what to expect from him, and on those days, it was always best to steer clear of him. Landon was nothing like that. He was always consistent of character and would never throw the tantrums Keifer was prone to when the mood struck him.

I quietly disappeared into the bathroom and turned on the oversized shower letting the bathroom fill up with steam. I got undressed and looked at myself in the mirror. I placed my hands over my abdomen and thought about the little person growing inside me. The concept seemed so foreign to me, so surreal.

My thick blond hair cascaded down my slender neck and fell over my petite shoulders. My size two waist that I strived diligently to maintain appeared as narrow as always. The thought of gaining twenty to thirty pounds brought tears to my eyes. The possibility of stretch marks scaring up my flawless alabaster skin was about enough to push me into full-blown hysterics.

It was not that I was a vain person. It was simply that I worked hard on my appearance. I ate healthily. I exercised daily. I did not smoke and rarely drank, if ever. Mainly on special social engagements and nowhere near as much as my peers. It seemed that in our group of friends at school, I somehow was always the designated driver. I'm not even sure how I got the role, but it wasn't nearly as challenging for me on Mondays as it typically was for them.

I climbed into the shower and let the hot water wash the stress away from my tense muscles. I was on the verge of hysterics — laughing or crying, I wasn't sure which, but one was about to burst through the fragile seams of my shell. I hated to think about the hell that was getting ready to rain down upon me.

My mother was going to go ballistic. That much I was positive of. My dad would not be thrilled, but the prospect of a grandchild to spoil would be too appealing to him for him to remain upset with me for too long.

I was honestly more concerned with Landon's reaction than everyone else. I knew Keifer would be thrilled. He has been wanting a son since the day we were married, and thus far, I have managed to delay that for several years.

But Landon …

Landon was a different story. We talked about having children years ago, not long after we became exclusive. We had both strongly agreed to wait until we were in our 30's and had completed our residency programs. And here I was, 23 years old, as was Landon. The timing of this pregnancy could not be worse for either of us.

I sat down at the bottom of the shower and thought about my conversation with Jocelyn and wondered if, with her support and that of her extended family and mine, I or we could possibly pull this off.

I wanted to think, wanted to believe that Landon was going to stick around and not abandon me. Or worse yet, demand I have an abortion. I am ardently pro-choice but only in instances where the mothers or baby's life was in jeopardy, or in cases of rape or incest. I felt strongly against it being used as a form of birth control or a solution to an untimely or unplanned pregnancy — such as my situation.

Still, as I sat there with the hot water slowly turning to cold washing down upon me, I didn't know if I was going to laugh or cry. I wrapped my arms around my knees, hugging them close to me and rocked slowly back and forth. It was an old habit from my early childhood that always gave me comfort. My mind was racing in a thousand different directions.

But in the true spirit of being my mother's daughter — weakness, fear, and self-pity were not options. Three things my mother loathed in any person, male or female. For she herself was the pillar of strength and expected nothing less of her children. Of course, some people took her demeanor as cold and impersonal, but she wasn't. She just had high expectations for herself and her children. She was a gifted physician and had an extraordinary bedside manner with her patients, somewhat with her staff and almost none with her family.

My siblings were both more like our father, laid-back, easy-going, quick to smile, and always determined to find the good in any situation. I had not been so blessed. Like my mother, I was a career-driven, type A personality, who worried about everything — big and small. I would lie awake in the dead of night, stressing over something that was beyond my control. It was just my nature.

I sighed audibly and stood back up, trying to pull myself together — if only for the next few days and if only for the sake and happiness of my dad.

⁓

Jocelyn, my brother's girlfriend, Liang, and I spent the afternoon getting poked, prodded, and stuck with pins as the final alterations were made on our bridesmaid dresses. We each took turns standing on a small platform surrounded by mirrors, making faces, and rolling our eyes at each other while an elderly seamstress named Dora worked her graceful fingers to make sure each of our pale sage, silk gowns with a sheer overlay, fit us snuggly, but not tightly. The dresses were very elegant with their spaghetti straps and soft fabric that glided over our bodies gracefully, stopping two inches above our knees.

It was Liang's turn up on the box. Jocelyn and I settled into the little loveseat and watched Dora turn Liang this way and that. It was sort of comical witnessing these two endure this simply because neither of them was overly girly.

Jocelyn preferred jeans and sweatshirts over anything else. Her fashion sense had improved much since her barrier depleted between her two worlds. Her *other* self, like mine, was extremely feminine — because she had no other option. But despite herself, that smidgen of her consciousness had bled over into this world.

Liang, on the other hand, was much different. Makeup made her nervous, and she rarely wore it. She dressed feminine but not girly and watching her struggle in our three-inch strappy heels was more comical than if Ethan would have been wearing them. But Liang didn't need makeup. She had such a natural radiance about her she practically glowed. Plus, her long ebony hair hung slightly beneath her collarbone in a long layered stylish cut that required little to no maintenance outside of some mousse and a hairbrush.

I was so jealous.

She also had the exact same look she did the first time I'd met her when Jocelyn and Jackson had graduated high school. Liang looked twelve then, and she maybe looked fourteen at the most now. That was pretty damn impressive for someone who just turned twenty-one last month.

"It was sweet of Patsy to include me in the ceremony, but we all know I'm going to break my neck walking down the aisle in these heels," Liang complained.

"We'll practice." I assured her.

"There's not enough hours between now and Saturday to keep me upright." Liang stated, making Jocelyn giggle.

Jocelyn knew Liang better than I did since they played together on the girls' softball team Jocelyn's senior year. Liang finally confessed later that she'd tried out for the team attempting to make peace with my sister. Apparently, the two didn't initially hit it off when Liang started dating our brother.

"You'll be fine." I said although I wasn't exactly as confident as I sounded.

"Sure, you will." My sister chimed in, still smirking.

I knew what my sister was thinking and elbowed her in the ribs to express it. But she only continued to smirk.

"Any idea what Dad has on the agenda for the rest of the day?" I asked, attempting to change the subject.

"No, he didn't mention anything else this morning. I think we might be off the hook until the rehearsal dinner tomorrow night." Jocelyn told me.

"That would be nice." Liang smiled.

"I hope so because I want to see Jenna and Caitlyn. I know they're both in town." My sister always wanted to visit them whenever she came home.

"That sounds fun. How are they doing?" I inquired.

"Jenna's in nursing school at IU, and Caitlyn is at Northwestern studying interior design." Jocelyn told me.

"I would imagine it fits her well." Caitlyn was probably the most elegant yet eccentric person I knew.

"She loves it. They both do actually." My sister grinned.

"Is Jenna still with Kyle?" I remembered the cute little geeky boy next door.

"No. They split up after their first semester of college. Jenna was at Indiana University, and Kyle was in Tennessee at TU. Managing a long-distance relationship along with school was just too challenging. Although I believe it was for the best because Kyle had met someone else and got married last summer to a girl from down there. In fact, they are expecting their first child next month."

"Wow. It's hard to imagine Kyle as a dad." It was even harder to imagine myself as a mom.

After lunch, Jocelyn and Liang left with their guys to visit friends. I took advantage of Landon being out on the golf course with my dad and decided I would take a nap. I was emotionally drained and desperately wanted some alone time.

4

FRIDAY, JULY 22, 1859

KEIFER CAME HOME LATE after delivering Mrs. Tarrow's fourth son in six years. She had to be one of the most fertile women on the planet. He handed his hat to our housekeeper, Marta, before pouring himself a glass of scotch from the decanter in the parlor.

"Rough day, darling?" I walked up behind him and touched him lightly on the shoulder.

"No. Not really. Mrs. Tarrow has a body built for having babies. However, I know she is a bit disappointed that it was another boy. She was really hoping for a girl this time." He sighed. "I just wish this heat would break. It is even more miserable after the sun sets than it was at noon." Keifer complained.

"Yes, it is. But hopefully, this heatwave will end soon." I tried to sound optimistic.

"I hope so." He finished off his drink and turned around. "Did I miss dinner again?"

"I had Naomi fix you a plate when I saw your carriage down the lane. I was sewing on the porch." I kissed him lightly on the cheek. "It should be waiting for you in the dining room."

"Thank you, darling." Keifer smiled and picked up the evening edition of his Boston newspaper, *The Liberator,* and headed into the dining room.

I watched him disappear out of the room and then sat down in the rocking chair by the hearth. I looked over at my basket of yarn and considered picking them up but dismissed it almost as quickly as the thought had entered my mind. I needed to tell Keifer about another baby that was on the way, and I knew he was going to be elated about this one.

Keifer had been stumped for years, trying to figure out how and why we weren't getting pregnant. There was no logical reason for it in his eyes, and he speculated over the last year that one of us was sterile. I could never tell him that I was using various natural remedies of herbs to combat his efforts.

I felt horrible deceiving him, but it was not like I could be honest with him. He had no knowledge of *EVE*, and Keifer was an intellectual, not the imaginative sort. He would never believe anything about the concept of *EVE*. He would be more likely to believe me to be mad.

I was positive my news was going to overjoy him. Therefore, I wanted the timing to be perfect. It was not something I could simply blurt out. Instead, I wanted it to be intimate and special.

But how?

An hour later I found Keifer in his study. He was looking through an old textbook. Something he was reading perplexed him as I noticed his face was all tensed up, and his brow was wrinkled.

"Excuse me, my love. Can I interrupt you for a moment?"

"Mmmm." Keifer didn't even look up.

"Keifer?" I said a bit louder.

"Sorry." His eyes appeared for the first time. "What can I do for you?"

"It's a beautiful evening. I wondered if you would like to join me on a walk." I started, but Keifer quickly cut me off.

"Sidney, I wish I could, but I am looking for something. Mr. Nichols is having abdominal pain, and I cannot figure out why. I need to look through this and several other books and see if I cannot find some sort of explanation." He looked tired.

"I understand." I leaned against the doorframe and switched tactics. "But darling, this is rather important as well. It has to do with something personal about my health." I tried to be as vague as possible.

"Summer cold?" He inquired but continued looking at the text.

"Not exactly." I let out a heavy sigh. "Would you please join me so that I may explain?" I held out my hand to him.

Reluctantly, and with a heavy sigh, he closed the book and took my hand.

The evening air was thick and sticky. The smell of freshly cut grass and jasmine hung heavy in the air. We walked down the dusty path between the fields silently hand in hand. The sun was on its final descent of the day, but not before brilliantly dressing the sky in shades of gold, purple, and red.

Keifer stopped as the path reached the riverbed. He turned towards me and took my other hand in his as well.

"Your silence makes me nervous. I fear this is serious." He stated.

"It is, I am afraid." A small part of me was enjoying toying with him. "But it should resolve itself before we break the fields to plant next spring."

"I don't understand." His forehead wrinkled in confusion.

"Your prayers have been answered, my love." I smiled lovingly into his beautiful hazel eyes.

A smile spread across his shapely lips, and his eyes shined brilliantly in the twilight.

"Are you saying what I think you are saying?" His grip tightened on my hands.

"We're pregnant." The words slipped out so much easier than I anticipated.

Keifer yelped and picked me up, twirling me around and laughingly wildly. By his reaction, you would have thought he was the first man to ever impregnate his wife. I couldn't help but laugh along with him. His enthusiasm was contagious.

He pulled me into a forceful embrace.

"You have made me the happiest man alive, Mrs. Marshall."

"I love you." I leaned up and kissed my husband.

"I love you more." He continued to smile.

There was a definite skip to Keifer's step as we began walking back towards the house. The hot, muggy air no longer bothered either of us. All my apprehensions slipped away with each step that carried us back to the home we dearly loved. I placed a hand over my abdomen, thinking about the tiny life growing inside me; wondering if it was a boy or girl. I truly didn't care so long as it was healthy.

"I pray we have a son." Keifer announced about halfway up the path. "And then the following year, we can have a daughter." He was grinning widely.

"Let's start with one." I laughed at his enthusiasm.

"You know you will have to take it easy." He stopped and turned towards me. "No more riding the horses, walking out in the afternoon sun to check on the workers. None of that. You let Casper handle it, or he can send Duncan." He placed his hand on my abdomen. "This child is our miracle. I feared we would never be blessed with a child. I am going to take such good care of you two and make sure we have the healthiest and fattest baby this side of the Mississippi." Keifer chuckled, but I quickly realized he was going to suffocate me over the next seven and a half months.

"I am not made of glass, darling." I assured him.

"I know, but sweetheart, we had such a difficult time getting pregnant, I fear something may go wrong." He confessed.

"We will be fine," I leaned over and kissed him softly. "I promise, I will protect our child."

"I have no doubt." Keifer smiled and took my hand in his before starting back towards the house.

5

FRIDAY, JULY 19, 2019

LIANG, JOCELYN, AND I HID upstairs in my third-floor hideaway most of the afternoon, getting ready for our dad's rehearsal dinner. We had the music turned up, singing slightly off-key, and danced around my childhood suite. My bed was littered with discarded clothes, and various shoes were scattered about the floor.

My old vanity table was littered with dozens of cosmetics that we passed amongst us, trying to decide what looked best for this special night. We had four different styles of curling irons, and a flattening iron blazing hot and ready for the next user.

"Is it just me, or does this feel weird?" My little sister turned towards us, holding a curling iron to the side of her head. "Going to Dad's rehearsal dinner."

"It's not you." I remarked, still sorting through the pile of clothes on my bed.

"But Shane seems so happy." Liang chimed in. "In all the years I've known him, I've never seen him this happy."

"He is happy." I remarked, pulling out a black skirt and grey blouse. I held them up to the ladies. "What about this?"

"That looks like you should be going to a funeral." Liang wrinkled her nose.

"Perhaps I am," I shrugged and tossed them back on the bed.

"Why would you say that? I thought you liked Patsy?" Liang put down the shoes she was trying on and narrowed her eyes and pursed her lips in a confused expression.

"I do. It's just that Dad marrying her simply means our parents will never get back together. It's just sad is all." I sat down on the edge of my bed. "You really didn't know my mom before their marriage went bad. She used to be a completely different person. She used to laugh and joke around." I sighed heavily, remembering how she used to be so radiant. "I miss those days."

"I know what you mean." Jocelyn put down the curling iron and leaned against the vanity table. "I wish I knew what happened between them. They used to be so happy together and in love. I wonder what happened to make all that disappear? It would kill me if that happened to Jackson and me."

"I don't know what happened between them. I noticed the change when I started high school. It was like they just stopped talking. They still did the grocery shopping together, or at least they did for a while, but then it got to where Dad would pick up whatever they needed on his way home or Mom would. They just sort of existed in the same house and only spoke to each other when necessary." Jocelyn said.

"Well, at least they're both happier now." Liang stated, shifting uncomfortably.

"True, Dad is anyway. I wouldn't know about mom. I never talk to her." Jocelyn's eyes landed on me.

"She's doing all right. She's dating another doctor. He's a pediatric surgeon at the same hospital she works at. His name is Dane, something or other. I can't pronounce his last name." I told my sister.

"Is she getting serious with him?" Jocelyn's eyes shifted down. I knew the strain in her relationship with our mother still bothered her a great deal.

"I have no idea. She doesn't confide in me. You know mom." I shrugged. "She never shares anything that she doesn't feel we *need* to know."

"True." Jocelyn muttered under her breath.

"You two still aren't speaking?" Liang asked in a soft voice looking over at my sister.

"Oh, we speak. She was kind enough to call me last Christmas." She smirked. "I haven't spoken to her since."

We were all quiet for the next few minutes. None of us knew what to say. So, we each just sort of began fiddling with what we were doing before the conversation started. Luckily, the next song that came on the radio was Imagine Dragons, *It's Time*, and before the second verse began, the three of us were singing and dancing, putting all thoughts of the conversation out of our heads.

The rehearsal hall was gorgeous, small, and intimate, filled with close family and friends. My father was glowing with happiness, grinning from ear to ear like some silly ol' fool. I was happy for him. I truly was. But it still hurt my heart. I reached down and took Landon's hand, squeezing it gently. He leaned over and kissed me lightly on the cheek and smiled.

My heart was consumed by the love I felt for him and my family surrounding me. I don't know if it was the pregnancy hormones starting to kick in or just me being overly emotional because of the wedding. Regardless of which it was, I could feel the tears welling up behind my overly emotional eyes.

TRANSCENDENCE

Hopefully, it was simply the wedding because if I had to put up with this raw emotional state for the next seven or so months, I was never going to be able to do my job, study, or keep my wits about me.

My dad stood up and made a toast to his new bride. His auburn brown hair, the same shade as my siblings, was recently trimmed and styled. I felt so proud of how handsome he looked in his burgundy dress shirt and black slacks. His dark brown eyes were glistening in the low light of the backroom of the hotel as he nervously cleared his throat.

Our dad's speech was lovely. His words were soft and tender as his eyes rested on his blushing bride-to-be. And Patsy was a beautiful sight this evening. She had allowed me to do her hair and makeup, and she was even wearing one of my dresses. It took some doing for me and my two cohorts to talk her into it, but we kept emphasizing how important it was. She struggled, kicked, and screamed, but in the end, she was breathtaking.

It truly amazed me how my dad went from one extreme of an ultra-feminine, high maintenance, career-oriented, type-A personality, lady like our mother, Amy, to a tomboy like Patsy. Perhaps that was Patsy's appeal for my father after almost thirty years with someone as demanding and girlie as our mother.

Ethan, fully recovered from his hangover and sporting a new haircut per our father's request, looked stunningly handsome. He was sitting beside Liang tracing his index finger over the rim of his wine glass, making it hum softly. I watched him for almost thirty seconds before Liang reached her limit with it and placed her hand over his and shook her head slowly at him like a mother correcting the behavior of a child. I smiled despite myself thinking that regardless of his degree, Ethan was still a child at heart.

My eyes locked with my little brothers for a moment. I could see the sadness buried in them barely hidden beneath the surface. He smiled at me briefly, but I could tell his heart wasn't in it. I couldn't help but wonder if the same thing that was bothering Jocelyn and me earlier was also the little voice whispering in Ethan's head.

As the evening wore down and the guests began to leave, I excused myself from the table and went to the restroom to freshen up. It had been an exhausting couple of days, and I kept reminding myself that I still had to make it through the wedding.

I exited the dining hall and walked down the small corridor to the facilities. I was digging through my purse, looking for my hairbrush when the sound of Patsy's voice caused me to turn my head towards another off-shoot hallway on the side.

"I will call your attorney on Monday, okay?" I stopped in my footsteps to listen, wondering who she was talking to.

"But the hearing is set for when you're going to be on your honeymoon." I immediately recognized Donnie's voice. "What am I supposed to do?"

"I will have your attorney file for a continuance. It's not a big deal. Would you stop worrying about it? I have everything under control. I am as good as married, and then all our financial troubles will be over." I heard her state confidently.

I stood frozen against the wall. I couldn't believe my ears. I could feel my face flushing with anger and my hands balled into fists at my side.

What a manipulative bitch!

"Don't worry, Donnie. By this time tomorrow, we won't have any financial problems ever again." I heard Patsy reassure her son.

"We shall see ..." I muttered under my breath and hurried back off into the main reception hall.

My dad was standing there surrounded by his closest friends, family, and colleagues looking happier than I had seen him in years. My heart broke, thinking of what I knew I had to do. There was no way I could let him marry such a despicable creature. But how in the world could I tell him on the eve of his wedding that his bride-to-be was a monster and only marrying him for financial security for her and her witless wonder of a son? It made me physically ill.

I sat down beside Landon and had a long drink of water. How I wished it was something stronger, but I knew I couldn't regardless of how much I wanted it.

"Are you alright?" Landon looked over at me with a troubled expression. He placed his hand gently on my arm.

"No." I went on to explain the conversation I'd overheard in the hallway. When I finished, Landon slumped down in his chair and folded his arms, dropping his head.

"Damn. This sucks!" He muttered. "You have to tell him."

"I know." I looked over at him with mournful eyes. "I can't believe this. Look how happy he is." I nodded over in the direction of my father. "This is going to destroy him. Not to mention the humiliation he's going to endure."

"Would you rather him marry that greedy low life?" Landon inquired. I shook my head.

"No. Of course not."

"Then you have to tell him the truth."

"I know. Where's Jocelyn?" My eyes scanned my room for my sister. I knew I was going to have to have her beside me if I was going to do this. She was much stronger than I could ever imagine, and she was closer to our dad than I was.

"She's over there with Liang." Landon gestured to the far corner of the room. "I wouldn't tell her about this just yet. She'll pounce on Patsy in front of everyone. Wait until we leave."

"I will." I knew he was right.

Jocelyn thought of the world of our dad, and she was going to see this as a personal deception against all of us, not just our dad.

"We need to find a reason to get him out of here." I stated.

"It's his rehearsal dinner, and all of his colleagues are still here." Landon pointed out.

"Do you really want to continue with this farce? Let him carry on this joyful evening in bliss so he can look back at it with even more regret and feel like an even bigger fool in front of his family, friends, and colleagues?" I reasoned.

"I guess you're right, but how are you going to get him out of here smoothly. It's going to take something big to make him leave his own rehearsal dinner." He stated.

"True." I sighed.

I knew nothing short of a family emergency was going to do it. Unfortunately, his entire family was here, and all fine.

I picked up my water glass, wishing again it was wine and took a sip. Then it dawned on me — I'm pregnant. I can fake abdominal cramps and make him leave with me. Even if I must slightly deceive Landon a smidgen, I knew my dad would never let Landon take me to the hospital without accompanying us there. I turned towards Landon in his seat and rested my head on his shoulder.

"Are you good with a small white lie to get him out of here even if you're involved in it?" I whispered in his ear.

"For this? Of course." The corners of his mouth turned up, and his eyes twinkled with mischievousness.

"Okay, just go with me and don't question my story." I told him.

"Never." Landon assured me. "What are you going to tell him?"

"I'm not going to tell him anything. You are." I said quietly.

"If I act upset that you're sick … I mean over dramatically upset and insist that you must go to the hospital. What am I supposed to tell him I suspect? Appendicitis? He's never going to buy that." He raised his eyebrows and looked at me questionably.

"No, he wouldn't. But if you tell him I'm cramping, and you fear I'm having a miscarriage, he'd drive us to the hospital." I informed him.

Landon looked surprised at the words that came out of my mouth. "You can't do that to him! That's mean." He tightened his lips and narrowed his eyes a bit. "Besides, your dad is never going to believe we were stupid enough to get pregnant!"

"Accidents do happen." I felt a small jolt from the butterflies in my stomach.

"Not to us…" I clearly heard Landon mutter under his breath.

"Please," I gently nudged him on the shoulder. "He'll understand by the end of the evening." I reasoned.

One of the perks about him being a med student was he would know exactly what to say to my dad to get his attention and alarm him just enough to get him out of here without a lot of fuss.

I watched Landon walk across the room towards my dad. I leaned forward just a bit in my chair with my arm across my abdomen as if I had cramps or pain of some sort. I didn't want to overdo it, but Jocelyn looked at me at the wrong time and hurried across the room by my side before Landon had even begun talking with my dad.

"Are you alright?" She squatted down in front of me. "Is it the baby?" She whispered. I was never any good at lying, so all I did was nod my head. "Are you spotting?"

"A little." I kept my eyes on the floor so they wouldn't betray me.

"We need to get you checked." She reached out for my hand. "Come on. I'll drive you to the hospital. Can you walk?"

Again, I shook my head.

"Okay," my sister stood up and scanned the room. "Damn, I wish Jackson were here." She muttered aloud.

"Where's Jackson?" I couldn't imagine him missing the rehearsal dinner.

"He's picking up his parents at the airport." My sister informed me. "Where did Landon disappear too?" She looked around. "Damn it, he's over talking to Dad." She looked over at me. "What am I supposed to say? Did you tell him?"

Before I could answer, my dad and Landon had come up beside me. Landon pulled my chair out a bit from the table and lifted me up in his arms. I rested my head against his strong firm chest and closed my eyes. I hated being this deceitful even if it was for a good reason.

I heard my dad holler at Ethan and Liang to explain their absence with a family emergency and to apologize to Patsy for him. He rushed ahead of us and pulled his SUV into the little roundabout in front of the club. He jumped out and opened the back door so Landon could put me in.

Jocelyn ran up and climbed into the passenger seat before I could say anything to her. Her face was stricken with concern, making me feel all the worse. I was hoping just to get my dad out of there and to a place where I could talk to him privately. Hopefully, having Jocelyn along would help give me the strength to be honest with our dad and cushion the blow a smidgen for him.

"Are you okay?" My sister leaned between the seats and asked. I nodded into Landon's chest. "Don't worry, I'm sure they're both going to be fine. I'm glad she finally told you. I've been bursting all day with excitement." She leaned over and put her hand on Landon's arm.

I shot my head up with an astonished look on my face hoping to make her shut up. Unfortunately, she had turned towards our dad. "If you take Washington, it will be faster." She told him.

"I know, my dear. I have been driving a little longer than you have." I could hear the nervousness in his voice.

"Sorry," Jocelyn apologized in a low voice.

"What did your sister mean? Is there something you need to tell me?" Landon leaned in close and whispered.

I closed my eyes and took a deep breath. This was not going at all how I envisioned it.

What the hell was I thinking? Appendicitis would have been so much easier.

I couldn't find the words to respond with. I could feel every muscle in Landon's body tense up as the full weight of Jocelyn's words fell upon him.

"You can't be." He muttered more to himself than to me. "We've been so careful."

"Accidents happen." My dad responded from the driver's seat. I wasn't even aware he could hear us.

I looked up at Landon's face. He had closed his eyes and rested his head back against the seat. He looked exhausted. And I knew he was. Our schedule: our lives as med students were so demanding we barely found the time to make love, let alone get pregnant.

"Dad?" I reached up and touched him on the shoulder. "Head to the house, please."

"What?" He slightly turned his head towards me. "Wait. No. We're going to have you checked out. I need to know that my grandchild and you are all right."

"Dad, I'm fine. Please just head to the house, and I'll explain."

"No. We're going to the hospital." He turned the corner sharply, and my stomach lurched. My dinner did a flip flop in my stomach and suddenly decided it wanted to be set free.

"Oh my God! Pull-over!" I reached for the door handle, pushing my weight against it, trying to open it before my dad stopped.

I hung out the open doorway, retching into the street. It seemed everything I'd consumed in the several hours came back up all at once. I felt horrible. Landon pulled my hair away from my face and gently rubbed my back. When my stomach was empty, a wave of drive heaves took hold of me until my throat was raw, and tears poured down my face.

"Here." Jocelyn handed me a water bottle. I rinsed my mouth out and spit into the street.

"Thanks." I gave her a weak smile sitting back against the seat again. "Can we please just go home?"

"I think we should get you checked." My dad looked worried.

I glanced over at Landon, whose face had paled considerably. Seeing me get sick somehow must have made it real to him more so than my sister's slip up. I heard him inhaling loudly as he closed his eyes and exhaled. I knew this was his way of struggling to keep his mouth shut. I couldn't imagine what was going on in his head, but I was positive I was going to find out as soon as we were alone.

"I'm fine, Daddy. Really. Please just head to the house." I begged.

"Fine, but I still think you should be checked." He pulled back onto the road and headed towards the house.

I felt drained and reluctantly opened my eyes as we pulled into the driveway. My dad parked in the garage and helped me into the house. I felt so bad I didn't object. Landon hung back a little, looking like someone had sucker-punched him in the face. I guess in a way, I had.

"You need to go upstairs and go right to bed. I need you to feel better tomorrow so you can stand up with us." He said as he walked me into the kitchen.

"About that, Dad. We need to talk." I told him.

"About what?" He started walking me towards the stairs and stopped.

"Can we sit down in the family room? There's something you need to know."

"Well, it can't be any bigger than the bomb you just dropped on me about the baby, so sure." He tried to smile, but I could still see the worry that haunted his eyes.

I couldn't respond.

Thankfully, Jocelyn and Landon followed us into the family room. I sat down on the couch, and my sister handed me a glass of ginger ale to ease my upset stomach.

"Here. Hopefully, it will make you feel better." She offered me a smile and sat down on the love seat.

Landon took a seat beside me, and my dad plopped down in his recliner. He leaned forward a bit and rested his elbows on his knees.

"So, when are you due?" He inquired.

"Dad, that's not what I want to talk to you about." I began. "It's something else."

"Okay, but first. I want to know when exactly you two were planning on telling me the great news. Was it going to be at the reception tomorrow?" Dad grinned from ear to ear. "How far along are you?"

"Dad?" Sometimes I wondered how he ever got anything done at work.

"Just tell me …" He wouldn't let it drop.

"Seriously, Dad!" I raised my voice ever so slightly.

"What? I'm just excited." He continued grinning like a fool. "All right, fine." He sat back in his chair and looked at me. "What is so important that you had to alter the entire evening? You realize that I'm going to catch hell for leaving the rehearsal dinner."

"No, you won't." I said numbly and leaned forward a bit. "I've got something to tell you, but I don't know how too." I struggled.

"You can tell me anything, you know that. Did you and Landon elope or something?" He leaned forward a bit, and Landon straightened in his spot.

"No." My boyfriend immediately responded. "We'd never do that."

"Well, after this one did it." He nodded over in Jocelyn's direction. "Nothing would ever surprise me."

"My mother would kill me." Landon said flatly.

"I know the feeling." Jocelyn said with a giggle.

"What did you expect us to do? Throw you a reception party?" Our dad looked over at Jocelyn with raised eyebrows.

I knew everyone had had several drinks this evening but, this was ridiculous!

"Dad?" I tried again. My head was pounding at this point, and I was feeling nauseated all over again.

"Sorry," He turned back toward me. "What were you saying?"

"You need to know what I overheard tonight." I began slowly.

"Okay."

I continued giving him a detailed account of the conversation I'd heard between Donnie and Patsy. With each word, my father's face became a little sullen, but Jocelyn's got red. She was fuming by the time I'd finished, and my dad wiped a single tear off his cheek. He sat back in his chair and never uttered a word.

"That bitch!" Jocelyn exclaimed.

"Jocelyn." I shook my head slowly at her. She, in turn, rolled her eyes back at me.

Several awkward long minutes passed as the four of us sat there in silence. I knew my father was absorbing it all and considering his options. He was not the type of man who took humiliation well, but he always respected someone who was honest and straight forward with him.

I kept waiting for him to tell me that I'd misunderstood their conversation or perhaps misinterpreted it, but he never did. It was almost as if he had been expecting something like this to happen, and it broke my heart to be the one to break the news.

"Now, are you going to tell me when you're due?" He finally broke the tension that had fallen over the room.

"Around Valentine's Day." I finally answered him. I also noticed Landon's head shot around and stared at me.

"Wonderful. It will give us something to celebrate. I believe I'll be coming to Boston because I could never miss my first grandchild's arrival." He smiled over at me. "I'm very happy for you both."

"Thanks, Daddy." I got up and walked over to him. I leaned down and hugged him tightly. "I appreciate that."

"Should I even ask if you're going to get married?" His eyes drifted from me to Landon as I stood up.

"We'll see." Was all I could come up with.

The front door opened, and there was an obvious intake of breath from everyone in the room. Jackson and his parents walked in, looking confused.

"Good evening," Robert walked over and shook my dad's hand as he got to his feet. "We went by the rehearsal dinner, and they said there was an emergency, and you had taken your daughter to the hospital. Then Jocelyn texted Jackson and said to come here. Is everything all right?"

Jackson sat down beside Jocelyn with the same confused look on his face as his parents. I saw him lean over and whisper something to my sister but just shook her head.

"I'm afraid there's been a snag in our wedding plans." My dad shifted his weight uncomfortably.

"I am sorry to hear that." Emily stepped forward and gave my dad a hug. "What can we do to help?"

"Thank you, but no. This is something I must take care of myself." My dad tried to keep his calm demeanor.

We heard the front door slam loudly and footsteps in the hall. Liang, Ethan, Patsy, and Donnie all filed into the room, setting their things down, acting like nothing in the world could possibly be wrong. I looked over at my dad, still standing there next to Jackson's parents, and saw him take another deep breath.

"Sidney, are you okay? Ethan told me they took you to the hospital." Patsy came over with a mask of concern on her face and placed her hand on my arm.

"No, I'm fine." I said coldly and rejoined Landon on the couch.

"Okay," she turned towards Ethan. "But you said…" her voice trailed off as she scanned the room, trying to figure out what was amidst. "What's going on, Shane?"

She narrowed her focus to my dad while my brother and Liang sat down on the couch on the other side of me. Donnie stood there, awkwardly next to his mother.

"Perhaps I should be the one to ask you that?" My dad said in a rough tone. "I would like to talk to you in my study."

"Why? There's nothing we need hide from the children, darling." Her voice turned sweet, and she reached out for my father. But he took a step back.

"All right. We can certainly discuss it here in front of them if that's what you want." My dad sighed heavily. "Would you care to explain to me the conversation you had with Donnie in the hallway during our rehearsal dinner?"

Patsy managed to keep her cool exterior, but Donnie's face was a dead giveaway, and we all knew it.

"What's going on?" Ethan leaned over a smidgen and whispered to me.

"Hush." I flashed him a dirty look. "Perhaps we should all get something to drink in the kitchen." I suggested and started to stand.

"Sit down." My dad said firmly.

I slowly sat back down and took Landon's hand. The room was deadly silent.

"Are you going to answer me?" He stood facing Pasty.

"I don't know what you're referring to." Patsy said as innocently as she could manage.

"Are you going to stand there and tell me that you said nothing about after tomorrow you would have no financial worries ever again? You never told your son that by this time tomorrow you will be set for the rest of your life because even if we divorce, you're entitled to half of everything?" He asked with such a calm demeanor that even I was nervous.

"I believe you misunderstood what I meant. I would never ..." Patsy took a step closer to my father, but once again, he took a step back.

"Would never what? Use me for my money? Take advantage of someone for what they can give you like status, security, a real home?" He questioned.

"Darling ..." Patsy attempted, but my dad cut her off.

"Don't. Just don't." He took another deep breath. "You realize that when I heard what you said tonight, it was the final straw. I've kept my mouth shut because I truly wanted to believe that you were with me because you genuinely love me. All those little things you tried to hide from me — I already know about them. I know how far in debt you are. I know you're barely getting by, and you've borrowed more money than you'll ever earn. I even know that Donnie was expelled from college for heroin and has charges pending. I also know that you're being sued because he had an accident while driving without a license and that he also lost his license for being caught not once, but twice for driving while intoxicated and with drugs on him."

The rest of us sat there with our mouths hanging open. Obviously, this was all news to us.

"Did you really believe I would never find out?" My dad asked.

"I never ..." Patsy failed to find the right words to dig herself out. "Shane?"

"Please, get your things," he turned towards Donnie, "both of you, and get out." My father said calmly.

"The wedding? People are coming." Patsy looked flustered. "Shane, don't do this."

"I didn't. You did." He sighed heavily again. "Please, just get out of my home."

"I have to pack." She stammered.

"Fine. There are plenty of people to help you both." My dad informed her.

"I will not have them touching my things." I could tell Patsy was on the verge of rage and tears from the humiliation.

"Well, you are certainly not roaming about in my home without an escort. I cannot trust you. You've both proven that. So, either one of them stays with each of you while you gather your belongings, or I can get you both a police escort. Your choice." I always knew my dad was a no-nonsense, kind of man, but I hadn't even expected this.

"I can't believe you're doing this to me." Tears rolled slowly down her cheeks.

"As I said, this is on you." He reiterated.

"But the wedding? Everyone is going to be expecting us." She pleaded.

"I will take care of canceling everything. After all, I was paying for it all." The irritation was now dripping from his voice.

"Shane, please. Can't we discuss this? I love you."

"Don't embarrass me, or yourself, any further. Just get your things and go." But Patsy just stood there. "Now or I will have the police escort you." he said calmly.

Patsy and Donnie walked slowly towards the stairs. She put her arm around her son's shoulders, but I didn't hear them say anything. "Ethan. Jocelyn. Please accompany them." My siblings rose and wordlessly followed them upstairs as my dad collapsed back into his recliner.

"Can I get you anything?" I approached him gently. He looked so sad and defeated.

"A beer would be great." He offered me a weak smile.

"Robert? Emily? Would you like anything?" I offered.

"No, thank you. I believe we will be turning in for the evening." Emily smiled sweetly yet uncomfortably.

"I'm sorry about the drama." My dad said to them.

"Think nothing of it. Please let us know if you need anything." Robert offered.

"I'm so sorry, Shane." Emily leaned over and hugged my dad.

"Thank you." My dad hugged her back. I knew he thought very highly of Robert and Emily.

"Goodnight, everyone." Emily smiled sweetly and took her husband's arm.

I watched them head towards the foyer to gather their luggage and head upstairs to the guest room. I couldn't help but hope that someday Landon and I would have a relationship that strongly resembled theirs. I knew they weren't perfect, but they were perfect for each other.

I hurried off to the kitchen with Landon right behind me. "We need to talk." He grabbed my sleeve. "Now."

"Okay." I swallowed hard and grabbed a beer out of the fridge. "Let me give this to him." I shook off his hold and returned to the family room. I handed my dad the beer, wishing I could have one myself, and I didn't even like beer. "Can I get you anything else?"

"No, baby. Thanks. I'm good." He barely nodded at me.

Jackson and Liang followed me back into the kitchen to give my dad a little bit of privacy. Jackson got out some glasses and poured him and Liang some wine. He offered Landon and me a glass, but I shook my head as Landon drug me out into the sunporch closing the door behind us.

"Are you?" Landon stood there, facing me with a hand on his hip.

"Landon ..." But words failed me.

This was not how this was supposed to go. I didn't want to tell him like this. In fact, I never wanted to tell him.

"Sid, I'm serious. Are you pregnant?" He looked on the verge of tears.

"I took a test this morning." I slumped down on the oversized cushioned wicker chair.

"And?" He pushed.

"First test I've failed since junior high."

"Maybe it's a false positive. We need to get a blood test done." He took a seat beside me.

"Three? Three false positives? You know how unlikely that is?" I looked over at him sadly.

"Have you thought much about what you want to do?" His words hit me like a ton of bricks. Perhaps I was seriously wrong about him. I suddenly felt all alone.

"Don't worry about it." I stood up. "It's not your problem." I walked back into the house, expecting him to surely follow directly behind me.

But he didn't.

"Are you okay?" Jackson asked as I passed through the kitchen. I nodded and hurried up the stairs. I knew that if I said anything, the flood gates would open, and tears would pour down my cheeks.

Damn hormones!

I brushed my teeth and ran a brush roughly through my hair. I stripped down into my panties and put on a tank top before climbing into bed. I curled up with an extra pillow listening to all the noise below me. Patsy and Donnie were gathering their belongings and not very quietly either. But the only sounds I wanted to hear were Landon's footsteps climbing the old stairs to my third-floor hideaway.

I don't know how much time passed while I laid there waiting patiently for him to appear. I needed him to tell me he loved me. I needed him to take me in his arms and tell me that no matter what, he was going to be beside me. I needed him now more than I ever had. I was scared silly, trying to imagine how I was going to balance my demanding schedule, workload, studies, and a baby. Doing it alone was terrifying.

6

SATURDAY, JULY 23, 1859

OPENED MY EYES and saw my beautiful husband lying beside me. Keifer was lying on his side, snoring peacefully with his arm over me and his hand resting on my hip. He had a slight smile across his lips. I smiled at him and wondered what he was dreaming about.

Most likely, it was the son he hoped I was carrying. He wanted a boy so badly. He talked about it all the time; long before I was pregnant. He wanted a son to take fishing, to teach, to play with, to someday pass along his medical practice.

I understood that. I was my father's only daughter. I knew he loved me in his own way, but I was nothing compared to the three sons he had with his second wife after my mother had passed away during my birth.

He and his new family had moved to Chicago shortly after his third son, Nicholas was born, and I rarely heard from them. It was for the best. He was happy with his new family, and I wanted to stay with my grandparents.

They had raised me after my mother passed, and when my father, Walter, married Bethany when I was seven, I couldn't imagine living with his new wife. Even then, I knew she didn't want me. I was constantly told how much I resembled my mother, and I knew she had a hard time looking at me because I reminded her that she was not the love of my father's life. My mother was.

Still, I missed seeing my little brothers. I felt like I didn't know them at all. My family was no more than a Christmas or birthday card dropped in the mail whenever my father remembered he had a daughter, which wasn't very often. There were periods throughout my life where I heard nothing but silence from the man who fathered me.

Perhaps, I was nothing more than a painful reminder of what he'd lost. Perhaps it hurt his heart, as my grandmother told me several times during periods of silence, to love me for fear that he would lose me too.

And that fear that was buried deep within me was now brought to the surface as I placed my hand over my abdomen and thought about the child I was carrying. I feared I may be fated to the same painful death as my mother when she brought me into this world.

I was terrified of giving birth.

I slipped into my petty coats and soft blue gown with white lace about the bodice and cuffs. I laced up the ribbons on my satin slippers and sat down at my vanity table. With long strokes, I brushed out my thick, wavy blond locks before gathering them up in a tight bun at the nape of my neck.

Keifer was still snoring peacefully as I tiptoed out of our room and headed quietly downstairs.

My grandmother was already seated at the table, sipping her morning coffee, and browsing through the morning paper.

"Good morning, darling." She looked up and smiled as I approached. "Did you sleep well?"

"Yes, grandmother. I did." I poured myself a mug of coffee and sat down in the chair beside her. "Did you rest well? How are you feeling?"

"Good." She reached over and patted my hand lovingly. "Did you talk to your husband last evening."

"Yes. And he was delighted." I giggled. "I do not believe I have ever seen him so excited. One would think he was the first man to ever impregnate his wife."

"Yes. Men always get excited. But their job is done, and ours is just beginning." My grandmother smirked.

"What is just beginning?" Keifer entered the dining room, dressed in black trousers and a white blouse.

"Good morning, sweetheart. Did I wake you?" I got up and placed a mug in front of him and poured him some coffee.

"No. No. Tis quite all right. I needed to get up." He smiled. "How are you feeling?"

"Wonderful." I leaned down and kissed his cheek.

"Oh, grandmother. Why are you reading the paper again? You know you should not trouble yourself with political things." Keifer playfully chastised her as he did most mornings.

"It is my sinful indulgence. Nathan tolerated my curiosity; you may as well too." She dearly enjoyed toying with him.

"Women have no business reading the newspaper. You have scores of books in the library. I would be more than happy to select one for you." My husband rolled his eyes at me as I took my seat.

"Select one for yourself. I am quite happy with the reading material in front of me."

"Suit yourself." Keifer added a second heaping teaspoon of sugar to his coffee.

"What are your plans for today?" I attempted to change the subject.

"I need to stop at the Tarrow's farm and check on how they are doing. Would you care to join me?" He offered.

"I would love too."

"Good morning, Doctor, Mistress, Mistress." Naomi entered the dining room carrying a tray of toast, fried eyes, and slabs of ham steak.

"Good morning, Naomi. Everything smells wonderful." Keifer beamed, but as the aroma hit my nose, my stomach flipped, and a wave of nausea gripped ahold of me.

"Are you all right, dear?" My grandmother reached over, placing her hand on mine. "You look green."

"Excuse me." I jumped from my chair and rushed to the back door.

I barely made it off the steps when my stomach turned inside out. Keifer followed me and rubbed my back gently. When I straightened up, he handed me a towel.

"Morning sickness is perfectly normal."

"I know." I wiped off my mouth and sat down on the steps. "It's simply not very enjoyable."

"It should subside by your second trimester." He said, taking a seat beside me.

"Does every woman experience this?"

"Most, but not all. It varies." My husband put his arm around me. "As you know, no two women are alike in their reproductive systems, so their bodies do not react the same to the hormone changes caused by pregnancy."

"I see." I rested my head against his shoulder.

"You seem worried, my darling. Is everything all right." I nodded.

We sat there in silence, gazing over the south fields. The sun was ascending over the silhouette of the tree line, shining brightly over the emerald grounds. The leaves on the old oaks and maples danced in the slight breeze in harmony with the morning bird's sweet song. There was smoke rising from the outbuildings where the workers resided, telling me they were enjoying breakfast as well.

"You are concerned about childbirth." It wasn't a question, but an obvious statement.

"Yes." I whispered.

"I can assure you that every woman is different, and simply because your mother was ill-fated in childbirth does not mean you will be as well." Keifer lightly kissed my forehead.

"I know, but I cannot help but fear it." I looked up at the sky, trying to detour the tears welling up in my eyes. "I'm sorry. I cannot help it. I want to be here with you and see our child grow up. I would love to someday have a large family and fill this house with their laughter. And I want to grow old with you." I brushed the tears off my cheeks and sighed heavily leaning on my husband's shoulder. "I want to spend our old age rocking on the porch covered in grandchildren."

"And so, you shall, my love." He assured me.

"I pray so." I looked up into his loving eyes.

"As do I."

"I am sorry, darling. But I really must be going. I need to see everyone before I pick up my sister at the train station at one." Keifer gave me a gentle squeeze.

"Eugenia has impeccable timing." I muttered without looking at him.

"I know. But she's lonely staying with Margaret. And my sister has been a saint for dealing with our younger sister. Margaret and Thad deserve a break." He reasoned.

"I understand, but you have other siblings she can stay with." I pointed out.

"You don't like Eugenia?" A small smile spread across his lips.

"Darling," I carefully selected my words. "It's not that I do not like her. It is just, well," I took a deep breath. "She can be a bit challenging."

"I know she can be critical and cynical at times." He raised his eyebrows at me. "Hopefully, she won't stay that long." He squeezed me gently.

"Let's hope." I muttered loud enough for him to hear me. "I love you." I quickly said and kissed him on the cheek.

"I love you too, darling." He chuckled and shook his head.

He held out his hand, helping me to my feet. We walked back in through the kitchen to his study. He picked up his medical bag and stuffed some papers into it.

"I should be home around two if her train is on time." He kissed me briefly.

"Please be careful." I followed him to the front door.

"I will. I promise."

I watched his carriage disappear behind the trees down our long driveway. I stood on the porch enjoying the cool breeze flowing through the trees. The green lawn stretched out before me. I leaned against the railing and breathed in the fresh air.

"Is Eugenia still coming in today?" My grandmother walked up beside me.

"Unfortunately." I turned towards her. "Keep your fingers crossed her train derails." I rolled my eyes.

"Let's hope." She held up her hands with her fingers crossed.

"I don't know if I have the strength for this."

"Of course, you do. You love your husband, and sometimes that means enduring the hurricane." She giggled and walked back into the house.

"Gee, thanks." I called after her.

Keifer and Eugenia arrived shortly before four in the afternoon. Her train had arrived over an hour late, and she was not in the most pleasant of moods when her brother commented that he had been waiting in the hot afternoon sun. They were still arguing as Keifer stopped the carriage in front of the house. My grandmother and I were sitting on the front porch reading when they arrived.

The afternoon was lovely up until that point. Keifer helped Eugenia out of the carriage, and she abruptly shook off his hand once both of her feet were steadily on the ground. My husband took a visible deep breath and retrieved her trunk. He set it on the ground where Preston, who took care of the horses and handiwork around the house, picked it up, looking to Keifer for instructions.

"Please put Ms. Eugenia's trunk in the east room." He told him.

"I prefer the north room. I don't like the morning sun blazing in on me." Eugenia quipped.

"As you wish." Keifer grunted through gritted teeth. Preston nodded and carried it into the house. Naomi held the front door open for him while balancing a tray of lemonade.

"How was your trip?" I asked my sister-in-law as she ascended my front steps.

"Hot and miserable." She huffed up the steps under her enormous weight. "We were late to leave and late to arrive. I do not know why I decided to travel this time of year. I thought it would be cooler up here than Savannah, but it is just has stifling up here." She paused on the porch and surveyed my grandmother and me before she took one of the glasses of lemonade from Naomi without thanks.

"I'm sorry, Eugenia." I smiled sweetly.

"It does not cool off for another month, I'm afraid." My grandmother informed her.

"Well, it will be welcome when it does." Eugenia gulped down her drink and placed the empty glass back upon the tray. "I am going to lay down for a while. Please let me know when supper is ready." She disappeared into the house without another word.

"She is delightful." I smiled at my husband.

"You did not have to spend the last hour with her listening to every ailment preconceived by mankind." Keifer sat down in the rocking chair next to mine. Naomi handed him a fresh drink. He smiled at her. "Thank you." My grandmother and I helped ourselves as well.

"How long does she intend to stay?" My grandmother inquired.

"She mentioned Christmas." Keifer muttered, rolling his eyes.

"Christmas? That's five months away." I declared.

"I know." He took a deep breath and let it out slowly. "Whatever you do, do not mention the baby. She will insist on staying until it is born, and I do not have the patience for that."

"What am I supposed to do?" I asked.

"I am sure you can think of something." He closed his eyes and leaned his head back.

"Darling. I was hoping to prepare the nursery. I would also like to share our good news with our friends." I explained.

"Keifer, do you really believe it is fair to your wife, in her current condition, to subject her to Eugenia's pleasantries, especially after how long you both have been waiting for a child?" My grandmother asked sweetly.

I almost snorted in my drink, knowing full well what my grandmother was thinking and doing. I loved her for it. I wish I had said it first. The very idea of having Eugenia at my home for the next several months made my morning sickness seem like a picnic.

Keifer opened his eyes and shifted in his seat. I could see him struggling to maintain his composure. The time with his sister and the heat were wearing on him.

"I realize that, Marissa. And no, I do not want her pleasantries to affect my wife or our child." He stated roughly.

"Sweetheart. It's simply that she can be a lot to take." I tried to explain.

"What would you like me to do? You know how she is." He looked exhausted.

"I know." I glanced over at my grandmother, who rolled her eyes and shook her head slowly.

"I need to do some research in my study. Please tell me when supper is ready." Keifer slowly got up and disappeared into the house.

"I don't know if I can be a gracious hostess." I turned towards my grandmother. "I cannot stand that woman. She is despicable in every possible way."

"I wonder how a conversation informing her as much would transpire. Maybe she would change her behavior."

"She would immediately go on the defensive and attack." I suspected.

"Most likely." My grandmother agreed.

"I dreaded this." I said flatly.

"What are you going to do?"

"As soon as she shows her true colors, I am going to say something to her, and if she does not like it, I will show her the door. And frankly, I could care less how upset the rest of Keifer's family gets with me over it." I smiled coyly.

"I am proud of you." My grandmother patted my leg. "But I must ask you for a small favor."

"Of course."

"Please make sure I am present when you do it." She smiled, and I laughed.

"I promise I will do my best."

After supper, Keifer, my grandmother, and I sat out on the front porch to enjoy the beautiful evening. The skies were clear and littered with stars. The humidity remained low and the light breeze floating across the fields enhanced the peaceful ambiance. Mr. Edmund Bennett, our nearest neighbor, and the owner of our small town's only bank, galloped up on his beautiful 2-year-old colt. He was a stout man with broad shoulders and long silver hair that rested just below his shoulders. He kept it tied back with a leather thong. His sideburns and mustache were always kept neatly trimmed.

Mr. Bennett owned about twenty acres adjacent to ours. He wasn't much of a farmer but claimed the work he did on his small farm was good for his health after being inside the bank for such long hours.

He was a handsome man with three grown sons. They had all gone to universities and were successful businessmen in their own right. Mr. Bennett's wife had passed away two winters ago of pneumonia, and I believed the only reason for his frequent visits was to spend time with my grandmother.

The two were not far apart in age. They were very cute and agreeable with one another. I knew my grandmother had never gotten over my grandfather's passing, but I could not help but hope she would find love and happiness again.

"Good evening, Doc." He dismounted his handsome colt and shook hands with Keifer. "Evening Marissa, Sidney." He nodded in our direction. "Wonderful weather we're having tonight. So, I thought I'd take a bit of a stroll." He sat down on one of the porch rockers.

"Would you care for some coffee?" I offered.

"That would be appreciated." He smiled broadly and relaxed back into his chair.

I went back into the house, followed closely by my grandmother. She claimed his interest in her annoyed her, but somehow, I believed she was utterly enchanted by him.

"I do not understand why he finds it necessary to stop by here every night." She grumbled along the way.

"Oh, grandmother. You're exaggerating. He does not stop by every evening." I rolled my eyes with a slight grin as we entered the kitchen.

"Almost." She argued.

"This is the third evening this week. I am sure he gets lonely in that house all by himself." I pointed out.

"Even so." She pretended to huff. "Tell him to get a dog if he wants company."

"That is not a very Christian way to behave." I teased.

"Oh, hush." Her eyes narrowed.

"He's sweet and has a crush. Enjoy it." I flashed her a quick smile over my shoulder as I set the tray with mugs, sugar, and the coffee pot.

"I am too old for such nonsense." My grandmother said abruptly.

"Oh, please. You are in your mid-sixties. Hardly what is considered old." I informed her.

"Perhaps not in *other places*, but *here* . . ." She replied in a low voice.

"Not *here* either."

"I am getting ready to be a great-grandmother." She raised her eyebrows at me but still followed me out to the front porch to join the gentlemen.

"I could not believe my own ears." Mr. Bennett was saying when walked back out on the porch and I placed the tray on the side table.

"What did you hear?" I asked, handing him a mug of fresh coffee with three sugars; just the way he liked it.

"Thank you kindly." He took a sip. "Perfect as always." He smiled. "I was just telling your husband about the abolitionist protesters in Boston that I encountered yesterday. They were making quite a spectacle of themselves."

"I see." I sat down on the swing beside my grandmother with my own mug.

"We have been seeing more and more of it not only in Boston but other cities as well. I was just reading an article on it." Keifer added.

"I was astonished when I saw multiple articles about the fights taking place in Washington and by those who are supposed to represent us." Mr. Bennett shook his head. "I heard Mr. Morgan say last week that his cousin, Senator Wilson, is now carrying a revolver and a bowie knife with him in the capital. He said he is not looking for trouble, but will defend himself, if necessary, against these hot-headed Southerners — no offense, Doc." Keifer shook his head not taking any offense to the words. "If they are not careful, they are going to split this country in two — more so than it already is." Mr. Bennett stated.

I choked on the coffee I swallowed and coughed at his words. My grandmother patted me several times on my back as I cleared my throat.

"Are you all right, dear?" Keifer sat a bit forward in his chair.

"Yes. I apologize. My coffee did not agree with me." I glanced over at my grandmother, who smiled dimly at me.

"Good evening." Eugenia said in her thick southern accent, walking out onto the porch.

"Mr. Edmund Bennett, I would like to introduce my sister, Eugenia. She is visiting with us from Savannah for a while." Keifer nodded towards his sister as Mr. Bennett stood up and shook her hand lightly.

"It is a pleasure, Ms. Marshall." Mr. Bennett smiled.

"Mine as well." Eugenia took a seat on the rocking chair beside her brother.

"How long are you visiting?" Mr. Bennett inquired.

"For a bit. I have not seen my brother in quite some time." She smiled at my husband, making me nauseated. "I heard you mention the hateful abolitionist protesters."

"Yes. They were stirring up people today in Boston." Mr. Bennett remarked.

"There was a crowd of them at the train station this afternoon." She folded her hands in her lap, but I could see the tension in her posture. "They seem to associate every Southerner with that wretched book, *Uncle Tom's Cabin*." Her voice took on a stern tone that everyone picked up on.

"I believe they are a nuisance." Keifer agreed. "Mr. Bennett, how are your crops handling this dry spell?" His attempt to shift the subject was obvious.

"We have been irrigating from the riverbeds. But a good soaking rain would be a blessing." Mr. Bennett seemed relieved to change the subject. "And how are Mrs. Tarrow and the new baby?"

"Both strong and healthy." Keifer smiled.

"Mr. Bennett, do you agree with these abolitionists?" Eugenia interrupted her brother, narrowing her eyes in Mr. Bennett's direction.

"Well, I … um." He began, but Keifer interceded.

"Eugenia, we prefer not to discuss politics." His tone told her to shut up, but she did not pertain the grace God gave her to take subtle hints.

"Nonsense. I am curious about the northern point of view." She smiled coyly at her brother.

"Sister, as I said, we do not discuss politics." Keifer's voice became sterner.

"Hush now brother, I am well aware of how you sympathize with these Northerners determined to destroy our way of life." Her voice took on the same tone as her brother's.

"Excuse me," Mr. Bennett seemed stunned by the accusation.

"You are a Northerner, are you not, Mr. Bennett?" Eugenia raised an eyebrow at him.

"Yes. Born and raised in Massachusetts." he said proudly.

"And what is your position?" My sister-in-law edged to the end of her seat leaning forward.

"Position?"

"Politically."

"Eugenia," Keifer flashed her a stern look which she promptly waved off with her fat stubby hand.

"Politically. I believe and support the great state of Massachusetts." It was obvious to everyone, but Eugenia, that Mr. Bennett was not willing to elaborate.

"So, you believe slavery is wrong and inhuman. You believe we beat and mistreat our slaves. You feel that slaves should have the same freedom and rights as a white American citizen." Eugenia went off on her tangent without actually asking any questions.

"Yes. I believe that slavery is wrong." Mr. Bennett said proudly, but politely. "I believe that the system is inhuman and that the tribes in Africa were wrong in kidnapping these people and selling them to profiteers who shipped them to a foreign continent where they do not know the language or have the ability to assimilate. I believe it is wrong to hold another person in bondage because of the color of their skin."

"And you welcome this man into your home, offer him coffee," Eugenia waved her hand at the mug Mr. Bennett was holding. "And allow him to insult your heritage?" she huffed. "Brother, I am ashamed of you."

My grandmother and I had learned to keep silent when such talk began. We knew what laid upon the horizon and how bad it was going to be. Not in actual experience, but we had both studied the American Civil War at length in our *other* times.

The fuse had been lit, and while it was still only smoldering, it was lit, nonetheless. In less than two years, the Southern states would declare their independence, and the worst war in American history would be upon us.

"Eugenia, you are right. This is my home and Mr. Bennett did not insult me or my heritage. I happen to agree with him, and he is always welcome in our home." Keifer set his mug on the table and turned towards his sister. "And if you have a problem with that, you can leave. But while you are here, you will kindly keep your political opinions to yourself." I couldn't stop smiling watching Eugenia's face pucker up in defiance.

Thankfully, Eugenia finally got the hint and shut her mouth. I let out a small sigh of relief, and Mr. Bennett shifted uncomfortably in his chair. I got the impression that he would not be visiting as often if Eugenia was staying with us.

I placed my hand protectively over my abdomen, scared at what this war would do to my young family. I knew Keifer would serve. He believed strongly in honor, duty, and country. And while he would not be on the front lines, he would serve as a military surgeon and be responsible for cleaning up and mending the battered and broken bodies of young men.

I feared the mental toll it would take on him and the reality that he would most likely spend the rest of his life struggling with post-traumatic stress disorder from it — just as many first responders do. I knew they carried the horrific images with them for the rest of their lives — those they tried to but couldn't save.

I also knew my brothers would be fighting in the Union army. Patrick, the oldest of my younger brothers, was a physician just like Keifer and would serve as a surgeon also. But Monte and Nicholas were not trained physicians and, therefore, would be on the front lines in the thick of the battles.

And although my sister in my *other* time, Jocelyn, has assured me repeatedly that all four of the men I love survive the war, I could not help but fear what it would do to them. Concepts such as post-traumatic stress disorder, combat stress, moral injury, and traumatic brain injury were not known on this plane, but still very much existed and were about to be experienced by countless soldiers.

The men droned on for a couple hours after Eugenia, bored and frustrated with the conversation, excused herself and retired. They began speculating as to what was to come if the Southern states declared their independence. Still, like most Northerners, they agreed that the Southern states had been threatening disunion for several decades without doing anything about it. They agreed it was simply nothing more than Southern posturing for power and chalked it up to another episode of the boy who cried wolf.

They couldn't have been more wrong — this time.

My grandmother and I participated appropriately but let the men ramble on. They each had strong feelings against war but also felt that slavery should not be allowed to spread into the new states or territories. It was a conversation I'd heard dozens of times and one that always ended with the same result; if the Southern states should leave the Union, then war was inevitable.

7

LANDON NEVER CAME upstairs. I woke up in the morning to find the pillow beside me empty. The sun was fighting its way through the small cracks in my blinds, arousing me from a deep, dreamless sleep. I rolled over and propped myself up on my elbow only to be greeted with a wave of nausea that swept over me like a tidal wave.

I leapt out of bed and ran to the bathroom to get sick. I couldn't imagine how; there was nothing left after last night's battle. But the dry heaves soon kicked in, and I felt horrible. I knelt beside the toilet and rested my head against the side of the cold porcelain. I couldn't fathom going through this for several more months or even another week. A soft knock on the door interrupted my misery.

"Sidney?" Jocelyn's voice echoed through the door. "Are you okay?"

"No."

"Can I come in?" she asked. "I brought you some saltines and peppermint tea."

"Sure." My sister opened the door and set the tray down on the vanity. "Thanks." I took the cup of tea from her and took a sip.

"Morning sickness?" I nodded.

"I hate this." I muttered between sips. "How is dad doing?"

"I don't think he went to bed last night. He gave me a list of guests: Emily, Liang, and I are going to call them all to tell them the weddings been canceled." She shrugged.

"Ugh."

"I know." She sat down on the edge of the tub. "I'm not looking forward to it, but I don't want him to worry about that of all things."

"What about the caterer or the hall?"

"I've got their numbers too. He gave me everything to handle for him." She shrugged and half-smiled. "Is there anything I can get you before I go?"

"No. But thank you." I smiled at her appreciatively.

"Okay, well, just text me if you do. I'll be in Dad's study for a couple hours making calls." She stood up and walked over to the door. "Holler if you need me."

"Oh, Jocelyn. Wait a sec." She paused just outside my bathroom door and turned back towards me. "Have you seen Landon this morning?"

"No. Not yet." Jocelyn paused, "I'm guessing he's not taking it well?"

"Hardly. From the way he phrased things last night, it looks like I may very well be on my own in this."

"You're kidding?" She walked back into the bathroom. "I'm so sorry, Sid. I never would have thought Landon would have reacted this way." She looked puzzled for a moment.

"What's wrong?" I questioned.

"Oh, it's nothing." She immediately wiped the expression off her face. "I'm sure everything will work out fine." She tried to reassure me.

"I hope so." I said although I had my serious doubts.

"Are you sure there's nothing I can get you?" She asked again.

"No. I'll be fine. Thanks for the tea and crackers."

I crawled back into bed, thankful my sister, Emily, and Liang were handling the phone calls. I stared at my phone, willing Landon to call me. I knew he knew no one in Chicago outside my immediate family, yet he'd managed to stay out all night. I was torn between grave concern and being furious.

I hastily brushed my teeth and splashed some cold water on my face. I pulled my unbrushed hair up into a messy bun and smirked at the reflection staring back at me. I took a deep breath and tried my best to muster every ounce of deep inner strength I processed before heading downstairs.

"You can do this." I whispered, sighing heavily.

Out of habit, I immediately headed for the coffee maker. I poured an oversized mug and went in search of my dad. He was sitting at his desk, staring at the pile of papers in front of him. I could tell by the look on his face he didn't see anything before him.

"How are you?" I sat down in the seat across from his desk.

"You really need to switch to decaf." His blurry eyes glanced up at me.

"I know. I will." I curled my feet beneath me.

"Has Landon returned?"

"No. Not yet." I fumbled with my words and took a sip of the morning brew. "I can't imagine where he is. He doesn't know anyone in Chicago."

"I'm sure he's probably held up somewhere thinking of how he's going to make it up to you for being an ass." My dad grinned. "We are good at that, you know."

"Being an ass?" I smirked.

"No, smartass. Making up for behaving like idiots." He chuckled softly, but the sound of it was hollow.

"We'll see." I said in a low voice more to myself than my dad.

❧

By late afternoon, I found Jocelyn and Liang, along with Ethan lounging in the family room. They looked exhausted. I felt bad that I hadn't helped with any of the wedding cancelations. I knew they all felt drained and had tap-danced around dozens of questions from family, friends, and venues.

"What's going on?" I plopped down on the sofa beside my little brother.

"Debating on dinner. Any suggestions?" Liang shrugged slightly.

"I'm not hungry." I leaned my head against Ethan's broad shoulder.

"No word from Landon yet?" He asked.

"Does everyone know he's gone AWOL?" I sighed heavily.

"Just us." Jocelyn assured me.

"Wonderful." I glanced down at my phone for the millionth time. No missed calls.

We heard the front door open and close briefly. Jackson and Landon walked into the family room together. I looked over at Jocelyn for some sort of explanation, but she merely shrugged.

The silence in the room was deafening. Jackson, always the peacemaker and most level-headed of the bunch, cleared his throat loudly.

"Anyway, I think I need a drink. Anyone else?" He nodded towards the kitchen.

"I could use a beer." Ethan rose from the couch, followed by Liang and Jocelyn.

"Subtle guys. Real subtle." I rolled my eyes as the troops strolled into the kitchen to eavesdrop.

"I'm sorry." Landon took the spot previously occupied by my brother.

"Where have you been?" I couldn't stop myself from asking.

"The Holiday Inn by the interstate." He reached over and took my hand. "I just needed a little bit of time to process everything." He admitted looking down at his hands. "I know this isn't what we planned, but life doesn't always go as planned." He looked up with a weary smile.

"No. It doesn't." I squeezed his hand gently.

"I love you, more than I ever thought I could love anyone. And I know we can do this. I'm not saying it will be easy, but we can do it." Landon leaned over and kissed me softly.

"I love you too." I kissed him once again and brushed the tears escaping from the corner of my eyes. "Damn hormones." I smiled weakly.

"Guess I best get used to them." He met my eyes. "We're going to have a gorgeous child."

"You mean an ornery child." I laughed.

"That too." He chuckled.

"I'm glad you came back." I confessed. "I was worried."

"About me or if I'd come back?"

"Honestly?" Landon nodded. "A little of both."

"I'll never leave you, Sid. I may be stubborn at times or maybe need a little space occasionally, but I will never leave you. I'm sorry that I put you through that." He wrapped his arms around me and pulled me close to him. "You have my word."

"I love you." I whispered.

"I love you too, always and forever." He whispered back.

8

MONDAY, JULY 25, 1859

FOUND MY GRANDMOTHER having her morning coffee on the veranda. She looked like a picture sitting amongst the roses and geraniums with the full green foliage across the backdrop. Her light grey gown reflected the early morning light, and I wished I could take a photograph of her.

My grandmother wore her in a loose bun at her neck. Her face and hands were careworn from years of love she continues to show to her family and friends. She sat there with the paper folded across her lap, her brow furrowed in concentration. I couldn't help but wonder what concerned her so.

"Good morning, grandmother. How are you feeling?"

"Fine." She said but did not look up from the morning edition.

"What has engrossed you so?" I sat down on the lounge across from her.

"Mr. Bennett was correct. Things are escalating throughout the country." She set the paper aside and picked up her coffee.

"We both know this already. It is not news." I said in a low voice and glanced around to ensure we were alone.

"Yes. Yes. I know. I simply hoped I would not be around to witness it."

"What is that supposed to mean?" I asked, slightly alarmed.

"My grandson's will be fighting in this war, maybe even my sons. Your husband will be gone, most likely for the duration, and we will have to survive without any protection, and you of all people should know what happens to women, their homes, their land during war." She took a deep breath.

"We will not be alone. We have Casper and Silas. Not to mention all our workers. They will not be fighting in this war." I reminded her.

"You know that Lincoln will sanction Negro soldiers before the end of the war. What if they decide to fight? What will happen then?" Her eyes looked fearful.

"I understand why you are concerned, but we will survive this. All of us. Jocelyn has assured me." I reminded her.

"I know. I apologize." My grandmother sighed heavily and reached for her hand fan. She opened it and began waving it about back and forth as if lost in her own thoughts.

"Grandmother, we can use our knowledge the best way we can and prepare for what is about to happen. And we can do all we can to ensure the safety of those we love. That is all we can do." I reached over and touched her arm.

"Good morning, my beautiful girls." Keifer approached us. "It is a lovely morning to have breakfast outside." He leaned over and kissed me on the cheek.

"Good morning, dear." I smiled at him. "Please join us. I saw grandmother out here enjoying her coffee and thought so as well."

"I have to several patients to look in on this morning, then I will be at the office this afternoon if you need me." he remarked, sitting down beside me. "Naomi is setting the table on the patio. I believe breakfast will be ready shortly."

"Wonderful." My grandmother recomposed herself. "And where is Eugenia this morning?"

"I saw her in the dining room before I joined you ladies. She prefers to have her breakfast indoors."

"Very well. I am going to check on everything in the kitchen." She stood up and straightened her gown before heading towards the house.

"Did I interrupt something?" Keifer looked concerned.

"No. She is just worried. Just as everyone else is." I reached over and took his hand. "All this talk about what will happen if the Southern states succeed from the Union and war should follow."

"Hopefully, it will not come to that." He looked out longingly over the fields.

"I am concerned it will. I am scared for my brothers; for you." I told him honestly.

"I won't be fighting." He stated a little too casually.

"No, but you will still be in the thick of it; mending broken bodies and trying desperately to save as many soldiers as you can." The textbook images flashed through my memory from my *other* world. "It will be a horrible war that will tear this country apart long after the battles are over."

"That is true with any war."

"This one will be different. This will tear families apart, destroy friendships." I knew he had friends from medical school who lived in the south, not to mention his entire family in Savannah.

"Let's just hope and pray it does not come to that." He glanced over this shoulder and saw Naomi putting breakfast on the table. "Come on, dear. Let's eat before it gets cold." Keifer stood up and offered me his hand.

❧

Eugenia kept herself busy throughout the morning in the parlor reading. I was thankful she avoided me and kept to herself. I believe she felt the same towards my grandmother and me as we did her. She said very little to us and preferred being alone. I attempted to talk to her, but her responses were short and abrupt. I was happy to leave her to herself.

I spent the remainder of my morning going over the ledgers with Casper and Duncan and discussing the upcoming harvest. Then I talked with them about building new storage cellars; ones that could be well hidden from unsuspecting eyes.

I had decided to use my knowledge of upcoming shortages to hide away as much and as many provisions as I possibly could. I took out a piece of paper and wrote down a list of things I wanted to fill the cellars with; coffee, sugar, flour, butter, oats, potatoes, smoked ham, dried beef, rum, wine, candles, matches, kerosene, leather, wool, shoestring, buckles, buttons, hairpins, lace. I scribbled down and handed the paper to Casper.

"We need to start stocking large supplies of these items. There will be more added to the list, I am sure."

"Matches?" Casper questioned reading through the items. "What are matches?"

"My apologies." I took the paper from him and scratched out the common word from my *other* world, and hastily wrote Lucifers. "Lucifers. I meant to write Lucifers." I corrected myself and handed it back to him with some coins. "We can put things in the current cellars and any overflow of items in the back bedroom until the new cellars are built, but they need to be started as soon as we find a suitable location. Please give it some thought today." I asked.

"Yes, Mrs. Marshall." With a nod, both men left the study to journey into town.

I put the ledgers back in my grandfather's old master desk and took out some fresh paper. I wanted to write a letter to Patrick to see how he and his family were doing and to share the good news of our own with them.

It was funny to think that my child was going to be born a few months after my niece, or my little sister — in my life *there*. If we lived closer to each other, they could have grown up together. The oddities of *EVE* were overwhelming at times.

"Do you think it wise to be so obvious? Or suspicious?" My grandmother stood in the doorway to the study.

"What do you mean?"

"The list you gave Casper. I had a look at it before he left." She walked over to the window and opened the drapes. "You need some sun in here. This place looks like a tomb. How you can work in the dark is beyond me." She remarked before taking a seat in the chair before the desk.

"I hadn't noticed." I shrugged.

"I guess you are as concerned as myself about certain upcoming events." She spoke with caution as the house staff moved about.

"Of course, I am. How could I not be?"

"I just thought after our conversation earlier." She let her voice trail off.

"What? That I wouldn't prepare?" I smiled, lovingly at her. "You know me better than that. I may not be able to stop this war, but I can make sure we come through it with our skins."

"What can I do to help?" Her eyes brightened.

"We need to build a couple more cellars, but not your typical cellars. I want these to be hidden from the unseen eye. They need to be kept safe for all of us." I leaned forward, crossing my arms over the top of the desk. "You and I both know of the extreme shortages that will soon occur and how despicable and brutal the scavengers will become."

"I recall." She nodded.

"I realize we are not in the direct line of any major battles — thankfully, we are a good distance from them, but still, I want to err on the side of caution. You can never tell what desperate people will do to survive." I pointed out.

"Very true. I would rather be safe than sorry." She agreed.

"Any thoughts as to where these cellars would be located?" I asked.

"I have a couple of locations in mind that might serve our purpose." A small smile spread across her lips. "Would you care to join me for a walk about the grounds before our evening meal?"

"Of course."

My grandmother and I strolled down by the densely wooded area beside the river. The ground was sparse with grass but heavy in sticks, mud, and underbrush. In this part of the land, it would be difficult for scavengers to find anything if they didn't know where to look since it was about four acres from the house and probably two from our docks and boats.

"This would be ideal for a couple large cellars and maybe even an icehouse depending on how close we can get to the river without breaking through." I speculated.

"Yes. I believe it would." I paced around through the broken terrain.

"What are you thinking?"

"That I should have become an engineer instead of a pediatrician." I chuckled with no humor.

"That would have been helpful." I could tell she was trying not to laugh.

"Anyway," I rolled my eyes playfully at her. "I suppose I could do a bit of research *there* and see what our best approach would be."

"Should we stock up on some burlap also? For the ice." She asked.

"Yes, I believe so." I shrugged. "I miss refrigerators. And freezers." I mumbled.

"I miss electricity and indoor plumbing." My grandmother declared with a smirk.

We started to walk slowly back towards the house. The air was cooling down as twilight moved closer to us. The sky was glowing with gold and purple amongst the scattered clouds. The air smelled clean and crisp, like nothing I ever encountered in my 21st-century life.

"I miss television and cars." I linked my arm with hers.

"I miss jazz, hot showers, and department stores."

"I miss toilet paper and tampons." I laughed.

"Me too." My grandmother laughed.

"And you know what I wish I had? Tupperware." I looked over at her and rolled my eyes playfully. "That would be nice about now."

We continued to banter on our short journey back to the house. She and I had become more than grandmother and granddaughter with the transition to living with *EVE*. The inherited gift had brought us closer and given us a shared bond of wonderment.

9

THE FLIGHT BACK TO BOSTON was just as nerve-wracking as the one out to Chicago. The morning sickness made it even worse. I had packed crackers in my purse, but even those weren't settling my stomach once we hit a patch of turbulence an hour into our flight.

It was difficult leaving my dad, Ethan, and Liang. My dad was still morose, and I felt horrible for him. Ethan was not the most sympathetic person, and I wished my sister, or I could have stayed home a bit longer with him.

But my dad insisted he was fine. Thankfully, he had the week off work because he was supposed to be on his honeymoon, but still. It gave him time to recollect himself before he faced the questions at work. I knew he was dreading it, especially since Patsy worked there as well.

We hadn't seen or heard anything from her or Donnie since the night they moved out. I could only imagine how she was going to justify her actions or explain why the wedding was canceled to the people at the hospital. I knew my father was a private man, so he would never say a word to anyone regardless of what that evil shrew said about him.

Jocelyn was especially worried about him. She was such a daddy's girl, she fretted, leaving him. I knew she'd be calling him every day for a while and probably driving him insane. But they were so close, I knew he'd secretly love it. I envied their relationship.

My mother and I used to be close before my parents got divorced. When she walked away from him, she pretty much walked away from all of us. We rarely talked now unless it was related to my classes in medical school, and I knew she spoke to my siblings even less. It saddened me to think of how upset she was going to be when I told her about my baby.

I looked over at Landon sitting beside me, and I knew he was dreading telling his parents as well. They were most likely not going to take it any better than my mother. I was happy that at least my father was thrilled at the prospect of becoming a grandparent.

I knew Jackson's parents — my adopted extended family, by marriage — would be elated. Emily and Robert were the most incredible people. I was so jealous that my little sister had married into such an amazing family. Landon's parents were nice, but not exactly the warm and fuzzy type.

We taxied down the runway, and I let out a deep sigh of relief. Landon rubbed his hand and flexed his fingers when I let go and reached for my purse under the seat in front of me.

"Sorry." I smiled at him.

"It's okay. I'm getting used to it." He smiled and slightly shook his head at me. "How are you feeling?"

"I'm okay."

"Yeah, now that's she's on the ground." I heard my sister mumble from the row behind us.

"Oh, hush." I looked back, teasing her.

"It's true." She raised her eyebrows at me and smirked.

"Even so." I turned and playfully stuck my tongue out at her.

"Very mature, doc." Jocelyn giggled.

We gathered up our belongings and eventually made our way towards the terminal.

Jackson's parents had left their Durango in long-term parking. We tossed our bags in the back of his SUV, and all squeezed in exhausted and anxious to get home.

I leaned my head against Landon's shoulder and closed my eyes. The last several days had been grueling. I wanted nothing more than to go home, take a hot shower, and curl up in my own bed.

"I feel so badly for Shane." I heard Emily remark from the front passenger seat.

"As do I." Robert replied to his wife.

"But it is still better he found out now before he married that woman than after." Jocelyn remarked.

"True. But I would imagine it will be a long time before he trusts another woman." Emily added.

"Can you blame him?" Jackson spoke up.

"No. Not really. But I hate it. My dad didn't deserve to be treated that way." Jocelyn quipped. "He deserves someone who treats him with love and respect; someone who will spoil him." She snuggled into her husband. "He has such a huge heart."

"I agree." I joined the conversation. "He would do anything for anyone. I hate to think of the embarrassment he's facing at work."

"Anyone who knows him will understand why he didn't marry her." Jackson stated.

"What did you tell people about why the wedding was canceled?" I hadn't thought to ask my sister before with all that was going on.

"I told them the truth — that dad came to his senses." My sister turned around in the middle seat and smirked.

"Are you serious?" I giggled.

"Of course." Jocelyn had a mischievous grin on her lips. "Why lie about it?"

"You are evil." I chuckled.

"No. I am honest. There is a difference." She stated.

"Do you think your father would appreciate that?" Emily looked concerned.

"What was I supposed to tell people?" Jocelyn asked.

"I had told the caterers, baker, and the venue and such that there was a family emergency and the groom had left for California on a red eye. That way, they could not question anything. Of course, he lost the deposit and had to pay for the food and cake, but it was a small loss compared to what he would have endured if he had married that woman." Emily informed us.

"That was probably a bit more tactful," My sister agreed, "but if I told the guests that they would have expected the wedding to be rescheduled and I could not leave my dad in that position after what she did to him."

"I understand." I reached up and touched her shoulder. "I would have done the same thing."

"Patsy is lucky he only threw her and that witless wonder of a son of hers, out of his house." Jocelyn sounded mincing.

"I believe Shane handled the situation with grace and style. Not many people could have kept such a calm demeanor." Robert added.

"I agree." Jackson smiled.

"Does anyone know where they went?" Landon asked. "I'm just curious."

"Don't know. Don't care." Jocelyn chimed. "I hope some gutter somewhere."

"You are sweet." I giggled.

We pulled into the driveway at Robert and Emily's. We had all left our cars here while we were gone. The windows downstairs were alight, and I wondered if Phoebe or Alex's wife, Leslie, had left them on for us.

"Would anyone care to come in for some coffee and something to eat before you head home?" Emily offered as Robert turned his vehicle off.

"That's probably not a bad idea." Jackson was the first to speak up. "It's only seven." He looked over at Jocelyn.

"I'm starving." She smiled, lovingly at her husband.

"Me too." I looked over at Landon, hopefully.

"Okay. I could use a bite." He held his hand out for me and helped me out.

"Thank you." I leaned up and kissed him on the cheek. "I am famished."

The men gathered the luggage and carried it into the front hall. The aroma was intoxicating as soon as the front door opened. Someone had been cooking, and my stomach growled.
"Welcome back." Leslie walked out of the kitchen, wiping her hands on a dishtowel. "I made some roulade and homemade egg noodles, peas and homemade yeast rolls." She was all smiles.

"Darling, it smells wonderful." Alex kissed his wife on the cheek.

"It smells delicious." Jackson headed straight for the kitchen with Robert and Landon directly behind him.

"Thank you, darling." Emily embraced her daughter-in-law. "I appreciate this."

"How was your trip?" Leslie asked.

"Eventful." Emily grinned. "We'll talk later." They walked into the kitchen together, followed by the rest of us.

The evening passed with all of us gathered around the island in the kitchen laughing, joking, teasing, talking —— this was my family. I watched Landon with them, and smiled to myself at how well he blended flawlessly in with them. My little sister married into this clan and got everything she ever wished for. And me — adopted and embraced by them; taken in and loved as one of their own due to marriage or by our united gift of *EVE*.

These are the people who are going to be the heart and soul of my child's formative years. I knew in my heart they were going to be the ones who were going to be there beside Landon and me, supporting us and loving our child. I felt so blessed to have them.

My hand rested on my abdomen as I looked about the room. This is precisely where I, or rather we, belonged. I knew there would be some difficult and challenging times ahead, but with their love and support, Landon and I could handle anything.

10

THE MORNING DAWNED WITH a brilliance that glistened over the dew-covered emerald fields. The sun flowed through the drapery flooding over the hardwood floor. I watched the light breeze lift them lightly as they fluttered with the wind. I yawned and stretched, not wanting to get out of bed. I was so comfortable and warm. It was a rare moment when the baby wasn't making me feel tired or nauseous.

I reluctantly climbed out of bed and put on my robe. I brushed out my long blond hair and brushed my teeth. I splashed some cold water on my face but still didn't feel ready to face the day.

Eugenia had been avoiding my grandmother and me, but she was bombarding Keifer every moment. He was barely able to speak with anyone after church services last Sunday as she monopolized every conversation anyone attempted with him. I finally was able to say two words to my husband once we reached the privacy of our bedroom.

As much as Keifer was annoyed, it did not compare to the anger I felt every time she walked into a room. She waltzed around my home, ordering my workers around, and demanding everyone cater to her needs.

I climbed into a burgundy gown and pulled my hair up into a low bun. I thought about my sister and my *other* life and the drastic difference between the two. Jocelyn would never allow Eugenia to treat her this way. She wouldn't even allow her to stay in her home.

I took a deep breath and smirked at the reflection staring back at me from my vanity mirror. I channeled some of my sister's strength and headed downstairs to greet the day.

My grandmother was reading the Boston *Post* newspaper on the veranda. I was relieved I didn't run into Eugenia on my way through the house. She was still avoiding me, to which I was truly grateful.

I sat down across from my grandmother and poured myself a cup of coffee from the tray Naomi had brought out.

"Good morning, grandmother. Anything interesting in the paper?" I inquired.

"Hello, darling. How are you feeling?" She smiled over at me.

"Much better." For once, I didn't feel nauseated. "Hopefully, it will last."

"Let's hope."

"Good morning, ladies." Eugenia appeared out of nowhere. Her mousey thin brownish blond hair was pulled up into a low bun and her oversized glasses were perched high on her pudgy nose. Her dark brown eyes were her only redeeming feature, but they were barely visible behind her glasses. The mud-brown plain gown she was wearing made her look even more like Mrs. Potato Head than she had before. For the life of me I could not imagine how she and my handsome husband shared the same parents.

I placed my hand up to my mouth, attempting to stifle the giggle that tried to escape as the thought passed through my mind.

"It didn't" I said, making my grandmother giggle.

Eugenia sat down at the end of the table and helped herself to some coffee. I tried to keep my composure and be as polite as I could muster. But there was something about her that challenged every ounce of patience I had.

"I was looking for Keifer. Do you know where he is?" Eugenia asked, putting her third teaspoon of sugar in her cup.

"He is at work. He will be home hopefully by supper." I sipped my coffee.

"I see." She took a long drink of her coffee while my grandmother and I exchanged knowing looks. "Is that a Boston paper?" Eugenia looked over at my grandmother.

"Why, yes, it is." My grandmother smirked.

"How can you read that dribble?" Eugenia looked as if a fly landed in her coffee.

"I find it quite intriguing." she responded, inhaling deeply.

"Personally, I found it full of hate towards Southerners." Eugenia pursed her lips.

"Just because we live north of the Mason-Dixon line does not mean we automatically dislike Southerners," I stated.

"I should hope not. You married one." Eugenia narrowed her eyes.

"Yes, I did. Although Keifer was raised in the South, I believe he's more of a Northerner now." I replied.

"Yes, a decade up North certainly has changed my brother — and not for the better." Eugenia grinned hatefully.

"Excuse me? My husband is an honorable man." She was testing my patience and graciousness.

"I believe so too. In fact, I am counting on it." Eugenia smirked.

"Counting on it?" I asked.

"Yes, well. I believe the Southern states will be seceding from the Union in the upcoming months. I pray they allow us to do so peacefully, but if they do not, then war could be on the horizon. I want to make sure my brother is on the right side should war break out." Eugenia shifted in her chair with an air of satisfaction.

"Did you come here to try to talk your brother into returning to Savannah?" For some reason, I wasn't surprised.

"Of course. Keifer only came North for medical school, but then he met you, and you convinced him to remain up here despite his family's wishes. Now it is time for him to return home." My sister-in-law glared at me.

"My husband is home, Eugenia. And this is where he shall remain." I told her bluntly.

"This is your grandparent's estate. Not yours. And certainly, not Keifer's. He shall inherit Gable Gardens. Our father's — our parent's plantation is his birthright. They are getting older and are not in the best of health. It is time for him to return." She smiled smugly.

"Terrace Falls is Keifer's estate." My grandmother stated in a harsh tone. "He and my granddaughter have inherited it from myself and my late husband, Nathan."

"Nonsense. You have a son in Chicago, I believe — your father, if I am not mistaken," Eugenia turned towards me for a moment, "who is remarried and has a young family — sons, who shall inherit before a granddaughter and her husband. It is their birthright. And what about your other son and his family. Or your daughter?"

"This estate is mine to will to whomever I decide to leave it too." My grandmother seethed.

"Our lives are none of your business, Eugenia. You have a great deal of audacity to come here and assume that my husband would want to leave everything he has worked so hard to build."

"He will. We are family." Eugenia continued to smile.

"I am his family." I placed my hand over my abdomen. "We are his family. And my husband would never leave us or his home." I stood and glared down at my sister-in-law, "And certainly not to live with someone as disagreeable as you. It is no wonder that you cannot find a husband. You are horribly unpleasant."

"How dare you speak to me with such disrespect." Eugenia's mouth hung open. "I shall speak to your husband about you."

"I hope you do." I spat before walking back up to the house.

I heard my grandmother giggle and her footsteps on the cobblestone walkway behind me. I didn't bother to turn around. I was afraid of what I would say, or worse, do, if I did.

I was in the study when Keifer came home. I heard him talking with Eugenia on the porch simply because she raised her voice several times. I knew he wasn't going to be happy with my behavior, but I considered my words very tame in comparison to what I could have said.

"Darling," My husband walked in, looking tired and in no mood to deal with family drama. "Do you have a moment?"

"Hello, dear. Please come in and have a seat." Keifer walked over and sat down in one of the chairs across from my desk.

Eugenia lingered in the doorway with a satisfied look on her face. I knew she was anticipating Keifer giving me a good bawling out for what I'd said to her.

"You do not have to linger in the doorway, Eugenia. Have a seat so you can hear everything." I said so curtly even Keifer seemed surprised by my words as I motioned towards the other chair beside my husband.

"Very well." She huffed but took the seat, nonetheless.

"I understand you two exchanged some unpleasantries this morning." Keifer looked irritated.

"I understand that your sister only came here to try to convince you to return to Savannah." I folded my hands upon my desk and narrowed my eyes. "Which you failed to mention to me."

"I did not mention it because it was a moot point. I told my sister that this is my home, and I have no intention of leaving it." Keifer turned towards his sister. "Why do you insist on causing trouble?"

"Keifer, you know very well that you are to inherit Gable Gardens. It is your birthright." Eugenia stated harshly. "It is time for you to come home."

"Eugenia …" Keifer began, but she cut him off.

"You know very well our great state is about to secede from the Union. When that happens, we could very well be met with hostilities from the Northern states. If that happens, we will need good physicians to take care of our men." She stated.

"And what about the soldiers who are not traitors to their country?" I asked.

"Southern soldiers are not traitors. They are honorable men who stand up for what they believe in — for what is right." Her hateful eyes turned towards me.

"Eugenia, the Southern states have been talking about seceding from the United States for the several decades if not longer. The notion has never passed. It is all simply talk." Keifer sighed.

"No. Not this time. I believe they will secede, Keifer." I said in a low voice.

"I know the issue of slavery and states' rights are a heated topic in government, but the issues will be resolved by Congress. They always are." My husband hated this topic.

Keifer was a Southerner at heart. He was born and raised in Savannah, Georgia, and his entire family still resided there. His decade in Massachusetts had made a Northerner out of him, and he had lost most of his Southern accent. But I knew the prospect of a war between the North and South distressed him terribly.

His family owned a large plantation called Gable Gardens. It was a breathtaking place with more than a hundred slaves. It was nearly five times the size of Terrace Falls, with over twice the amount of help. I had been there several times and had fallen in love with the place. But even so, this was our home, and this place was a part of me. I could never imagine living or raising my child anywhere else.

"This war, if it should come," I carefully added, "will not be fought over slavery. It will be over the issue of states' rights." I said casually.

"The federal government needs to understand that we will not be told what we can do in our own states." Eugenia added.

"Each state when they joined the United States, agreed not to ever take up arms against it or to leave the United States — except Texas. Texas is the only state who has it written into their agreement when they joined, that they are free to leave at any time without reprisal." The look on Keifer's face told me I had said too much.

"How did you know that?" He asked.

"I believe I read it somewhere." I stated clearly.

"That shows how misinformed you are." Eugenia spat. "This is about keeping our way of life. Our rights. Our slaves. Nothing else. We will not be told what we can do by some *Black* Republican in Washington." The term black republican had taken root in the last several years to describe any republican who was anti-slavery.

"You are incorrect again, Eugenia. If a war does occur, it will be over states' rights. Not slavery." I corrected her.

"Are you going to sit there and tell me you are unaware of the Underground Railroad that provides assistance to runaway slaves?" My sister-in-law fumed.

"I have heard it mentioned." I smiled at her.

"And you dare to say that this is not about slavery?" She asked.

"I am sure you believe it is." I smirked.

"Keifer, I told you how difficult it was for me to travel up here. It is getting dangerous for Southerners to venture so far North these days. Now is when you need to come home. Times are changing, and you are greatly needed at home."

"We already discussed this. I am home. Margaret and Thad are taking care of Gable." My husband sighed heavily.

"You must understand, we need you. The county is already calling for militia troops. The governor in South Carolina has already raised ten thousand troops." For the first time, her voice took on a nervous edge.

"I do understand. And I am sorry. My place is here." Keifer tried to explain.

"Because your wife is now with child?" Eugenia's hateful glare rested upon me again.

"Yes." He answered plainly.

"I find that very convenient that she should find herself in a family way just as you are needed to return to your true home." She shifted her weight back towards her brother. "After years of trying with no success, can you not see this is her vague attempt to keep you here? She is a Northerner. She is not one of us, brother."

"Funny. I thought we were all Americans." I stated hatefully.

"Brother," Eugenia placed her hand on Keifer's arm. "Please. You must listen to me. You do not want to be on the wrong side of history." She implored him.

Keifer remained silent, but I could tell he was struggling with his temper. He could only hold it for so long before he would speak his mind. His sister was dancing along his last nerve, and I knew it was only a matter of time.

"Do not trouble yourself, Eugenia. He won't be." I tried not to chuckle but failed miserably.

"A Southern gentleman can lick a dozen Yankees." She spat hatefully at me.

"How?" I smirked. "You have no industry to speak of in the South. You have only a couple of factories. Hardly any railroads and only a few ships, none of which are military vessels. Everything you use is supplied by the North." I stated proudly.

"That does not matter." She scoffed.

"I am afraid it is going to matter a great deal to a great many Southerners." I chimed.

"That shows what little you know." She rolled her eyes at me and straightened her back in a show of superiority.

"I know the North can cut off your supplies — that includes weapons and gunpowder and textiles. I know we can tear up your railroads, leaving you unable to move troops and blockade your harbors so that no one or nothing can get in or out. And that any cotton the South stores away for higher prices in Europe in hopes of purchasing arms, will rot in Southern warehouses because Europe will never recognize the South as a sovereign nation." I retorted.

"You arrogant little wretch." Eugenia raised her voice. "How dare you!"

"You stupid fool. You come into my home, insult me, and challenge my beliefs, my home, and my integrity." I scoffed.

"Eugenia, would you please excuse us. I would like a word with my wife." Keifer gripped the arms of his chair until his knuckles turned white.

Looking quite proud of herself, my sister-in-law stood, turned, and heavily walked out of the room, closing the door to my study loudly.

"Sidney," Keifer began.

"Do not scold me, Keifer." I was too irritated to think straight.

"I was going to tell you that I had not realized you were so well informed. You had addressed topics I had not heard entertained under this roof." He leaned forward. "Care to tell me what you have been reading or with whom you have been speaking?"

"I can think for myself, darling." I replied. "I know enough of geography to know the South has little factories, railroads, or ships. Certainly, I am not the only one who has thought of this?"

"No. I simply had not expected you to be considering such things. You know how I feel about you and politics." He reminded me.

"This has nothing to do with politics and everything to do with our survival. I do not want or desire us to be caught unawares." I pointed out.

"Do you really believe it will come to war?" His eyes implored.

"Yes. Unfortunately, I believe so." I reached across the desk and placed my hand over his.

"I pray you are wrong." He half grinned. "This could tear our country apart."

"I know." I whispered.

"I was afraid Eugenia was going to pressure me when she initially wrote to say she was coming." Keifer admitted. "I had hoped I was wrong."

"She has been horrid since her arrival. I want her to leave." I told him.

"You realize that I love Gable Gardens just as much as you love Terrace Falls?" His eyes dropped.

"I know." I stood up and walked over to the window. The sun was sinking behind the west fields, and twilight was well upon us. We were late for supper, but that didn't matter right now. I placed my hand on the glass feeling the coolness seep into my palm. "I am so sorry, darling. I cannot imagine being in your shoes right now. If you really feel you should return . . ."

"My place is right here beside you." Keifer walked up behind me and wrapped his arms around my waist. I felt his hot breath on my neck as he leaned his cheek against me. My heart broke knowing how this was tearing him apart.

11

SATURDAY, OCTOBER 5, 2019

NDIAN SUMMER WAS LEAVING US. Its brief appearance had been a welcomed reprieve and a gentle reminder that warm days were going to allude us until next May. I was sad to see it go, but fall was my favorite season.

I loved the bonfires, the crisp air, the hoodies, and, most of all — the brilliance of the colors of the leaves. I loved taking long walks in the woods with Landon. We'd stroll down broken trails littered with fallen leaves and talk about our future. With our hectic and demanding med school schedules, those moments were few and far between. I treasured them when they occurred.

Landon had warmed up to the idea and was now getting excited about the baby. He insisted on being at every appointment and continuously teased me with outrageous baby names. We had agreed to wait to find out the sex of our child, which not only aggravated our family, but also our friends and classmates.

We had turned my home office study into an elegantly decorated nursery with a lot of help from Emily. It was divine; something I could never have created without her help. Her special gift was a glider rocker that sat beside the window overlooking the small garden below.

A large birch tree stood outside providing ample shade to the room. Landon had hung a hummingbird feeder on one of the lower branches and each morning dozens of hummingbirds visited for their morning meal.

The nursery had become my favorite place in our apartment. I spent countless hours sitting in the rocking chair reading textbooks aloud and studying my notes in a soothing voice for our child. I wanted our child to know my voice in a calm manner rather than the sometimes hectic and demanding voices typical of the outside world.

Landon and I were working part-time on the weekends at Massachusetts General Hospital. As medical students with only a pre-med bachelor's degree in science, we were basically unskilled labor working emergency room admissions and occasionally — rarely encountered patients outside of just entering their identification and insurance information.

I finished up a twelve-hour shift at 6 o'clock in the evening. I was tired and sore from sitting behind the partitioned counter all day without a break and only a couple quick dashes to the bathroom. We had been swamped and flu season, with the weather change in full swing. I walked slowly to the parking garage thinking only of taking a long hot shower.

I unlocked my car and climbed into the driver's seat. I started up the car and rolled down the window to let the cool evening air replace the stale in my car. I sighed heavily and reached into my purse grabbing my phone. I turned it back on after leaving it turned off in my locker all day, per hospital policy. It immediately began buzzing alerting me to missed calls, voicemails, and text messages.

Strangely, I had seven missed calls — two from my mother, Amy, four from Jocelyn, and one from Landon. I had four voicemails, and three text messages. I clicked on the first voicemail from my mother and immediately her voice filled my car.

"Hi honey, I imagine you are at work. Give me a call when you get off. Talk to you soon."

Second message from mom, *"Hi hon, it's mom again. Call me."*

Third message from Jocelyn, *"Hey Sidney, don't go home. Mom is waiting to ambush you. She's at your apartment. Landon is trapped there with her. Come to my in-law's."*

Fourth message from Landon, *"Hey Sidney, it's me. What the hell. Get here asap before I tell your mother what I really think of her."*

This was not what I wanted to deal with this evening. I couldn't fathom what my mother was doing in Boston. I had not spoken to her in months. She never called or emailed me.

I knew I should call Landon, but instead I hit the button that would connect with my sister. Jocelyn answered her phone on the second ring.

"Oh my God, Sidney. Where are you?" Her anxious voice flooded my car.

"I just got off work. I'm in the parking garage and just checked my messages. What the hell is going on?"

"Our brother has a big freaking mouth!" Jocelyn declared. "He told mom about the baby."

"Oh, crap." I exhaled loudly. "Why would he do that?"

"Because he's an idiot." Jocelyn said angrily. "He is lucky he's still in Chicago."

"Good Lord. I imagine she's here to give me an earful." I put my car in reverse and pulled out of my parking spot. "And that is just what I want to listen to after a long day of dealing with screaming patients, disgruntled nurses, and irritated doctors." I pulled out of the garage and fought my way through the early evening traffic.

"Where are you headed?" she asked.

"Home." I pulled onto the freeway and merged into traffic. "If I don't, I don't believe Landon will ever forgive me." I chuckled without any humor.

"Do me a favor," she cooed. "Keep your phone connected and slip it into your pocket so I can hear this."

"Why do you want to hear this? It's just going to be a lot of screaming." I admitted.

"Because I just want to know what I have to look forward to in a few years when Jackson and I decided to have kids." Jocelyn confessed.

I pulled back onto the side streets and navigated my way to our apartment. I parked just outside our building and went to turn my car off but hesitated just a moment. I knew things were going to get nasty really quick.

"Are you sure you want to hear this?" I asked my little sister.

"Yeah. I have you on speaker. Phoebe is sitting here with me."

"Hey Pheb's," I snorted. "Wish me luck." I turned off the car and dropped my phone, still connected to my sister and best friend, into my pocket.

"Good luck," I heard their voices ring out just before I climbed out of the car.

I unlocked our door and stepped inside. Landon was leaning against the breakfast bar. His hair was disheveled, his shirt untucked, and his expression told me he was at his wits end.

My mother was seated on the couch dressed in Khaki dress slacks, brown boots with four-inch spiked heels, and a light burgundy sweater. She wore a long gold chain around her neck that accentuated her earrings. Her legs were crossed, and her back was straight, almost ridged. Her expression was anything but welcoming.

I walked over to Landon before I said anything. I kissed him on the cheek and whispered, "I'm sorry" before turning towards my mother. "Mom, I got your messages. I didn't expect to see you hear."

"I would image not." She stood up and crossed the room. She hugged me briefly and stepped back, her eyes staring at the tiny bulge in my abdomen. "So, it's true. You're pregnant." She said it as a fact, not a question.

"Yes." I glanced over at Landon. "I heard Ethan told you."

"And why did I have to hear it from your brother and not you?" She raised her eyebrow at me while placing her hand on her hip. "I would have appreciated a phone call from you."

"To say what exactly? That I disappointed you? That I did something even worse than your other daughter? Why would I ever doubt that you would not cut me off for letting you down just like you did with Jocelyn?" I stated calmly.

"I did not cut your sister off. She made her choice. She chose Jackson and his family over her own." Amy's eyes narrowed a bit.

"Funny for you to say that when you are the only family member who no longer has a relationship with her."

"Your sister is a spoiled brat who eloped in high school because I refused to pay for her chase a boy, she'd just met halfway across the country to attend college." Amy declared with righteous indignation.

"I have no doubt that is how you view it." I snorted.

"That is the truth. Not a view." Her voice took an authoritative tone.

"And remind me again why I should have called you?" I scoffed.

"Because I am your mother. I have a right to know if I am about to be a grandmother." She stated flatly.

"No. No, you do not have a right to know. You have a desire to know." Landon jumped in. "Sidney is an adult. You have no say in the decisions she, nor I make."

"Landon," Amy confronted him. "Why don't you make yourself scarce so I can talk to my daughter alone."

"Because I want him here. This is his home, and you are the uninvited guest." I reminded her.

"Uninvited?" She huffed with disbelief. "I am uninvited. I do not need an invitation to visit my eldest child."

"A phone call – which I remind you works both ways, would have sufficed." I rationalized.

"I did not take time off work and fly all the way to Boston from Seattle to be treated this way." She walked over and picked up her purse.

"What did you expect when you ambushed my boyfriend out of the blue while I am at work." I explained.

"How was I supposed to know you were at work. I don't know your schedule." She exhaled loudly, putting her purse on her shoulder.

"That's because you don't talk to me." I shook my head in disbelief. "You don't know my schedule or anything about my life because you don't bother to call."

"You know my schedule. I am always working. I live at the hospital and it's not like you're ringing my phone off the hook." She tried to turn the tables.

"So, this ambush is my fault?" I glanced back at Landon to see if he was just as baffled as I was at this crap. He was.

"I'll bet your parents know about this baby." Her eyes turned towards Landon as well.

"Of course," Landon shrugged casually.

"And how do they feel about it?" She inquired.

"They are thrilled about the baby, but not about the timing." He confessed.

"I feel exactly the same." My mother eyed me closely.

"And you flew across the country to accomplish what? To chastise me for being stupid for getting pregnant in med school? To tell me how difficult I just made my life. How I let you and dad down? How disappointed you are in me?" I raised my voice for the first time. "You can't possibly say anything to me I have not already voiced to myself and Landon. So, say what you came to say because I don't have enough self-loathing to what this has done to not only my life and the life of the man I love." I hastily brushed the tears off my cheeks and put on a brave face.

"Well, I suppose you covered it all." Amy set her purse down on the stool beside Landon and wrapped her arms around me. "I'm so sorry. I was just so mad." She kissed me on the cheek, stood before me still holding onto my forearms. "I just don't want you making the same mistakes I made." She smiled sweetly.

"What is that supposed to mean?" I couldn't believe my ears.

"You know what I mean." She rolled her eyes. "I got married before I had completed my internship and had you right away. Jocelyn came two years later followed immediately by Ethan. Then I was fighting to balance my residency with three small babies and a husband who was consumed with building his own career. Your father never considered how difficult those years were on me." She complained. "I just want you to understand the challenges ahead of you."

"I do understand." I took a small sidestep towards Landon. "We are aware. Plus, I have a lot of support." I reminded her.

"Yes. Your sister's extended family." Amy let out a deep breath leaning against the arm of the recliner. "I am well aware of Emily replacing me in the lives of you and your sister." She scoffed.

"Phoebe is my best friend, and my sister is married to her brother. So, yes, we all spent a lot of time together."

"I figured as much." She casually rolled her eyes.

"Do you plan on seeing Jocelyn while you're here?" I could not help but ask.

"I would like to, but she didn't answer when I called." She shrugged.

"She's probably studying." Landon pipped in.

"Maybe," Amy fidgeted with a ring on her left ring finger for a moment bringing it to my attention. I bit my lip trying not to say anything knowing I did not want confirmation of what I was looking at. "Anyway," she continued. "I don't believe your sister wants to see me. She never calls, texts, or emails. At least you email occasionally. Ethan is the only one who calls regularly."

"You and I both know why that is." I pointed out.

"Regardless," as always, she dismissed her role in the status of our relationship. "Despite popular opinion, I only want my children to be happy. But I also want them to learn from my mistakes."

"But in doing so, you have always judged us to harshly for anything we do that you do not approve of." I reasoned. "Do you really think you will be able to repair your relationship with Jocelyn?"

"I'm trying," she huffed.

"Mom. Try harder." I plainly stated. "Did you know she's made the Dean's list every semester?"

"Um, no." She awkwardly continued fidgeting with her ring.

"And she's working part-time at Robert's law firm learning as much as she can."

"Well, I am glad at that. I wondered if Robert and Emily were supporting her and Jackson." She smirked.

"No. They are not. Jackson is also working at his dad's firm." However, I failed to elaborate further because things about Jackson's presence in our lives during my sister's senior year could only cause them problems.

"Wonderful," her lack of enthusiasm was evident.

"How long do you plan on staying?" Landon spoke up.

"Just tonight. I fly home tomorrow evening."

"But you just got here," I was surprised by her short visit.

"Yes, I arrived at three, and just rented a car. I must be back in the office on Monday morning." Amy explained.

"You couldn't have taken more time off? A week perhaps." I couldn't believe her. "We haven't seen you in more than a year and you're only staying in Boston for twenty-six hours?" She was unbelievable.

"Unfortunately, this was a last minute, ill-planned trip. I was hoping that perhaps we could all get together for Christmas. What would you think of coming to Seattle for the holidays?" She said hopefully.

"You mean all of us? Me and Landon. Jocelyn and Jackson. Ethan and Liang."

"Yes, of course. You have all never flown out to see the life I've created in Seattle. Plus, I would like you all to meet Dane. He is someone who has become very important to me." Amy was suddenly all smiles.

"That will be difficult to say the least." I turned towards Landon for help. "Landon and I will be working at the hospital. We don't have any seniority to request time off around the holidays." I explained.

"But surely if you explain," my mother started but Landon quickly interceded.

"Dr. Timmons, you know how short-staffed the hospitals are around the holidays and two lowly med students don't have a prayer of being granted time off."

"I suppose," she sighed heavily. "Thanksgiving?" She raised her eyebrows at us.

"Finals," Landon and I answered in unison and then laughed.

"Ah yes, of course." Amy smiled. "I suppose we'll wait until the spring."

"Well, why don't we all have dinner together this evening. I'll call Jocelyn and see what she and Jackson are doing?" I offered.

"That would be lovely."

"Alright," I excused myself and stepped into my office.

I pulled my phone out of my jacket pocket curious if Jocelyn and Phoebe were still eavesdropping. I could hardly imagine them listening to such a boring conversation for the last thirty minutes. But I was wrong.

"You there," I hit the speaker button.

"I am not wasting a Saturday evening with that woman." Jocelyn's voice filled the room.

"You must. You cannot leave me alone with her." I declared. "I can't afford bail."

"I've got you covered." Phoebe snickered.

"Thanks," I laughed. "I appreciate that. And you are going."

"Jackson will be so thrilled." The sarcasm in my sister's voice was evident.

"We'll pick you both up shortly. Are you still over at Robert and Emily's?" I asked the obvious.

"Yes. And thanks for the warning." Jocelyn seemed less than thrilled.

"Don't pout. I'm starving." I smiled.

"You realize the only justification I get out of spending a miserable dinner with that woman is the fact that you are gaining weight and will soon lose that perfect little figure of yours." My sister teased.

"You're so sweet. I love you." I said sweetly. "See you soon."

"Can't wait," Jocelyn chimed back before disconnecting the call.

∾

The dinner was as uncomfortable and awkward as possible. Jocelyn said probably a dozen words all evening to our mother and Jackson simply said, 'good evening' and 'good night.' Landon was not much better. He and Jackson exchanged unspoken words throughout the meal with their side glances and eye rolling.

I knew neither of them cared much for my mother and she had done little to nothing to endear herself to them. She had never been shy about his disdain for Jackson and after her ambushing Landon regarding my pregnancy, he had quickly joined Jackson's way of thinking.

Amy had got herself a room about fifteen minutes from our apartment. Although he didn't say it, I knew Landon was thrilled she had not asked to stay at our place. We really did not have a guest room, but our couch pulled out into a sofa bed. However, it was terribly uncomfortable, and Amy would never consider subjecting herself to such a night.

Amy had guilted Jocelyn into going shopping with her the next day since I had to work. The look on my little sister's face told me I was in for an earful for it later. My mother and I parted ways in the parking lot of my apartment. As I hugged her goodbye, I was surprised by the lack of emotions I felt towards her. I admired her. I loved her. I was proud of her. But I cannot say that as a person, I liked her.

I snuggled into bed beside Landon and rested my head upon his chest. It was after eleven and I had to be back at the hospital at six in the morning for another twelve-hour shift. I was so tired I don't even remember closing my eyes.

12

MY STAYS FELT UNUSUALLY TIGHT this morning as I tried to focus my attention on Paster Lawerance Belville's sermon on loving thy neighbor which seemed particularly fitting given the current climate. I was seated between my husband and grandmother while Eugenia was perched on her pedestal on the other side of Keifer.

Eugenia and I had barely spoken since her last outburst. She continued to ignore my grandmother and I, for which we were both grateful. However, she continued to berate and speak condescendingly to our workers. Keifer made excuses for her and repeatedly apologized to them on his sister's behalf, but I was at my wit's end with her behavior.

After services concluded, we made our way to the front steps of the church. It was a cloudy day, but still relatively warm. The morning fog had lifted but the humidity clung to the air. A warm breeze floated around us as we stepped down to the courtyard in front. The trees scattered about before us were beginning to change their colors to welcome in the new season.

Our neighbors were milling about catching up on the latest gossip and news. Everyone was dressed in their Sunday best. Ladies adorned their best bonnets and gowns. Their wide hoop skirts were maneuvered around so neighbors could shake a gloved hand.

"Lovely service, Brother Belville." My grandmother shook our paster's hand.

"Thank you, Marissa. You are looking quite well." He smiled gently.

"I am feeling well." She beamed and moved down the church steps.

"Good morning, Sidney."

"Good morning, Brother Belville." I greeted him briefly before following my grandmother down the steps.

"Good morning, Dr. Marshall. I see you brought a guest with you today." I heard our Paster speak over my shoulder.

"Please allow me to introduce my sister, Eugenia. She is visiting with us." Keifer's voice was light and pleasant.

"Hello, Miss. Eugenia. We are pleased to have you with us." Brother Belville said politely. "I hope you will join us again before you leave."

"Thank you." I took a deep breath hoping Keifer would move her along down the steps before she said anything further.

Our house had been in an uproar the night before when Eugenia asked if she could join us this morning. My grandmother and I were adamantly against it fearing she would pull another stunt like she had with Mr. Bennett. Regardless of tradition that house guests attended services with their host, thus far we had not invited Eugenia to join us. She was of the Methodist faith while Marissa, and I were Southern Baptist – to which Keifer was now also.

Eventually, Keifer relented and agreed that Eugenia could attend services with us only on the condition – that she behaved herself and keep her political opinions to herself. She sweetly promised her brother to be on her best behavior. But my grandmother and I did not believe it possible.

Thankfully, she moved on without another word to our Paster. I looked over my shoulder and saw Keifer with a hand on her elbow guiding her down the steps. He wore a pleasant and forced smile on his face telling me she must have muttered something under her breath he had overheard.

"Good morning, Sidney." Our neighbor, Mrs. Charlotte Morgan approached us. "Hello, Mrs. Timmons." She was holding her baby girl, Adelaide who was born last spring, on her hip.

"Charlotte, how are you?" I reached over and touched Adelaide's chubby little arm. The little girl giggled and took ahold of my finger. "And how are you, Miss Adelaide? You are growing too quickly." She was a beautiful baby with bright blue eyes and a headful of blond curls like her father.

"Little Miss here started crawling this week and is quickly learning the word no." Charlotte chuckled.

"It is a touch lesson to learn, isn't it?" Little Adelaide cooed and giggled in her mother's arms.

"Sidney, I hate to impose on you and your family, but is there any chance your husband could look at Evan's tooth this afternoon. I believe it is infected. He has been up the last two nights in pain. He cannot rest." Charlotte explained.

"Yes, of course. Why don't you all join us for supper this afternoon. I know we have all been so busy we have hardly seen each other since summer." I offered.

"That would be lovely. We will head over directly after dropping the children off with Kezia." She beamed.

"Wonderful. I am looking forward to a nice long visit with you." I patted Adelaide's back gently before Charlotte scurred off to find her husband.

"Me too. We shall be there shortly." She smiled back at us.

Keifer and Eugenia joined us, and I told him about the Morgan's joining us for supper. He and Evan were close in age and got along splendidly while Charlotte and I had also become close friends after she and Evan were married.

Evan and I had grown up together. He met Charlotte when was clerking for his uncle's law practice in Ohio. She was friends with his cousin, Miriam, and he had started courting her shortly thereafter. They were married the following year and moved back to his hometown that spring. Evan was a prominent lawyer in Braintree and Boston. He had made a nice living for his growing family.

I informed Naomi upon our return about our guests and helped her and Marta quickly rearrange the table for everyone. I was hoping Eugenia would stay in her room and allow us to have a pleasant afternoon with our friends. But I knew she would never skip a meal or eat in her room. And Keifer reminded me it was rude to ask when I half suggested it to him.

I saw the Morgan's carriage coming down the long dirt pathway to our house. I hurried to the front parlor to let my grandmother know they had arrived and found Eugenia sitting on the chaise lounge trying to look engaged in a book.

"Grandmother, they will be here momentarily. They are coming up the drive." My grandmother nodded, but Eugenia smiled over at me leaving me with an uncomfortable feeling.

I opened the front door and Preston was already assisting them out of their carriage at the foot of the front steps. Charlotte was wearing a lovely burgundy gown trimmed in ivory lace and ribbons. Her thick dark hair was swept up in a curled bun on her crown adding to the angelic look portrayed on her face. She was a beautiful young woman in her mid-twenties and still maintained her hour-glass figure after having two children.

"Good afternoon, Sidney." Charlotte took her husband's arm and ascended the porch steps.

"Welcome," I greeted them happily. "Please come in."

We joined my grandmother and Eugenia in the parlor. Marta brought in a tray of tea and announced supper would be ready shortly. Keifer and Evan excused themselves and retreated into Keifer's office so he could examine Evan's tooth privately.

"I do not believe we met this morning," Charlotte extended her hand towards Eugenia. "I understand you are Keifer's sister visiting from Savannah."

"Yes," Eugenia touched her hand as if she were forced to touch a spider.

"It must be so nice visiting with your brother and spending time with Sidney before the baby arrives." Charlotte's voice was sweet and sincere.

"Yes." Eugenia rudely did not place her book aside.

Charlotte smiled over at me and continued, "I know it was a great comfort to me to have my sister with me when my children arrived. I do not know what I would do without her." She laughed lightly. "Of course, now we have Kenzia to help with the little ones and she is an absolute God send." Charlotte sipped her tea and sat down across the room from Eugenia next to me on the sofa.

"Who is Kenzia?" Eugenia asked.

"She is our nanny. She came to live with us after our son Levi was born almost three years ago." Charlotte looked nervously at me.

"And you pay her?" Eugenia inquired.

"Of course," Charlotte looked oddly at Eugenia. "She works for us, also lives with us."

"How many children do you have?" Eugenia asked.

"Two," Charlotte beamed proudly. "Levi is almost three and Adelaide is almost eight months old."

"You choose beautiful names for your children." Eugenia surprisingly complimented my friend.

"Thank you," Charlotte smiled.

"I never understood where your name came from, Sidney. Before you, I had always thought it a strictly male name. What is your middle name?" A smirk spread across Eugenia's thin lips.

"Harper," I stated proudly.

"Sidney Harper." Eugenia physically winced. "Not a feminine name. Where did it come from?"

"My son was certain she was a boy throughout his wife, Julia's pregnancy. So, he wanted to name his son, Sidney Harper after his grandfather who had passed away three months before Sidney was born. When her mother passed away during delivery, her father decided to go ahead with the name they had agreed upon." Marissa explained the history of my name.

"I cannot help but wonder why he did not name her after you or her mother. Sidney Harper is a male name." Eugenia had a disgusted look on her face.

"I think it is very unique." Charlotte chimed in. "Just as the lady herself."

"That we can agree upon." But Eugenia certainly did not mean it in the complimentary way Charlotte did.

"Supper is ready," Naomi announced from the parlor entryway.

"Thank you," I nodded towards her and turned to my companions. "Shall we?" We rose and walked into the dining room.

Evan and Keifer were waiting for us with our chairs pulled out when we entered. The gentleman assisted us politely before they took their own seats. Evan did not look overjoyed but had a painful look on his face.

"Is everything alright?" I inquired.

"Yes," Evan nodded. "Doc is going to take out my back molar after supper. It's infected. But he wants me to eat something since I will not be able to for the next several days."

"I said you will not be able to eat solid foods. You can have broth and lots of hot tea, but no coffee for the next seven days." Keifer grinned across the table at his friend.

"You will be fine, my love." Charlotte reached over and took her husband's hand.

"Let us pray," my grandmother spoke up. Everyone joined hands and bowed their heads. "Thank you, Lord, for bringing us all together on this beautiful day. Thank you for this delicious food to nourish our bodies. Watch over us Lord, protect us and our loved ones. In Jesus name we pray. Amen."

"Amen," we all answered in unison.

Naomi placed a smoked ham, candied yams, corn on the cob, green beams, and yeast rolls on the table. The steam rolled off the dishes and filled the air. The smell was intoxicating. Keifer served the ham while the other dishes were passed around the table.

My grandmother and I were unusually quiet having been off-handedly insulted by Eugenia over my birth name. My sister-in-law looked smug as she sat across my dining room table eating my food and it made my stomach turn. I wanted nothing more than to get this woman out of our home and take her toxicity with her.

"Mr. Morgan, I understand that you are the attorney who represents this county to the state assembly." Eugenia sliced up her ham nonchalantly.

"That is true," Evan answered politely.

"Do you enjoy that type of work?" Eugenia's poker face to those around the table appeared innocent enough except to those of whom knew better.

"Yes, I find it very satisfying and rewarding." Evan dipped into his yams. "I believe in a small way I am making a difference in my community and state."

"In what way?" Eugenia stirred her coffee, eyeing Evan carefully.

"Eugenia," Keifer warned, but Evan waved him off as if he was ready or expecting this.

"Ms. Eugenia, your opinion, and words to Mr. Bennett have become well known in our community. If you believe you are going to entice me into a heated debate regarding the current climate in Washington or the North, you are mistaken." I almost laughed at the expression on Eugenia's face.

"I beg your pardon, Mr. Morgan. I thought attorneys enjoyed a good debate and I was only curious on your perception of current political issues. But if you feel you are not up to it, I certainly understand." Eugenia said arrogantly.

"Well then, what do you think of Kansas passing their state constitution? Looks like they are going to enter the Union as a free state." Evan smirked.

"I think its abhorrent what the abolitionists did sending all those northerners to settle the territory just to fraud the vote." She spat.

"So, you are telling me only Southerners are allowed to move into new territory in this westward expansion to expand their system of oppression? That hardly screams equality, does it?" Evan was enjoying himself.

I glanced over at my husband hoping he would say something to end this before it got out of hand. But Keifer looked as if he was amused by it as much as Evan.

"I understand your narrow point of view, but that is hardly what happened. Can you explain to me why it was Southerners who were slaughtered by these Black Republican abolitionists?" Eugenia pinched her lips.

"If I recall correctly, there were multiple atrocities committed by both sides. No one's hands are clean." Evan stated as a matter of fact.

"That being said, are you excusing or better yet, justifying the actions – the murders committed by these Black Republican abolitionists. There is a reason the last decade has become known as Bleeding Kansas." She raised her eyebrows at Evan.

"I am not excusing nor justifying anything – let alone murders." Evan leaned forward and rested his forearms on the table. "You are simply not willing to concede that the chance of Kansas becoming a slave territory or state ended with the death of the Lecompton Constitution." Evan informed her. "Unfortunately, many in the southern Kansas territory thought taking up arms was a better solution." Evan shook his head. "No one wins in that situation."

"And do you believe it will end there?" Eugenia questioned. "The federal government put so much emphasis on popular sovereignty in the Kansas – Nebraska Act. They wanted – rather demanded the territory to define itself. Correct?" Eugenia tilted her head to the side, and I could sense where she was going with this line of questioning.

I look over at the faces of the other three gathered around our table. Each of them was engrossed in the heated, and false pleasant debate occurring across the table. Charlotte was completely enthralled as I believed she was hearing most of this information for the first time. Keifer appeared to be impressed with both parties' abilities to hold their own and focus on facts. Marissa was wearing a self-satisfied smirk that visibly broadened with each quick-witted response Evan came back with.

"Yes. I believe the purpose of the Kansas – Nebraska Act was that the federal government wanted the citizens residing within the territory to decide what they wanted." I cringed just a bit knowing what Eugenia was going to focus on next.

"Then you agree that state's rights are more significant than federal rights." Evan quickly realized he had played right into her hands.

"That is not what I said." Evan chuckled fully aware of her ploy. "The federal government respects the rights of states, but ultimately, they have final say. Our democracy is designed that way for a specific reason – hence county, state, and federal levels of government."

Eugenia chewed on the side of her lip for a moment contemplating her next response. Evan smirked over at Keifer who openly expressed his admiration for his friend while cutting his ham.

"And if we are speaking of fair play, I suppose you condone the actions of Southern representatives? It was South Carolina's Congressman Preston Brooks who caned Massachusetts Senator Charles Sumner in May of 56' because Sumner's speech on 'Crime Against Kansas' upset his disposition, correct?" Eugenia's face turned deep red. "I suppose caning an elderly unarmed man who is pinioned behind a desk that is bolted to the floor, while having your companions holding back anyone who could stop it, is the Southern way to conduct a debate." Evan chuckled and popped a piece of roll in his mouth enjoying the stunned look on Eugenia's face.

"You sir are greatly simplifying what occurred between them. Sumner insulted the South for two days in his continual rant full of lies and deceit. The man should have gotten worse." Eugenia spat.

"Eugenia," Keifer was astonished by her words. "The man almost died on the Senate floor." He shook his head in disbelief. "I cannot understand any rational for Brooks' behavior. I do not care what Sumner said."

"Every Southerner believes Sumner asked for it, and if there were any justice, he would have gotten worse." Eugenia declared sticking out her chin with Southern pride.

"Brooks violated the rules of congressional combat in every possible way." Evan stated. "He should have been permanently expelled and banned from office. Thankfully, he died before he could do much more damage. The world is for the better for it." Eugenia's eyes narrowed at Evan, but he continued smirking happily satisfyingly at her. "Didn't he die from a cold?"

"Brooks passed away from a respiratory infection." Eugenia said through gritted teeth.

"So, a cold." Evan snorted and shrugged towards Keifer who accidentally snorted in his coffee.

"Excuse me," My husband wiped his mouth his napkin. He placed it back on his lap and attempted to recompose himself. "I think we can all agree that both sides have behaved poorly."

A silence fell over the dining room and hugged everyone like a strait jacket. My grandmother and I exchanged knowing glances and had an unspoken conversation with our eyes. I tried not to laugh or even smirk over Evan's remark, but it was challenging, and I was unsuccessful.

"On a happier note, have you and Doc decided on names for the baby?" Charlotte quickly changed the subject.

"After his father if it's a boy." I smiled at my husband.

"And if it is a girl?" Marissa grinned over at me.

"Keifer and I have decided to name her after my mother, Julia Grace." I said proudly.

"Why would you do that?" Eugenia wrinkled her nose.

"What do you mean?" Keifer interrupted.

"I mean, it is morbid, isn't it? Naming a child after a deceased woman who died in childbirth." Eugenia explained.

"I believe it is a loving tribute to a lady who sacrificed her life to bring her beautiful daughter into this world." Charlotte explained.

Thanks to Charlotte shifting the topic, the remainder of the meal was delightful. She talked about the joys and headaches of early motherhood and how watching her children grow was the greatest joy she has ever experienced. It was easy to see how much motherhood agreed with her.

They left for home before twilight. Evan was holding a rag wrapped around a chunk of ice up to the side of his face. I advised Charlotte to have him put some tea leaves over the area inside his mouth to help with the bleeding and Marissa confirmed it worked like a charm. I reminded her that he would be uncomfortable for the next several days and possibly swollen. Evan grunted at Keifer when he told him again to stick to a liquid diet.

Overall, I was thrilled with how well the afternoon went. Keifer and I settled in front of the hearth letting the heat take the chill out of the air. Marissa was reading quietly in her rocking chair and Eugenia had not been downstairs since dinner. She was irritated that her point didn't cause as much ruckus as she hoped.

13

I **WAS EXHAUSTED. I WAS TEN** hours into my twelve-hour shift when I finally found fifteen minutes to sneak into an on-call room and rest. I was beginning my seventeenth week of pregnancy, and it seemed I was tired all the time. My feet were beginning to swell after long shifts, but thankfully, I really wasn't showing much.

I had only gained five pounds thus far, causing Jocelyn to give my child the nickname of Smurf. My doctor assured me that everything looked good, and it was not uncommon in young women as active as I was. I was still working out several days a week, and despite my knowledge, I was practically bathing in lotion twice a day out of fear of stretch marks.

I kicked off my sneakers and crawled beneath the blanket. I closed my eyes and snuggled down into the pillow. Every part of my body was worn-out, and my feet were killing me.

"Sidney?" A soft knock at the door broke my peace. "Sidney?" The light from the outdoor corridor broke into my sanctuary. "I apologize for bothering you." The triage nurse, Paula, said in a weak voice. "We have an incoming trauma; a GSW to the chest. It's about five minutes out."

"Okay. Thank you, Paula. I'm coming."

I reluctantly swung my legs over the side of the bed and slipped my feet back into my sneakers. I picked up my scrubs jacket and put it on as I walked back out into the bright hallway lights.

"Two minutes, Sidney." Marti, one of the interns, shouted over the noise coming from the emergency room.

"All right." I jogged towards my station to await information from one of the law enforcement officers.

I could hear the roar of the sirens off in the distance growing closer by the second. I reached into the pocket of my jacket and pulled out a hairclip. I twisted my hair into a French knot and waited anxiously with Marti and two other interns.

The ambulance pulled into the bay, and the rear doors flew open. The paramedic hopped out and began listing all the vitals. The patient was a large man wearing nothing but gym shorts. He was in restraints with bandages over his right shoulder.

The residents and physician on-call, Dr. Bradley Hoffman began working diligently on the patient and rushing the gurney inside. The gurney was quickly followed by two officers and a paramedic hollering off the patients' stats to the physician.

"What happened?" I asked Tiffany, the paramedic I've gotten to know well in the last couple of years.

"Officer-involved shooting." She nodded towards the officer as he followed the residents.

"Wonderful." I rolled my eyes behind them. "What happened?"

"I suspect this guy is on PCP. It took six officers to restrain him after he was shot in the shoulder after he shot a known drug dealer and an innocent child and their mother who happened to be in the same laundry mat at the same time." One of the officers shouted over this shoulder.

The medical team put the suspect in trauma room three. He was shouting and cursing, fighting against the restraints. Marti turned towards me with a discouraged look on her face.

"The officer should have had better aim." she muttered.

"I agree." The officer stated, roughly only loud enough for her to hear me.

"How are we going to get him off the gurney? Can we tranquilize him?" Marti asked Dr. Hoffman.

"Not yet." He grabbed a syringe of Narcan.

Dr. Hoffman approached by the foot of the bed to hand the syringe to a resident who was closer to administer the medication, but one of the interns — a gangly young man named Norman who was brilliant with medicine but lacked an ounce of common sense — had loosened the foot restraints on the suspect.

The suspect screamed out a barrage of profanity and kicked his way loose, flailing about wildly. His foot kicked out the moment I passed and caught me directly in the abdomen. I went flying back into the cabinets, cracking my head into the countertop.

Everything went black.

I woke up to a blinding bright light blaring down at me. My head was throbbing, and there was a stabbing pain in my stomach. I tried to double over and groaned softly. I felt hands gently nudge me over to my back.

"Lie still, Sidney." Marti's voice spoke softly.

"It hurts," I moaned.

"I know." She smoothed the hair away from my face.

"Landon, I want Landon." I closed my eyes, trying to block the pain.

"I already called him. He's on his way." Her hands felt cool on my face.

"Sidney, how are you feeling?" I recognized the voice of Dr. Jarbo, an attending obstetrics and gynecology physician.

"My baby," my hands roamed gently over the small bulge in my abdomen.

"I need you to lie still." His soothing voice was of little comfort to me. "You've suffered a blow to your abdomen."

"The gunshot guy," I muttered.

"Idiot boy loosened the restraints." Marti stated.

"I didn't think he'd lash out. I was only trying to move him over to the bed." Norman's nasal voice whined.

"My baby?" I looked over at Dr. Jarbo.

"You have some bleeding. We're going to do an ultrasound as soon as Landon gets here. I'm hoping it's just a little distress." He took my hand and leaned in towards me.

Tears welled up in the corners of my eyes. I wrapped my arms, protectively across my stomach, and closed my eyes. This couldn't be happening. I wanted this baby more than anything. I tried to calm myself and whispered internally to my child for it to move — to give me some sort of signal that it was still residing comfortably within my womb.

But nothing happened.

I felt nothing.

I rolled over on my side and silently wept.

A half-hour later, Landon rushed into the room. It was his night off, and he had thrown on a pair of jeans and a T-shirt. His hair was a mess, and he had a days' worth of stubble on his face.

"Sidney?" Landon sat on the bed beside me. "Baby, are you okay?" He ran his fingers through my hair.

"No." I wrapped my arms around his neck and curled up into him. "I haven't felt our baby move since I got kicked." The tears started rolling down my cheeks again and crashing on his shirt.

"I'm sure our little monster is fine." He tried to reassure me. "He's a tough little booger."

"Yes, she is." I couldn't help but smile.

"Sweetheart, I know you're worried, but I'm sure everything is fine." Landon squeezed me gently.

"Landon, thank you for coming in. Dr. Jarbo will be in shortly." Marti walked over to my side of the bed. "Can I get you anything, Sidney?"

"No. Thank you, Marti. I appreciate it." She rubbed my arm gently.

"How are you feeling, Sidney?" Dr. Jarbo pulled back the curtain and approached us as Marti exited.

"Still breathing," I muttered.

"It's a start." He grinned at my sarcasm. "We're going to move you upstairs where you'll be more comfortable and have more privacy."

"I'm being admitted?" I turned towards him with a look of disgust. "Can't Landon just watch me at home?"

"Is Landon an obstetrician?" Dr. Jarbo inquired.

"Not that I'm aware of." I looked up at Landon's face. "What did you say you were specializing in?" I joked.

"Enough of the remarks, Sid. You're staying here tonight."

"You're mean," I grumbled.

"I try." Dr. Jarbo pulled the curtain back a bit. "Marti is going to take you upstairs."

A half hour later, I was resting in the maternity ward in a private room feeling apprehensive. Landon got me tucked in tightly after listening to me complain multiple times over the revoltingly, thin gown the nurse forced me into.

"Don't make such a fuss. I'll call Jocelyn and have her stop by our place. She can pick up a pair of pajamas for you and your toiletries." Landon kissed my forehead.

"Fine. But you know you are going to cause alarm if you call her." I warned.

"Jocelyn doesn't overreact, except in hostile situations." He chuckled.

"True." I shrugged. "But she's so excited about this baby. I have never seen someone so attentive."

"I agree. It's a bit abnormal." He sat down on the corner of my bed. "I don't understand why she and Jackson haven't had a baby yet. She's completing her final leg of school. Have they even started trying yet?"

"I believe they are talking about it. I know they are both eager to start a family." That was a mild understatement.

"I hope they get pregnant soon." Landon muttered as he picked up the bedside phone and dialed Jocelyn's cell.

Even though I wasn't holding the phone, I could hear every word Jocelyn said, including the panic in her voice. Landon did his best to soothe her and tell her what things I needed from our apartment.

Knowing my sister, as soon as she hung up the phone, she'd be calling our father, Uncle Nicholas, Phoebe, and her in-laws. We were a close family, united by our rare gift. It was only a matter of time before they all showed up here fussing over me and driving the staff insane.

⚘

Dr. Jarbo came in, pushing a portable ultrasound machine. My heart leaped into my throat. I still hadn't felt our baby move since I woke up. I would have given anything to feel that little flutter that always warmed my heart and brought a smile to my face.

"There's no need to worry, Sidney. We just want to make sure everything is all right since you had a lot of bleeding with the trauma."

"I know, Dr. Jarbo." I barely said.

"Please, call me Keith. After all, we're colleagues." He smiled sweetly.

I rested back against the pillow, and Landon pulled up my gown to expose my abdomen. He took hold of my hand as Dr. Jarbo applied the gel to my stomach.

"Oh, that's cold." I shuttered briefly.

"Sorry," Dr. Jarbo smiled and moved the wand over my womb.

"Well?" All our eyes were glued to the monitor.

I wasn't fluent in obstetrics, but I knew enough to know an empty womb when I saw one; as did Landon. Tears welled up in my eyes, and none of us said a word.

"I'm so sorry," Dr. Jarbo said in a low voice.

"Are you sure?" I asked, even though I already knew.

Dr. Jarbo nodded slowly.

"No," I cried and reached for Landon.

"I'll schedule the D&C." Dr. Jarbo said in a small voice.

"Thank you." Landon choked out.

Landon wrapped his arms around me as I buried my face in his chest and wept. I could feel his body shaking alongside mine, and I knew he was crying too.

Dr. Jarbo quietly left the room.

14

WEDNESDAY, OCTOBER 12, 1859

SUMMER FADED INTO FALL and the hot, muggy days drifted seamlessly into cooler ones. The daylight hours shortened; the nights grew longer. Harvest was upon us.

Casper and Duncan spent most of their time in the fields overseeing the workers and progress. The details on the cellars were coming along, but I soon realized we would not break ground until after the spring thaw when we started planting for next season.

Still, we had begun stockpiling goods, as much as we could afford bit by bit. We had started stacking crates in the back bedroom. Keifer chalked my behavior up to a worrisome, expected mother.

I laid there in bed as the early morning sun rose over the brightly colored tree line, running my hands across my abdomen repeatedly. The images of my *other* life and the events that had transpired *there* in the last few days.

I closed my eyes and felt the joyous little quiver in the pit of my stomach. I put a little pressure on my abdomen and rubbed my hands across it again. Once more, the small quiver pushed back against my fingers.

My heart filled with joy, but I still had the lingering emptiness in my heart from the trauma *there*. I sat up quickly and tossed the covers aside. Thankfully, Keifer had already left for the office.

I looked down between my legs. There was no blood on my gown, nothing on the bed. I knew I had lost our baby *there*, but then why was I, or could I possibly still be pregnant *here*?

I climbed out of bed and slipped off my gown. I climbed into the layers of undergarments and pulled on my navy-blue gown. After struggling with the laces, I tied up my satin slippers and brushed my hair out before tying it into a low bun.

I hurried down the stairs, searching for my grandmother. She must have some explanation for this oddity of time. I finally found her out on the veranda with a thick shawl wrapped tightly around her shoulders and her morning coffee emitting steam from her mug.

"Good morning, darling. How are you feeling?" She shivered.

"Good morning, Grandmother. Why on earth are you sitting out here? The morning air has quite a bite to it?" I sat down in the rocking chair beside her.

"Eugenia was in the dining room, and I did not have the strength to deal with her bitterness this morning. I cannot wait for her to hop back on her broomstick and fly South for the winter." My grandmother stated.

"She avoids me unless Keifer is around. Then she makes her presence known is the most despicable ways." I sighed heavily. "I hope she leaves soon."

"Is that how you really feel?" Eugenia's voice snuck up behind me.

"Oh, dear Lord," I muttered, turning around in my chair. "You realize it is polite for people to announce their presence rather than eavesdropping on other people's private conversations."

"That is beside the point. I heard you say you wanted me to leave. Is that how you really feel?" She stood there with her hands on her hips in a menacing fashion.

"Eugenia, it is too early in the morning to have this conversation. I have not even had my coffee yet. Plus, I sought my grandmother out this morning because I have something important to discuss with her. Your insignificant issue can wait until later." I was in no mood for her pettiness.

"Well, I never." Her face turned red and puffed up like a blowfish.

"Well, now you have." I stood up and faced her. "Please, go bother someone else and ruin their peaceful morning." I turned my back to her and sat back down, smoothing out my dress, and smiling at my grandmother.

"I will have a talk with your husband about your rude behavior." She scoffed and stomped back towards the house.

"You do that." I hollered over my shoulder with a laugh.

"You know, Keifer is not going to be happy with you." My grandmother warned me.

"Keifer will forgive me. He has not been too thrilled with her lately, either. Especially since she argues with Mr. Bennett and Mr. Morgan every time they visit. Have you noticed Mr. Bennett's visits have decreased from three or four evenings a week to only once a week to ten days?" I pointed out.

"Yes, and I hate to admit I do miss him." she admitted. "And it's not like I can visit his home. The scandal that would cause would be horrific."

"I understand," I huffed. "I am simply going to have to be direct with her and ask her to leave. There is no other way for any of us to have peace."

"That will be a blessing. Can I be there when you tell her?" My grandmother giggled.

"Like I would deny you that pleasure." I smiled.

"Anyway, what is it that you wanted to discuss with me?" She refreshed her mug of coffee and poured me one also.

"Something happened on Sunday *there*, that greatly impacts my world *here* . . . I think." I placed my hand protectively across my abdomen. "I had waited to say anything because I wanted to make sure everything was alright *here* first. And apparently it is." I rubbed my fingers over the small bump once again.

"Explain, please." She added cream and sugar to both our mugs and handed me mine.

"It was toward the end of my shift, and we had a patient brought in with a gunshot wound who was suspected to be under the influence of drugs. He was in restraints but . . ." I continued to recount the events that had transpired in my life *there* and broke down when I told her about my beloved baby. "But I don't understand. If I lost my baby *there*, why am I still pregnant *here*?" I sobbed.

"That is perplexing." She paused for a moment, appearing deep in thought. "I wonder if that would explain why Patrick and Shane did not inherit *EVE*." Her lips perched in concentration. "Do you know their birthdates?"

"Their birthdates? I know Shane's. He was born on September 15, 1964. He was 30 when I was born *there*." I fiddled with my mug. "I know I was seven when Patrick was born, so that would have been in 1840. I believe he was born right around Christmas that year, but I do not know the exact date."

"But Bethany didn't have the gift of *EVE*. Monte and Nicholas inherited the gift from Walter." She pondered for a moment. "I wonder if Bethany had a miscarriage and then got pregnant again shortly thereafter. That would explain why the child didn't inherit the gift."

"But I thought the gift was passed through the mother." I asked. "That is what Nicholas speculated." I recalled my Spring Break visit to his home in Bloomington, Indiana, years ago when I first learned of *EVE*.

"I suppose he could be mistaken on that account." She shrugged. "Do you recall what your grandmother's name was on your father's side *there*?"

"Irene. She passed away shortly after Ethan was born. I barely remember her." I racked my brain, trying to recall her. "I seem to remember she spoiled us, but I'm not sure." For some reason, I had a vague memory of her at my birthday surrounded by lots of gifts. I wasn't sure if they were from her or not.

"Has Shane told you much about his parents?" She inquired.

"Not much, but I could ask Nicholas tomorrow." I felt exasperated. "What does this mean?"

"If Irene or Bethany had a miscarriage and then got pregnant again shortly after that, wouldn't that have affected the gift of *EVE*?" Grandmother speculated.

"I would imagine so, but I don't know." I slumped down in my chair, disheartened. "What does this mean for my child? Would my baby only be with me *here* and not *there*?"

"I believe so." She shrugged, slightly.

"I wish I could be certain. But this doesn't make any sense." My head began to ache.

"What doesn't make any sense?"

"Walter, my father *here*, has the gift of *EVE*. Nicholas told me that he told them tales of King Williams War. That was back in what. . . " I searched my brain for the date. "The mid-seventeenth century? If he travels back from this time, then who was the father of my father and uncles *there*?"

"What was your grandfather's name?" She looked down in concentration or confusion. I wasn't sure which.

"From *there*?" I was trying to figure out where she was going with this.

"Yes."

"Ralph. But then how does he fit with the inheritance of *EVE*?" I wondered aloud.

"Ralph? Are you sure?"

"Yes. Why?"

"Because my youngest son in my *other* life is named Ralph Miller after my father." My grandmother looked surprised.

"Then he would be the father of Shane, Monte, and Nicholas." I speculated.

"My goodness." She sighed heavily. "This is unbelievable."

"So, my child will not have the gift of *EVE* because I lost my baby *there*, but other children I have will inherit it?" I placed my hand over my abdomen.

"I believe so." She smiled. "You must remember that *EVE* consists of a great deal of speculation and not many definite answers. It's hard to say anything for sure."

"But it certainly is enough to give one a raging headache." I rubbed my temples.

"Have you eaten anything this morning?"

"No." I confessed.

"But you've consumed three cups of coffee. It is no wonder your head hurts." She stood up and adjusted her shawl. "Come on. Let's go to the kitchen and see if we can find you something to eat." She took a hold of my arm and led me back into the house.

We made it through dinner without Eugenia confronting me about the words I spoke earlier on the veranda. However, I knew it was merely a matter of time before she got my husband alone and tattled on me like a small child. She spent the entire meal giving me dirty looks across the dining room table. The awkward silence was noticed by all. Still, no one said anything.

Thankfully, Mr. Bennett stopped by just as Naomi brought out the coffee. We adjourned in the parlor, where Eugenia took the seat next to my husband. I smiled, coyly at my grandmother, and rolled my eyes. She stifled a giggle in her handkerchief.

"It is so nice to see you, Edmund. We have missed your visits." I smiled at him, taking a seat beside my grandmother.

"My apologies. I have been keeping myself busy." His eyes glimpsed over towards Eugenia before he smiled at me.

"I understand." I tried not to smirk.

"Yes. We certainly do." My grandmother echoed my sentiment eyeing Eugenia noticeably, causing Mr. Bennett to almost choke on his evening coffee.

"How are things at the bank?" Keifer made himself comfortable.

"Good. Busy. The turmoil and unrest in Washington are bleeding further across the country." Mr. Bennett noted.

"Yes. I hear a lot of it from my patients as well; both in the office and on my house calls." My husband admitted.

"Have you begun harvesting yet?" I attempted to change the subject before my sister-in-law decided to begin one of her infamous rants about States' rights and their right to own slaves again.

"Yes, I am happy to say I should have it finished up this weekend if the rain holds out." Edmund informed us.

"How wonderful for you. You must be so pleased." I remarked.

"Yes, well . . . " He looked slightly uncomfortable.

"What are people saying about States' rights?" Eugenia piped up.

"Please. Not this evening." My grandmother took a deep breath. "I do not believe I have the strength for another of your tyrants."

I could not help but smile. For my grandmother to be so blunt only meant she was truly at the end of her rope. I held my breath and waited for the fallout to begin.

"What is that supposed to mean?" Eugenia's tone rose up a notch.

"It means I am sick and tired of your opinion." My grandmother stated as matter-of-factly.

"Grandmother now is not the time nor the place." Keifer warned.

"Hush now, Keifer. I would like to hear what she has to say." Eugenia spoke up.

"Well, it is getting late. I must be getting home." Mr. Bennett placed his coffee mug on the end table.

"My sincerest apologies, Edmund." Keifer rose from his chair.

"Sit down, Keifer, and do not apologize for me." Eugenia said roughly. "Your grandmother-in-law and wife have been utterly deplorable to me since my arrival, and this morning I heard them talking on the veranda saying they could not wait for me to leave."

I looked over at my grandmother, who snorted into her coffee, making me chuckle aloud.

"Perhaps you should not eavesdrop on private conversations, because when you do you may hear something, you may not like." I retorted.

"See," Eugenia waved her napkin in our direction. "What did I tell you?"

"Let me tell you something, Eugenia. You have been horrid since you stepped off the train. You have made everyone in this house miserable. You have our staff walking around on eggshells. My lovely grandmother and I have done everything to make you feel at home and welcomed, and in return for our hospitality, you have gone out of your way to be rude, disrespectful, and cruel to her and myself. Plus, you have used everything from guilt to manipulation to force your brother out of the life he has worked so hard to build." I snapped.

"Sidney," Keifer looked shocked.

"What did I tell you." Eugenia pointed at me.

"My apologies, Keifer." I stood up and straightened my gown. "But a person can only take so much before they reach their limit, and she has pushed long beyond mine. Now if you ever loved me, you would put this horrid creature on the first train to Savannah tomorrow. Good evening, Mr. Bennett. Grandmother." I nodded at each and made my way upstairs to my room.

Thirty minutes later, Keifer walked into our room and closed the door behind him. He remained silent as he undressed and prepared himself for bed. I rested against the pillows and watched him, waiting for him, to give me a good tongue lashing for my unladylike outburst.

"Do you feel better?" Keifer sat down on the side of his bed.

"Yes, I do, actually."

"I blamed your outburst on pregnancy hormones." He looked over at me. "But I have a feeling you would have said it with or without the pregnancy." I saw the corner of his mouth twitch.

"Most likely, but one can never tell." I smiled sweetly.

"Well, you will be happy to hear that my sister has decided to travel home tomorrow."

"Are you serious? She's leaving?" I sat up abruptly.

"Don't look so distraught. It's unbecoming, my dear." He smirked.

"Keifer, you know she has been dreadful to me, and my grandmother since her arrival. She has done everything possible to make us feel unwelcome in our own home. Not to mention how she has tried to make you feel guilty about your parents' poor health to convince you to return to Savannah." I reasoned.

"I know." He turned towards me and rested his hand on my leg. "You are right. I am sorry she has been this way. I was hoping she would behave herself, but knowing her history, I should not have expected so." Keifer shrugged slightly.

"I am sorry, my dear. I know how much your family means to you." I reached down and took his hand.

"You are my family too, you know; the most important part of my family." Keifer crawled up beside me and kissed me. "I am sorry. I know you have been very tolerant these last couple of months."

"I tried." I sighed. "I am afraid I was not entirely successful." I laughed just a bit.

"I am proud that you tried." My husband chuckled as he turned down the oil lamps.

"I love you, darling." He climbed back into bed and took me in his arms.

"I love you, too." I whispered, kissing him passionately.

15

OPENED MY EYES IN THE DIM hospital room. My head was resting upon Landon's chest, and he held me tightly in his arms. I could feel the strong rhythm of his heartbeat against my cheek. There was still a dull ache in my head that would not allow me peaceful sleep. I squeezed Landon gently and closed my eyes once more, feeling safe and secure.

I could hear the rain falling outside my window. It was another rainy, gloomy October day. It felt perfect to me. I wished I was at home, curled up in front of the fireplace with a hot cup of coffee and a good book. I wished I was anywhere, but here.

There was a gaping hollowness in my chest. My arms felt empty for the child I would never get to hold. I longed for the face I would never get to see *here*. I wondered if the child I gave birth to *there* would have looked like the child I would have had *here*.

I knew those of us with this oddity of *EVE* looked the same on both planes, but what if my child was an exception. My body ached; my heart shattered. I wanted to scream, to cry, to shout. I wanted my baby.

The thought of going back to our apartment and seeing the newly decorated nursery; the bassinet we'd bought two weeks ago in our bedroom to keep our baby close to use at night — it was just too much.

Jocelyn, Phoebe, and Emily had bought so many little onesies, booties, and blankets. We had adorned the nursery with everything any baby could possibly need. Now it would remain empty.

Tears leaked from the corners of my eyes onto Landon's shirt. I could not help but wonder if he was experiencing the same whirlwind of emotions as I. I closed my eyes tightly and tried to focus on the fact that I was still pregnant *there*.

It was of little comfort.

Images from *there* flooded my mind's eyes. My conversation on the veranda with my grandmother replayed itself. I needed to get in touch with my Uncle Nicholas. I needed answers. I needed to know what was happening to my unborn child.

If my child did inherit *EVE*, what would happen to his or her soul now that they no longer have a body on his plane? How does this affect them? Do they still have a soul on that plane?

The questions consumed me, and all I could think of was talking to my Uncle Nicholas or Jackson's parents. They must have some answers for me. If I could just piece together what happened with Patrick and Shane, perhaps that would provide me with some insight as to what was happening with my own child.

"Good morning, Sidney." Lindsey, one of the OB/GYN nurses, lightly touched my arm. "How are you feeling?"

I moaned, turning towards her.

"I felt okay until I moved." I gave her a weak smile.

Landon stirred and stretched beside me. He gave me a gentle squeeze and sat up.

"Are you cramping?" Lindsey asked, taking my vitals.

"Yes."

"That's most likely from the D&C." She stated.

"Yes, I'm aware."

"Right." She smiled warmly. "I forgot. I'll get you something for the pain. Are you hungry?"

"I'll get her something." Landon spoke up. "I'm not about to subject you to the food in this place." He kissed my forehead lightly.

"Thank you." I grimaced and rolled onto my side.

"Einstein Bagels?" He climbed out of bed and slipped into his shoes.

"That sounds wonderful. And can you please get me some real coffee? I'd love a pumpkin spice latte."

"Of course. You can have anything you want."

"I love you." I reached up for him. Landon leaned over the bed and kissed me sweetly. "Help me up, darling. I need to use the restroom and brush my teeth."

"Do you feel up to it?" Lindsey asked, taking a hold of my arm.

"It's not a matter of want; it's a necessity." I gave them the best smile I could muster.

"Just take it easy. I'll wait out here for you. Holler if you need me." Lindsey guided me over to the door.

Landon waited to leave until I came back out of the bathroom. He helped me into bed and took a seat on the edge of it.

"I'm going to stop by the apartment to get cleaned up if that's okay with you." He asked.

"That's fine." I tried to make myself as comfortable as possible.

"I'll be back shortly." Landon grabbed his jacket, and with a quick kiss, he was gone.

"I'll get your meds, and Dr. Jarbo should be by shortly. Is there anything else you need?" Lindsey asked.

"No. I'm fine. Thank you." She left the room, closing the door behind her.

Finally, alone, I picked up my phone and began scrolling through my contacts until I reached Uncle Nicholas. I tapped on his name, and it began ringing.

"Hello sweetheart, how are you?" His voice was soothing.

"Not well." I choked.

"What happened?" I could hear the concern in his voice.

"Did Jocelyn call you?"

"She did, but I was in class. She left me a voicemail, but I have not called her back yet. Are you alright?"

"We had a gunshot victim high on something. He was in restraints, but this idiot intern undid his leg restraints, and he kicked me in the abdomen." I sobbed. "I lost my baby." I barely got the words out.

"Oh, Sidney. I am so sorry." Uncle Nicholas said in a low voice. "Where are you?"

"At work. I am up on the OB/GYN floor."

"I have classes until three this afternoon. Is it all right if I come by afterwards?" He asked.

"Uncle Nicholas," I struggled. "I'm still pregnant *there*. What's going to happen to my baby's soul? What does this mean?" I wept.

"Calm down. Your baby is fine, I promise." He paused. "I'm going to cancel my classes for the rest of the day. I'll be there shortly. What room are you in?"

"2358."

"All right. I will see you soon."

"Thank you." I whispered and brushed the tears off my cheeks.

"I love you." Uncle Nicholas said warmly.

"I love you, too." I hung up the phone and dropped it beside me.

Lindsey came in a few minutes later and administered some pain medication to my IV. She didn't ask why I was curled up in a ball crying. She already knew. She left quietly without uttering a word to me. I was thankful for it.

The world seemed to be spinning out of my control. I felt completely helpless in it. I could not shake this feeling of emptiness deep inside me. I felt hollow; like a part of me was ripped out, and nothing could ever replace it.

I was angry. I wanted to lash out at someone; anyone. I wanted them to hurt as badly as I did. I wanted to grab that idiot intern and bang my fists into him. This was his fault. His stupidity cost me my child.

Deep down I knew it was an accident. I knew Norman didn't do it on purpose. But I couldn't help it. I was so hurt, so angry. I wrapped my arms around a pillow and wept uncontrollably.

I felt a kiss on my cheek and fingers brushed my hair gently away from my face. I felt the weight of someone sitting down on the bed.

"Darling, are you okay?" Landon's voice brought me back from a dreamless sleep.

"Hi," I opened my eyes and pulled myself up in a seated position. I leaned back against the mountain of pillows.

"I'm sorry it took me so long. I didn't realize how hard it was going to be going back to the apartment." It was then that I noticed the red circles and puffiness under his eyes.

"I understand." I reached out and took his hand. "I don't want to go back there either." Tears started rolling down my cheeks once more.

"I'll pack it up before you come home." Landon leaned over and wrapped his arms around me.

"No. Not yet." I whispered with my head against his shoulder. "I need to say goodbye." I could feel his nod against me. "I'm so sorry, Landon."

"Sorry for what? You didn't do anything wrong." His voice cracked.

"I lost our baby." I choked on the words. "I'm so sorry."

"Sidney," He leaned back and looked at me. "Sweetheart, that was not your fault. It was an accident." He had tears running down my face. "I don't blame you." He shook his head slightly.

"I keep replaying it in my head. I wish I could have handed it off to someone else; stayed back away from him. Something. I don't know." I rambled.

"I know," he whispered.

"Sorry for interrupting." Uncle Nicholas knocked softly on the open door.

"Uncle Nicholas," I brushed the tears away. "Please, come in." I tried to smile as best I could.

"Hello, Uncle Nicholas." Landon sat up and hastily brushed the tears aside.

"How are you feeling?" He handed me a small bouquet of white lilies in a pink vase.

"You remembered." His small gesture brought about a fresh round of tears.

It seemed everything was making me cry as this emotional rollercoaster never seemed to end.

"For you," Uncle Nicholas smiled softly and sat down in the chair beside my bed. "How are you two holding up?"

"We're getting there." Landon stood up. "Your breakfast sandwich, and your lattes on the tray. I'm going to give you two some privacy." He leaned down and kissed me. "I've still got to call my parents and tell them what's going on." He sighed heavily. "I've been putting it off." He shrugged. "I'll be back shortly." Landon left the room, closing the door behind him.

Uncle Nicholas moved from the chair to the foot of my bed. He reached out and lovingly placed my hand on my calf, patting it briefly.

"How are you really feeling?" He asked as I unwrapped my sandwich. I didn't have much of an appetite, but I knew I needed to eat something simply to counter all the medication they were pumping through me.

"Numb." I took a bite but tasted nothing. "It doesn't seem real." I told him.

"And *there*?" He asked.

"I have been holding my breath for a couple days. When I woke up yesterday *there*, the first thing I did was rub my abdomen. I did everything I could to make the baby move. Finally, it did. I felt it." I explained.

"And then what did you do?"

"I got dressed and found my grandmother. I was frightened. I still am. What's happening to my baby? If this child was supposed to inherit *EVE*, what happens to it now?"

"What did Marissa say?" He inquired.

"We talked about Shane and Patrick. My grandparents — your parents. Their birthdates." I took another bite and then set it aside with no intention of finishing it. "Do you realize they are several months apart in age. Is that why they do not have *EVE*. Did Bethany have a miscarriage? Or Irene?" I speculated.

"I have never asked them. There is almost a decade between my eldest brother and me. My mother never mentioned a miscarriage to me on either plane, and honestly, I never asked. It was never something we discussed. Times were much different, and parents, especially mothers, did not discuss such things with their sons." Uncle Nicholas said in an almost apologetic tone.

"True. Even now, I do not believe that would be something my mother would ever discuss with Ethan today unless he asked her directly." I admitted.

"Amy is a bit more refined than most women." He chuckled.

"My mother is not the most affectionate person." I finally smiled. "I still cannot believe she flew all the way out here just to tell me she did not want me to follow in her footsteps. Like I needed a reminder." I scoffed.

"Does she know about what happened?" My Uncle raised an eyebrow.

"That I was attacked by a patient? No." I perched my lips together.

"The miscarriage?"

"No." I shook my head. "I don't want to hear the joy in her voice. I know she will be thrilled, and it makes me ill."

"So, you're not going to call her?"

"No."

"Why is that?"

"Do you really need to ask?" I tilted my head to the side.

"She is your mother, Sidney. She loves you."

"My mother's love has the tendency to be very conditional. You recall what she did to Jocelyn. Their relationship has never recovered." I reminded him. "And Jocelyn is probably livid with me, or she would be if this hadn't happened because she had to spend time alone with Amy on Sunday because I had to work. I'm afraid to ask Jocelyn how it went. She hasn't mentioned it yet because of all this, but I know I will hear about it eventually." I chuckled without humor.

"But you were always so close with your mother before she moved to Seattle."

"That is only because I was her golden child." I scoffed. "Look at me?" I snorted. "I look like her. I have always been an A student. I was a cheerleader all through school and my undergrad studies. I followed in her footsteps and am becoming a pediatrician." I laughed half-heartedly. "I am every parent's dream. When she found out, she looked at me as if I was her greatest failure." Tears leaked from the corners of my eyes.

"And here I thought she reserved that position for Jocelyn, even though Ethan's been flirting with it for a while now." My uncle laughed.

"She read Landon the riot act and rained hellfire down on him while I was at work. He handled her like a champ and didn't put up with her crap." I tried to make light of it by smirking through my tears. "And she wonders why I didn't tell her. Amy is the only person I know who could reach through the phone, grab me by the neck, and within seconds I would be standing in front of her in Seattle with her hands around my throat."

"I could see her doing that." My uncle laughed.

"She is definitely that good." I joined his laughter.

It felt good. I needed it.

I love my mother dearly, but I knew how she was. I had witnessed all that she had and continues to bestow upon my sister for not following the path she had designated for her. My mother has never forgiven her for it and after all these years, I do not believe she ever would.

My uncle took a deep breath, cleared his throat, and smiled lovingly at me.

"As far as Shane and Patrick; I believe there must have been a miscarriage. Shane is what — four months older than Patrick, so Bethany must have had a miscarriage. With birth control being what it was back in the nineteenth century, she must have gotten pregnant again within a couple months of losing the child that connected Shane's spirit." Uncle Nicholas rubbed his chin and speculated in deep thought.

"So, if I got pregnant again *here* before I give birth *there*, that child would not have *EVE*? Is that what happened to Shane and Patrick?" I pulled my knees up to my chest and wrapped my arms around them tightly, trying to hold myself together.

"I believe so."

"But the child I would have — on either plane — they wouldn't be the same; just like Patrick and Shane." I stated more than asked.

"Preciously." His head leaned slightly to the side in a curious sort of manner. "Can I ask you something?"

"Of course."

"I thought this pregnancy was unplanned."

"It was."

"Are you planning on trying for another child right away?" He asked.

"I don't know." I rested my cheek against my knee. "If someone had asked me this question six months ago, I would have said no way. But now; now I don't know." A tear escaped out of the corner of my eye. "This child wasn't planned, but it was dearly loved, and we were so excited about it."

"I know, darling. I honestly cannot imagine what you and Landon are going through. You must be devastated." He looked upset.

"I cannot even find the words." I shook my head and brushed the tears away. "I feel empty; like a part of me is gone, and I don't know what to do."

"I hope you can take comfort in the fact that your child is safe in your *other* life." He took hold of my hand.

"But that child will not be able to travel with me now. He or she will be stuck on *that* plane." I wasn't sure if it was a question or a statement.

"No, sweetheart. Your child will spend its entire life on one plane and has no way of inheriting *EVE*."

"And my other children that I may someday have?" I asked, hopefully.

"They have the possibly of inheriting the gift of *EVE*." He explained. "And they would be with you on both planes."

"I really hate this gift." I said, stubbornly burying my face in my knees.

"Sidney, look at me." Uncle Nicholas reached out and touched the top of my head. I looked up at him. "You and I believe this child was your husband, Keifer's." He whispered. "You should take comfort that you will be able to raise this child with him."

"Unless I follow in my mother's footsteps and do not survive childbirth." I remarked solemnly.

"And that weighs heavily on your mind, I believe."

"Very much so." I perched my lips together for a moment. "With me only being pregnant *there*, what happens to my soul if I should die *there*?"

"The same thing that happened to your Uncle Monte when he left his life *here*, I believe. However, I cannot be sure because one time is before the other. But that is not going to happen to you." He smiled. "You are forgetting one important element in all of this, my dear."

"What is that?" My tired and medicated brain was not processing much.

"You visited Jocelyn in 1879 in Chicago. You were there when my brother, Monte was killed in a freak accident." He explained.

"You're right." I let out a huge sigh of relief. "I was not even thinking. How could I forget something like that?"

"Intense situations play tricks on the mind and memory. Not to mention, you are on some wicked pain medication." He chuckled. "I am not surprised you did not recall the event. It was several years ago. You were alive and healthy. You and Keifer both were."

"We were old." I laughed. "Keifer and I grow old together."

"Yes, you do."

"That is wonderful to hear." I reached out and hugged my uncle.

"What is the wonderful news?" Landon walked back into my room.

"I am up for tenure." Uncle Nicholas said joyously.

"That is wonderful news." Landon came over and hugged my uncle. "I'm very happy for you."

Over the last several years, the two of them had developed a great friendship. Landon was very fond of his eccentric personality, as he put it. He saw my Uncle Nicholas as my quirky uncle who loved his historical research, gardening, and healthy eating. He found my bizarre uncle charming, and the two discussed gardening tips often.

"Thank you, Landon. I appreciate that."

"And I have some good news for you too." He took a seat on the other side of my bed. "I ran into Dr. Jarbo in the hallway. He'll be in shortly, but he said there's a good chance you'll be able to come home tomorrow. Of course, you're not cleared yet to return to work, but it will at least get you out of this place."

"What about school? I have already missed a week of classes." I had been trying to study whilst in the hospital, but the pain medication was affecting my ability to retain much material. I was anxious to get back to my classes.

"You have been cleared to go to class next week, but you cannot lift anything over ten pounds for the next two week." Landon patted my leg lovingly with a hopeful smile.

"Landon, I'm not sure I'm ready to go back to our apartment yet. I'm not sure I can face it." I admitted.

"I know. I've already spoken to Robert and Emily. We're going to stay with them for a while until you're ready to go back to the apartment." Landon began.

"But honey, I don't want to impose."

"You know the long hours we put it. It will ease my mind knowing you will have Emily there with you when I'm working." Landon pleaded with me. "Please, do this for me."

"Okay," I nodded. I was happy I was going anywhere but our apartment.

"Well, I guess I best get going. I will stop by this weekend and see how you are doing." My uncle leaned over and kissed me on the forehead and gave me a hug. "You take care of yourself and that wonderful man of yours."

"You take good care of our girl." Uncle Nicholas told Landon as he walked him over to the door.

"You have my word." Landon hugged him goodbye.

Landon turned out the bright overhead light and crawled up in bed beside me. I curled up beside him and rested my head upon my chest. I put my arm across his chest and closed my eyes.

He turned on the television and began flipping through the limited channels. I heard him settle on an episode of *The Flash*. It was one of his childish indulgences that I loved to tease him about. Under different circumstances I would have. But today, I was thrilled he was here with me.

I dozed off peacefully in his arms.

16

FRIDAY, OCTOBER 21, 1859

THE DARK CLOUD THAT HAD hovered over our house had finally cleared. There was a noticeable tension drop not only in the house but in the outlying cabins as well. It was the first time in months that I heard voices about the house instead of whispers. There was even singing in the kitchen when I came down for my morning breakfast.

"Good morning, Naomi. Isn't it a glorious day?" I joined my grandmother at the dining room table as Naomi poured me a fresh cup of coffee.

"Yes, mam'. It certainly is." She smiled and returned to the kitchen.

"You do realize it is pouring down rain outside." My grandmother smirked.

"Yes. I know." I grinned over the top of my mug.

"What are your plans for today?"

"I have not given it much thought. Keifer left early this morning and said he would be home by supper."

"And Landon? How is he doing?" She leaned in and asked.

"He is putting on a brace face in front of me, but I know he is in as much pain as I am." I looked down at the French toast Naomi had prepared. My appetite disappeared.

"I am sorry." She reached across the table and took my hand. "Right now, perhaps, we should rejoice in the knowledge that we still have our baby *here*."

"I know. I keep telling myself that, but the emptiness I feel *there* is overwhelming." Tears well up in my eyes. "I don't know what to do."

"Take it one day at a time. That's all you can do."

"I am trying."

"It will get better; with time."

"Guess who came by to see me?"

"Who?" She picked up her coffee and took a sip.

"Uncle Nicholas. We discussed Shane and Patrick. Or rather, their birthdays."

"Did he share our speculation?"

"Yes. While he does not know whether Bethany had a miscarriage, it is the only explanation as to why they are four months apart in age and why neither of them has the gift of *EVE*." I explained.

"My grandson is a very bright man." She smiled with pride.

"You realize how bizarre it is to have a close relationship with him *there* as my uncle who is in his 40s and turn around to a young man *here* that I barely know." I shook my head in dismay.

"I imagine it would be." She snickered. "I am glad he was able to ease your fears a bit. I know it might not be exactly what you want to hear, but at least it is a plausible explanation and a much better one than we had."

"I know. You are right." I tried to see it from her side. "It is so unsettling, but yes; it is plausible."

"So, what do you plan now?" My grandmother inquired.

"What do you mean?"

"Are you planning on getting pregnant again *there* as soon as you are medically cleared?" She raised her eyebrows.

"No." I shook my head slowly. "I'm not ready. And I cannot put Landon through that." My voice was barely above a whisper. "He has been through hell and back in the last couple of months. I have put him on an emotional whirlwind of highs and lows. I cannot ask any more of him. I believe we both need time and emotional stability for a while."

"I am so proud of you." She squeezed my hand lovingly. "You have grown into such a strong young lady."

"Plus, as much as I hate to admit it, we both need to reach our goals first before we journey back down the road to parenthood." I stared at the food on my plate and quickly wiped the tears off my cheeks. "I hate this." I muttered.

"I know. But you are doing the right thing. For you and for Landon." My grandmother whispered.

"I know."

Later that afternoon, Keifer and I were walking through the garden. Even his step seemed much lighter now that his sister had departed. I didn't want to point it out to him because it was obvious by the lighter tone of his voice and the smile on his face, that he was as aware of the transition within Terrace Falls as the rest of us were.

I took his arm and stepped down the cobblestone pathway. The fallen leaves crumbled under our feet and swooshed about beneath the edges of my dress. The leaves that still clung to the trees were a brilliant array of gold, reds, orange, and yellows. The sky was still a hazy gray, and a cool breeze blew through the strands of my hair that escaped my bun.

We walked in silence for a while, enjoying the peace and quiet. The final leg of the harvest would be completed as soon as the rain stopped for more than a day. I pulled my shawl closer around me and leaned in closer to my husband.

"How are you feeling?" Keifer inquired.

"Much better now that the morning sickness seems to have passed." I gently squeezed his arm.

"I am happy to hear that."

"I love this time of year." I remarked, passing beneath the trestle.

"I remember," he smiled down at me.

"I love the smells, the mild days and chilly evenings. I love the colors of the leaves, the peacefulness of it all. It seems like it's the long sigh before a deep winters sleep."

"The holidays are right around the corner." Keifer said as we crossed the little bridge into the densely wooded area. "Our last one alone. Next year we will be sharing it with our beautiful child." He smiled broadly.

"Won't it be wonderful." I boasted. "I cannot wait to see his or her little face and to hold them in my arms."

"His face." He jokingly corrected me.

"By the grace of God, my love." I playfully smirked at him. "You know what I would love for Christmas this year?"

"You may have anything you wish, darling."

"I would like to take a trip to Chicago to see my father and little brothers."

"Are you serious?" My husband stopped and looked at me.

"Yes."

"Why?"

"Keifer, they are my family too." I implored.

"Darling. By Christmas, you will be in your third trimester. It would be ill-advised for you to travel anywhere, let alone Chicago."

"But, Keifer." I started.

"No." He shook his head. "I am sorry, but perhaps we can go next Christmas and introduce your father to his first grandchild. That may soften the frozen heart of Bethany." He snorted.

"Nothing could thaw the heart of the Snow Queen." I stated. "I learned that one a long time ago." We continued our stroll through the woods.

"Me too." He muttered. "You could invite them here if you like. Didn't your oldest brother just have a baby? Another boy, right? Their fourth."

"Yes. I believe they named him William." I recalled Annabelle's last letter with the announcement.

"It looks like you will be the last female in the family." He shrugged slightly.

"You forget Monte and Nicholas are not even married yet." I reminded him.

"True, but you rarely speak to them. I understand they are your brothers, but it is not like you really know them. If it were not for Annabelle's letters, you would never know anything about them." Keifer stated the truth.

"I love that she feels such a strong sense of family. She is a lovely lady. Patrick is blessed to have found such a wonderful woman to share his life with." I squeezed my husband's hand.

"And they just had their fourth child? Patrick certainly did not waste any time, or Annabelle is the most fertile woman in the world." He chuckled. "How old were they when they got married?"

"Patrick was seventeen and Annabelle sixteen, I believe. Remember? We were there." I reminded him.

"Sorry, I had forgotten. You have so many brothers." Keifer smirked. He never hid his feelings about my father and his new family, as Keifer put it.

"Hardly," I nudged him playfully. "Only one of them is married."

"Are you saying we will have to visit Chicago for the other two?" He raised his eyebrows at me.

Imagines of my Uncle Nicholas; his kind eyes and quirky sense of humor flashed through my memory. The fun we had at his Victorian home in Bloomington when I first met him, and he told me about *EVE*. His patience, generosity, and the love he had for his family.

Although he really did not know me *here* and was still a teenage boy, completely ignorant of *EVE*, he was my favorite brother. I tried to recall what he looked like at Patrick's wedding. He was a child then, and very mischievous.

In my mind's eye, I was picturing the middle-aged professor. I was curious to see what he looked like as a teenager. It was difficult for me to fathom.

"I would love to be there when Nicholas gets married." I said off-handedly.

"Nicholas? He is the youngest one, right? The one that knocked the wedding cake off the table?" Keifer laughed whole-heartedly. "I thought Bethany was going to have a stroke. I have never seen someone turn that shade of purple before."

"It is a shame she didn't have one." I muttered and smiled sweetly when Patrick giggled.

"You have a bit of a mean streak in you." He snorted.

"Bethany brings out the best in me." I winked at my husband.

"As does Eugenia." I rolled my eyes.

"That is hardly fair. You know I get along well with the rest of your family. I love them. They have always been very kind to me."

"My parents and other siblings adore you. I cannot wait until they hear about the baby. I am sure the letters will be pouring in." Keifer kicked some scattered stones out of his way. "I was thinking if we're going to visit Chicago next Christmas with the baby, can we also spend some time with my family in Savannah?"

"We could go next fall before we go to Chicago." I suggested.

"I was thinking afterward. That way, we could avoid some of the harsh Boston winter and enjoy the mildness of January and February in Savannah." He suggested.

The idea of being a Northerner deep in the South in the spring of 1861 did not sound appealing at all. I knew the battle at Fort Sumter didn't begin until April of 1861 — April 12th, I believe, but I couldn't recall exactly. I made a mental note to look up the details on the internet *there*.

I knew things in the South were growing more hostile by the day. I also knew that Southerners did not want Northerners in the South, and they were very vocal and physical about it. They were harsher on men than women, but some did not differentiate. It would be dangerous for us to go in the fall, and almost suicidal in the spring.

What Keifer wasn't considering was the election. Abraham Lincoln was going to win the presidential election next year. What he also didn't realize was that Jefferson Davis was going to be elected President of the Confederate States before Lincoln and South Carolina would lead the way to Southern secession.

The changes that were to come over this next year would open the gates for an unsurmountable loss of life that would saturate American soil with the blood of its men and the tears of its women.

Standing beneath the canopy of autumn leaves, smelling the crisp, clean air that only occurs after a long rainfall, I listened to the surrounding silence with a mournful heart. The peace and serenity I found on this land was about to be blown apart as our nation would be ripped in two.

The knowledge of what was to come was unbearable. I didn't know how to explain it to him. I couldn't tell him the twenty-four-hour battle of Fort Sumter would only be the beginning of the next four years of living hell.

Sadly, I knew nothing of the outcome of Keifer's family after the Civil War. I truly didn't even know how to find out. I figured I could do some digging on the internet and hoped that certain sites could possibly provide me with some information.

"Darling," I stopped and held his hands. "I am afraid that the tensions in the South over the next year are only going to increase. It may not be safe for us to travel down there."

"Are you forgetting, Sidney. You are married to a Southerner." He grinned. "Besides, I am sure things will be settled long before then anyway."

"Do you really believe that?" I wondered aloud.

"No." His face looked solemn. "But I want to remain hopeful. I know war is brewing. You know it too." He placed his hands on my face. "I saw the plans for the new cellars in the study, and you have been stockpiling goods that are most likely to become shortages." He pointed out.

"I am afraid of what is to come." I admitted.

"As am I." My husband leaned down and kissed me. "And if I must leave you to take care of our men, I promise you I will return — to both of you." He placed his hand gently on the small bump of my abdomen.

17

JACKSON'S PARENTS WERE THE perfect hosts. I was tucked away snuggly in their guest bedroom. It was stylishly decorated in light greys, taupe, and cornflower blues. It was simple and elegant — much like Emily herself.

The canopy bed was cherry wood draped in cornflower blue; the bedding a light taupe with paisley blue designs matching the drapes. There was an ivory chaise lounge by the window with a small round cherry wood table. It adorned a small reading lamp and a bouquet of violets.

I sat on the chaise, reading Emily's latest romance novel. She had received several copies of her book before it was slated to hit the shelves in two weeks. I asked her about it the first evening I arrived, and she was kind enough to let me have a sneak reading of it.

The wind howled outside the window and rain pattered down on the roof. It was a lazy day, perfect for a hoodie and flannel pajama bottoms with fuzzy socks. My hair was pulled up in a messy bun, and I hadn't bothered with makeup in days.

I tossed a throw blanket across my legs. I simply wanted to get lost in words and let the world around me disappear.

Landon was staying with me at the Chandler's. He had Jocelyn and Jackson retrieve clothes and essentials for us so we could have a bit of time to heal before facing an empty nursery and bassinet.

"Knock. Knock." I looked up to find my little sister standing in the doorway. "Can I come in?"

"Please," I placed my bookmark and set the book on the little table.

"How are you feeling?" She came over and sat down on the corner of the bed.

"Better, I guess. When did you get here?"

"Just now. Jackson is downstairs with Landon and Robert watching football highlights." She rolled her eyes. "We may never see them again or at least until after the Super Bowl."

"I thought you liked football." I half grinned.

"No. I enjoyed watching my husband and little brother play football. The NFL holds nothing for me." She fiddled with the tiebacks on the canopy drapes.

"I see your point." I patted the spot beside me, and my little sister flopped down. "By the way, I am sorry I missed your birthday Tuesday. Did you get our gift?"

"Yes, thank you very much." She leaned over and hugged me. "I know you did not feel like celebrating, but you missed a wonderful dinner."

"What did Jackson get you?"

"A beautiful necklace, an old-fashioned turntable, and a couple records." She laughed at my face. "What? Blame dad. It's his fault I prefer vinal."

"You're such a dork." I teased as she rolled her eyes at me.

"What are your plans for the day?"

"I don't know. I was just going to read Emily's new book." I nodded towards the novel.

"Care to go shopping?"

"No. I'm not up for it." I adjusted the blanket.

"Of course. I'm sorry." Jocelyn looked down at her hands.

"Can I tell you something?"

"Always. What's going on?"

"I only lost the baby on this plane." I whispered. "I'm still pregnant *there*."

"Are you sure?" I nodded. "That's wonderful." She brightened briefly, but then her smile disappeared. "Oh, I'm sorry. I didn't mean . . ."

"It's okay. I spoke with Uncle Nicholas." I went on to recount my conversation once more for her.

"Did you mention this to Robert and Emily?"

"Yes. We talked about it yesterday after I returned from my classes and Landon was at the hospital."

"And what was their take on it?" She leaned forward with curiosity.

"They agreed that Bethany must have had a miscarriage and gotten pregnant again almost immediately."

"That would explain why Patrick and Shane did not inherit *EVE*." Jocelyn considered.

"I don't know how I am supposed to feel about it." I admitted.

"How do you mean?" She asked.

"*There*, I will have a beautiful baby. But *here*, I long for my baby. How am I going to feel when my child arrives *there*? How can I face Landon?" I admitted.

"Are you afraid he will think you are over it? The miscarriage you mean when the baby arrives." She asked.

"I guess. I don't know what to feel." I placed my hand over my empty abdomen, feeling lonely.

"I know it's going to be difficult. But I know you are a strong woman. You are highly intelligent, passionate, and compassionate.

You handle every challenge you encounter with grace and style." She smiled at me lovingly. "You are my big sister, and I look up to you. You are my mentor."

"You are wonderful. I love you for saying that. Especially considering I feel like a hot mess." I exhaled loudly.

"Can I say that I am loving this new look of yours. You look like you raided my closet." Jocelyn giggled.

"Thanks." I rolled my eyes at my little sister.

"I didn't even know you owned flannel pajama bottoms and fuzzy socks."

"It gets cold in Boston." I confessed. "I have several pairs now."

"I would have never guessed."

"You're mean." I smirked at her. "I am not some princess." I stated.

"Yeah, right. Since when?" She loved teasing me.

"Fine." I got up. "Let's go shopping."

There was a police car and a car we did not recognize sitting in front of the Chandler's house when my sister and I turned down their street. I looked at Jocelyn as she turned towards me. She reached over and took my hand. Neither of us said a word.

Jocelyn barely got the car stopped before I hopped out and ran towards the house. All I could think of was Landon. My heart raced as I ran up the steps and opened the front door. Fear gripped every ounce of my body.

Jocelyn almost collided with me in the foyer. An officer in uniform and one in business clothing were standing just inside the parlor talking with Robert and Emily. I took my sister's hand and stood there staring at these two strangers.

"Miss. Timmons?" I recognized the uniformed officer as the same one that had accompanied my assailant to the hospital on that horrible night.

"Yes," I answered nervously.

"I'm Officer McCoy, and this is Detective Warner from our homicide unit. We would like to get a statement from you about the night I brought the suspect into the hospital." The man uniformed officer in his mid-thirties informed me. "Is there a place we can talk?"

"Please feel free to use the parlor." Emily gestured to them to have a seat. "Can I get either of you something to drink? I just made a pot of coffee, or perhaps some iced tea?" she offered.

"No, thank you." The detective answered, taking a seat in one of the armchairs.

"A cup of coffee would be nice." Officer McCoy smiled, having a seat in the other armchair.

"Cream or sugar or both?" She asked.

"Both, please." He took out his notepad.

"Would you mind staying please, Robert." I touched his arm lightly. He nodded and took a seat beside me on the sofa.

"Are you, her father?" Detective Warner asked him.

"No." Robert said.

"And what is the nature of your relationship to the victim?" Detective Warner inquired. "Is she your daughter-in-law?"

"No. Sidney is my daughter-in-law's sister and my daughter's best friend. She is family."

"And she and Mr. Harrison have been staying here since she was released from the hospital?" the detective asked.

"Why does that matter?" I interrupted.

"I apologize. I just need to know where you are staying in-case I need to contact you for further details. I was not trying to upset you.

I am simply trying to access how you are doing or rather coping." The detective replied.

"Physically, I am fine. Emotionally, I am devastated." The detective jotted something down on his little notepad, and for some reason, it really ticked me off. "Tell me Detective, how would you feel a week after your baby was murdered?"

Emily walked in carrying a tray and glanced around, obviously feeling the tension. She set it down on the coffee table and handed the mug to Officer McCoy.

"Thank you, kindly." He smiled.

"You are very welcome." Emily smiled sweetly as she took a seat on the other side of me and took hold of my hand. "As you can imagine, this has been a difficult time."

"My apologies. I meant no disrespect." Detective Warner shifted in his chair. "If you're staying here with your sister's in-laws, I just thought. . ."

"First of all, my family is in Chicago. Landon and I moved to Boston for medical school at Harvard. I am at the top of my class, as is my fiancé. My sister and her husband's family used to live across the street from us in Chicago. When they moved back to Boston, they were kind enough to adopt me as family since I had no one here. We are staying with them because neither of us can bear to go back to our place where we have a fully decorated nursery and an empty bassinet next to our bed." I explained through the sudden rush of tears and getting to my feet. "Now that you know my life history, if you have anything further to ask me, you can ask my attorney's." I gestured around the room. "These are the best in Boston!" I stormed out of the parlor and ran upstairs to the room we had taken over.

A few minutes later, there was a knock at my door. When I did not respond, it got a bit louder.

"Jocelyn. Not now. Please." I called from the bed.

"It's not Jocelyn." Robert's voice called back.

"Oh," I scrambled off the bed and opened the door. "I'm sorry." I stood back, hastily brushing the tears off my cheeks and let him enter. "I'm sorry about my outburst." I shook my head and flopped back across the bed. "I just could not listen to him ask such stupid questions."

"I know." He sat down beside me. "I blamed it on the pregnancy hormone imbalance to which my wife was kind enough to give me a dirty look." He chuckled.

"Thank you." I couldn't help but smile. "So, what happens now?" I turned around and sat up.

"Well, the man who attacked you, a Tyrone Williams, was charged with aggravated assault on you and manslaughter for causing your miscarriage." Robert stated. "In addition to the charges he was originally charged with."

"What does that mean exactly."

"That you are going to have to speak with Detective Warner. You need to give a statement about what happened."

"Why? I don't know anything. Everything happened so fast. I just remember flying across the room. They would be better off talking to Marti or that incompetent intern, Norman. They were conscious through the entire thing, not me." I informed him.

"Either way, because you are the victim, they need a statement from you."

"And that will be the end of it?" I asked.

"No. Unfortunately not. You will also have to provide a formal deposition, and if this Williams character does not accept a plea deal, then this will proceed to trial where you will also have to testify." He saw the terrified look on my face. "Try not to worry." He took my hand. "We will all be there with you."

"I know." I took a deep breath. "Still, I cannot help but hope this Williams SOB accepts a plea, so I don't have to testify in open court."

"I hope so too." I looked over at Robert and smirked. "Let's just hope he can't afford an attorney like Phoebe to represent him."

"I believe she has met her pro-bono quota for the year." He chuckled.

"I certainly hope so."

Emily and Robert prepared an elegant dinner for us, and Jackson and Jocelyn couldn't resist joining us. Landon was still on shift at the hospital and would not be home until late. It was the joy of being a broke medical student and trying to support yourself.

The five of us sat down Emily's infamous homemade chicken and noodles. She had spent the afternoon making the noodles from scratch along with yeast rolls that were baked to a golden brown and melted in your mouth. It was the perfect antidote for a blustering rainy day.

"Emily told me about your conversation with Nicholas." Robert mentioned catching me off guard.

"Yes. He stopped by the hospital to see me." I tore a piece of the corner of a roll and popped it in my mouth.

"I spoke with him last night after Emily shared with me your conversation with him." He continued.

"What did I miss?" Jackson spoke up.

"Jackson!" My sister elbowed her husband in a not-so-subtle manner.

"It's all right." I grinned at Jocelyn. "I was concerned about how my miscarriage *here* affects my baby's soul *there*." I did my best to get the words out as nonchalantly as possible.

"I am sorry. I did not mean to upset you." Jackson's emerald, green eyes looked mournful.

"I know. I am fine." I tore off another piece and then another piled them on my napkin absentmindedly. "Uncle Nicholas speculated about Patrick and Shane being born several months apart and neither of them having the gift of *EVE*."

"I never thought to ask about their birthdays." Jackson noted.

"It seems Shane was born in September, and Patrick was born in December." Emily informed him.

"I guess that does explain a lot." Jackson raised his eyebrows.

"Bethany must have had a miscarriage and gotten pregnant shortly thereafter." I dismembered another roll.

"I am guessing you are still pregnant *there*?" Jackson asked.

"Yes. It is not easy. I feel so torn." I confessed.

"That is understandable." Emily empathized.

"I can see why that is, but you must try to remain focused on the bigger picture. Despite the pain you are coping with *here*, you can rejoice that you and Keifer will be celebrating the birth of your beautiful baby *there*." Robert tried to explain something there were no words for.

"I am trying. This whole situation is impossible to explain or comprehend." I looked down at my meal.

"I am sorry you must deal with this. The entire situation is horrible." Emily patted my hand.

"You know, I am not sure what is worse." I finally took a bite of Emily's fabulous cooking talents. "Having a child *here* while still in med school and juggling a hectic schedule or having a baby *there* on the eve of the worst war in American history."

"How bad are things in Boston?" Robert asked.

"Tense." I tried the roll. It melted in my mouth. "How were they in Chicago?"

"The same. We have abolitionists protesting daily; stirring up people and shouting their beliefs from the top of their lungs." Robert announced. "These people had no idea how bad it is going to get. The country will never be the same. Many believe a war will fix the issues, but they were completely oblivious to the years of reconstruction that will follow the war."

"We are having the same demonstrations. You would not believe who is making frequent appearances in Boston trying to raise funds for his cause?" I asked Robert.

"Who?"

"John Brown." I informed my captivated audience. "He has been mingling with many Boston elitists. Of course, they have no idea about the Kansas massacre he is responsible for or at least most of them don't."

"Who is he spending time with?" Robert leaned forward with intrigue.

"My goodness let's see; Thomas Wentworth Higginson, who is part of the Brahmin society and connected with Emily Dickinson. There's George Sterns, the wealthiest man in Medford. Brown was even the house guest of Henry David Thoreau, Bronson Alcott, and Ralph Waldo Emerson."

"Wow. Are you sure?" Emily asked. "I never would have thought."

"That is incredible." Robert looked impressed. "I had not realized you ran in such circles."

"I met a few of them very briefly with Keifer through Dr. Samuel Gridley Howe. It was a dinner party celebrating Dr. Howe's work with the blind and various other philanthropies." I explained.

"That must be exciting." Jackson seemed elated. "I cannot imagine meeting Dickenson, Emerson, Alcott, or Thoreau. You must have been ecstatic."

"I was nervous." I chuckled. "Okay, I was terrified." The rest of the table laughed at me. "Can you imagine? These names are notorious in reforming education and American Literature. I never dreamt I would ever dine with them."

"Did you meet John Brown?" Robert quipped.

"We were introduced briefly. I did not speak with him. But I will say I was completely in awe of him. He appeared as what we imagine as the picturesque frontiersman. He was not formally dressed and even carried his bowie knife in his boot." I told my mesmerized audience. "He was quiet, but you could see he was calculating. His eyes were unsettling."

"I cannot imagine what it must have been like to stand next to him." Jackson shook his head slightly. "Just knowing what he is capable of and what he is planning — it chills your blood because there nothing you can do about it."

"Believe me, I know." I confessed. "It is incredibly frustrating." I sighed. "There are so many things about the upcoming war that make me want to scream."

"Did you know that Nicholas is at West Point? He was in the infamous class of 61." Robert said.

"West Point? He never mentioned West Point to me before?" I was astonished. "Of course, he's never really spoken of the war."

"You are forgetting. When I stumbled across Uncle Monte's journals, he made several references to Nicholas being listed as missing in action." Jocelyn reminded me.

"I had completely forgotten that." I admitted. "It is no wonder he never discusses it."

"Monte said Nicholas was imprisoned down in Georgia at the Confederate prison camp called Andersonville. I researched the camp out of curiosity after we met Uncle Nicholas, and the conditions there were deplorable. He is fortunate he survived it. Most soldiers did not." Jocelyn told us.

"It is not surprising he never discusses it." Emily said in a sympathetic voice.

"I have never asked him anything about the Civil War. Now I am glad I haven't." I stated.

"That is probably for the best." Emily empathized. "I am sure it causes painful memories for him."

"I did not serve with Nicholas. I was with Monte for a while, but we got separated after I got wounded the first time. The second time I got hit I encountered Patrick at a field hospital when I was wounded by shrapnel after a battle in 63. I hardly got a chance to speak with him. I was too busy screaming as he dug the metal pieces out of my leg." Robert wiped the corner of his mouth with a napkin. "But I do recall him saying that Monte was fine, but they had not heard anything from Nicholas. I remember him being very concerned."

"I did not know you were wounded twice." Jackson looked over at his dad.

"Yes. Well, it was a long time ago." Robert shifted uncomfortably in his chair.

"How long were you in for?" Jocelyn asked.

"The duration. It was not that I wanted to be, but men on both sides were leaving at an alarming rate. I cannot say I was not tempted as well, but my honor would not allow me to go home." Emily smiled lovingly at her husband. "Still, I feel like I missed out on a lot at home. I know the war was very difficult for Emily and the kids. I tried to write as often as I could just so she would have some source of comfort that I was alive."

"It was a comfort even though I worried excessively for four years." Emily remarked.

"That must have been hard." I turned towards Jackson. "You were — what three years old when the war started. So, you would have been about seven when it was over? Phoebe and Alex were what nine and twelve when you returned?" I looked back at Robert.

"I missed a lot. I only saw them twice during the war." Robert's eyes dropped down to his plate.

I felt bad about bringing the subject up. Robert, like Nicholas, never discussed the war. Much like other veterans I have known, it was a difficult topic for them to discuss.

"I'm sorry." I felt horrible.

"No. It's all right." Robert stood up and began clearing the table.

"It's a very sensitive subject for him." Emily leaned over towards me and whispered when Robert exited the room. "Please, don't worry about it." She smiled.

Emily followed her husband into the kitchen. I looked over at my sister and her husband. They both looked as uncomfortable as I felt.

"I really did not mean to upset them." I whispered.

"My parents went through a lot during that time. Neither of them talks much about it. I have never pushed it with them because they shut down almost immediately." Jackson said softly. "Perhaps it is best to only discuss other aspects, but not their personal experiences."

"I understand." I wanted to sink into the floor.

I excused myself and retreated upstairs to my room. I could not have felt worse about how dinner had ended. I took a long hot shower and put on my comfy pajamas. I crawled into bed, picking up the romance novel and wished for Landon to come home soon.

"May I come in?" Emily knocked softly on my door.

"Please," I set the book aside.

"Are you alright?" She came over and sat down on the edge of the bed.

"I am so sorry about dinner." I began.

"Sidney, I know you three felt a bit uncomfortable, and I apologize for that."

"I overstepped."

"Nonsense," Emily curled her legs beneath her. "Robert and I hate the fact that you are walking into the same reality we lived a couple decades ago." I saw her tear up. "I remember it like it was yesterday."

"It is like the atmosphere has changed. The air is filled with tension. People are choosing sides, even in our free state. But it is not so much over the act of slavery, it is the abolitionists who are stirring up trouble. People like John Brown and the like." I explained.

"Yes. I recall how they were. They had a unique ability to cause turmoil. There was also a prisoner camp just outside of Chicago during the war. It was a horrible time. Most people today have no idea how truly horrific it was."

"Yes. Today it seems people want to glorify the Civil War. They want to envision it as simply North vs. South, Blue vs. Grey, and they memorize battles by statistics. I hate to think about what awaits on the horizon." I confessed.

"And the reenactments. Those creep under my skin. I know they are harmless and meant to educate, but they have no idea what it felt like to wait on the lists to see if your husband and loved ones are still alive." She shuttered.

"I know Keifer and Patrick won't be with the infantry, but Robert, Monte, and Nicholas will be. And even though I know they all survive it; I am sure there are others from home that will not. I have not done research on Keifer's family in Savannah. His brothers, cousins, and childhood friends — they are all going to fight for the Confederacy." I shook my head with dismay.

"What does Keifer think about what is going on?"

"He blames my stockpiling essentials on pregnancy hormones." Emily laughed wholeheartedly. "But deep down, I believe he is aware of what is coming. He has already said he will enlist as a physician for the Union. Still, I know the horrors he will see, and it will change him forever."

"It changed Robert. He used to be very quick to smile, laughed easily, and we used to tease each other playfully all the time." Her eyes welled up with memories passed. "After the war, he was solemn. He saw his friends blown apart; some died in his arms." She brushed the lone tear off her cheek. "He has never fully recovered. He had nightmares for years. The only way I could get him to sleep was to rub his back. It got so I would wake up every time he stirred, and I would rub his back to bring him out of whatever nightmare he was lost in." Her voice dropped.

"It must have been hard on both of you."

"It was," she paused. "And it still is. Robert has never fully recovered, and the nightmares still occur occasionally."

"I am sorry."

"Post traumatic stress disorder is horrific, not only on the soldier, but on the family as well. It is difficult for us to relate when most soldiers cannot discuss what they have experienced." Emily shared. "But I can tell you what helped Robert more than anything."

"What is that?" I wondered.

"Talking with other soldiers who had similar experiences. Robert confided in Monte and Nicholas after they all returned home, and it helped a great deal. Knowing they were not alone helped them cope with their shared traumas. I spoke with Vivian and Lydia — Monte and Nicholas' wives in their *other* lives, and they noticed the differences their bond made on their behavior and said that it had helped a great deal with the nightmares."

"So, for Keifer, the friendships he has made with our neighbors will be even more important to him after the war." She nodded. "I truly wish he had Robert and my brothers to help him."

"You could always move to Chicago." Emily shrugged.

"Or you could move to Boston." I pointed out.

"We do; just not yet." She patted my leg reassuringly.

"I know."

"Little does Keifer know how bad it is going to get. Granted, it is nothing in comparison to what the Confederate states are going to endure. But the prices of everything will go up to ten times their normal rate. Most people will not be able to afford anything. And the farmers will suffer greatly under the weight of scavengers and the Union garnishing crops." She recalled.

"My grandmother and I, along with our foreman and a select few trusted workers, have designed several hidden cellars acres away from our home in a dense part of the woods by the riverbeds to hide necessities. It is simply another thing Keifer attributes to my pregnancy paranoia." I chuckled.

"You know I am always here for you. I have been in your shoes, and I know exactly what you are going through — all the trials and tribulations, the apprehensions. It is going to be rough on you and all your loved ones. If you want to talk or simply need a shoulder, my door is always open." Emily leaned over and hugged me tightly. "Robert and I love you and Landon very much. You are family."

"Thank you so much, Emily. That means the world to me. I love you both so much."

"Well, I had best let you get some sleep." She stood up and walked over to the door. "You have sweet dreams, darling."

"Sweet dreams, Emily."

I set the book on the nightstand and turned off the lamp. I snuggled down beneath the duvet in a fetal position and closed my eyes. Emily's words gave me great comfort. I knew the next several years were going to be the worse years of my life. I couldn't be more thankful for the love and support from Emily and Robert.

18

SATURDAY, OCTOBER 22, 1859

MY GRANDMOTHER, KEIFER, AND I was finishing our breakfast when we heard hooves outside in front of our home. It was unusual for anyone to stop by this early. A moment later, a rapid knock came from the front door. Casper stepped over to open it.

"Hello Casper, is the Doc available?" Mr. Morgan's voice sounded from the foyer.

"Yes sir, he's havin' his koffee." Casper responded.

"Fine, thank you." Mr. Bennett's voice was followed by the sound of his heavy footsteps on the hardwood.

"But sir," Casper called out, but Mr. Morgan ignored him.

"Doc," his voice drew closer. "Morning, Doc." Mr. Morgan paused in the doorway realizing my husband was not alone. "Beg your pardon, Mrs. Timmons. Mrs. Marshall."

"Good morning, Mr. Morgan. Would you please join us." I welcomed him.

"Thank you, ma'am." He took a seat beside my grandmother who promptly poured him a cup of coffee.

"My goodness, Evan. What has you up in arms this morning?" My grandmother inquired.

"I am on my way back to my cousin's place. I was there until after midnight last night." He finally took a breath and sipped his coffee. "This raid on the Federal arsenal at Harper's Ferry is a disaster."

"What does our good Senator Wilson have to say?" Keifer asked, buttering another piece of toast.

"He just returned from Washington. As you can imagine, the Southern representatives are in an uproar. As if Brown's actions in Kansas, the massacre of the pro-slavery settlers near Pottawatomie Creek in 56', was not bad enough." He reached for a piece of toast and hastily began smothering it with strawberry jam. "I tell you, Doc. This is going to be bad."

"With everything that has transpired in the Capital over the last ten years, how could it possibly get worse?" Keifer wondered aloud.

"I know everyone is carrying a pistol, bowie knife, or both even before entering the Capital. Neither side trusts the other and the newspapers are only adding fuel to the flames. The Southern papers declare there was no insurrection because despite initial claims, not one slave joined Brown and his men. The only Blacks that were involved were free Blacks from Northern states. From what I understand, the South is pointing out that even though Blacks from multiple surrounding farms were incited to participate in this revolt and given the opportunity to kill their master's, not one did. In fact, they refused. They are saying this is proof that slaves are treated well by their owners." He rolled his eyes. "Can you imagine?"

"Some are very close to their master's and treated very well." Keifer defended. "The South could have a point." He lightly shrugged before sipping his coffee.

"That may be so in some cases, but not all of them." Evan reasoned.

"That is true." Keifer admitted.

My grandmother and I knew this was a touchy subject for Keifer. His family were responsible for more than a hundred slaves that lived and worked on his family's plantation. His family was well respected and highly regarded throughout Savannah and further. Although Keifer knew it was an inhuman and outdated institution, he was still not sure how it could be peacefully resolved.

"I believe the North is using this work of a mad man to further their own agenda. By claiming it was a slave insurrection than they are saying that the slaves are dissatisfied with their mode of life and are willing to shed blood to achieve it." I shook my head knowingly. "I am sure that there are some who feel that way. In fact," I looked directly at my husband. "I am positive of it." I turned my attention back to Evan. "But when we visited Gable Gardens last year, I got the opportunity to speak with several there and they are more worried about what will happen to them if they are freed."

"How so?" Evan wrinkled his forehead.

"Well, most cannot read or write. So, how will they get jobs to support their families? They have no place to go. If they are freed, they cannot stay in the south because they will be hated, nor can they go north because most do not want that either." I pointed out.

"I see what you mean." Evan scratched the scruff on his chin before pulling out a folded piece of paper from the pocket of his jacket. "I wanted to show you this, Doc because I thought, being from the South, your take on this situation could be invaluable." He flattened out the paper. "You know my cousin is an ardent abolitionist and as well as most in his hometown of Natick."

"Yes, he has made that clear each time we have encountered one another." Keifer chuckled. "I am afraid Henry will never forgive me for being born in the South."

"Probably not," Evan agreed. "The residents of Natick, as you know sent supplies to support '*Free Soil*' Kansas settlers over the last decade."

"Yes, I recall you mentioning it before." Keifer seemed intrigued to where Evan was taking this.

"Well, after news of the raid became public my cousin asked me to join him last evening for the Natick Republican Club meeting where they are hailing John Brown as a hero." Keifer sighed heavily but nodded. "And this was the result," he handed the piece of paper over to my husband. "The Natick Resolution."

"What does it say," my grandmother and I looked between the two men for answers.

"It is a letter to the Richmond Enquirer written by Henry Clarke Wright and dated yesterday. It begins, Sir — a large and enthusiastic meeting of the citizens of this town (the residence of Hon. Henry Wilson) was held last evening, called to consider the following resolution:

> "Whereas, Resistance to tyrants is obedience to God; therefore, resolved. This is the right and duty of the slaves to resist their masters; and it is the right and duty of the people of the North to incite slaves to resistance, and to aid them in it."
>
> This was adopted; ad though a United States Senator (Hon. Henry Wilson) and a United States Postmaster were present, not a dissentient voice was raised against it. The resolution utters the thought of Massachusetts, of New England, and of New York."[1]

Keifer tossed the paper hatefully back towards Evan. "This is complete rubbish. Do they have any idea what they are doing?"

"I warned him." Evan folded the paper and placed it back into his pocket. "What irritates me is that Wright claims there was not a dissentient voice raised against it." He scoffed. "What he fails to mention was most folk do not support violence as a means to end slavery."

"They might as well dissolve the Union right now if they believe this is going to go over well with any Southerner, slave-owners or not." Keifer's ears were bright red showing exactly how upset he truly was.

"I tried to reason with my cousin, but he was adamant." Evan finished off the rest of his coffee. "I apologize if I upset you, Doc. But I figured it was only a matter of time before you heard about this, and I wanted to personally come by and show it to you. I also wanted to assure you that I tried to prevent it."

"I appreciate the gesture." They both rose from their seats.

"Good day to you Mrs. Marshall, Mrs. Timmons." Evan left the dining room followed by my husband.

"Good day," my grandmother and I answered in unison.

"What in the Sam's hell are they thinking? I have never heard of the Natick Resolution before, have you?" I learned forward towards my grandmother.

"No," she shood her head. "Therefore, we can presume that it was not important enough nor significant enough to make it into the history books. Which I must say, is a relief."

"Yes, but ninety percent of what is going on has never been mentioned in our history books. I do not believe people have any inkling about what all transpired to cause this Civil War." I felt that I was even more ill prepared for this war than ever before.

That afternoon I was lounging on the chaise beside the hearth gazing out the front window. The porch swing swayed gently in the breeze. The hazy cloud-covered sky held the threat of rain that would most likely arrive before nightfall. The trees stood bare of their leaves which were now cluttered about the ground in a full array of colors soon to decay into to soil.

Evan's words echoed in my head. I could not believe how drastically different the reality of living through this time differed from all those lessons I had learned in school. Even the course I took in college outside my American History course that focused on the events leading up to the American Civil War and the Civil War itself never covered a tenth of the reality the nation was living in.

I felt very ill-prepared for what I knew was coming within the next eighteen months. The atmosphere was nothing like that depicted in our history books. They taught students that only the fanatic anti-slavery Northerners were considered abolitionists and that most Northerners did not care about what was going on in the South. However, nothing could be further from the truth.

I knew I was going to need to do a great deal more extensive research in my *other* life that ventured beyond what was taught in the classroom. I wanted to wade into newspaper articles published on both sides of the Mason-Dixon line and discover more than hearsay. I was only exposed to one side of this equation, and I knew I could not simply be like the other ladies in our small corner of the world.

19

THE SMELL OF BACON AND COFFEE filled the air and awoke me from a restless slumber. Landon was snoring peacefully beside me looking like a blonde angel. I carefully climbed out of bed and put on my robe. After visiting the restroom, I made my way downstairs in search of coffee.

Cheerful voices flowed from the kitchen of family members laughing and teasing each other. I entered the kitchen to find Phoebe there with her little son, Wallace – or Wally as we all called him. He was in kindergarten and full of energy. He was sitting at the breakfast bar playing with his scrambled eggs and bacon.

"Good morning," I greeted my hosts and poured myself an oversized mug of coffee.

"Morning, Auntie Sid." Wally grinned with a mouthful of breakfast.

"No talking with your mouth full." His mother playfully chastised him while tasseling his dark curls.

"Sorry," he grinned at me.

"How's my favorite little man?" I leaned over and kissed the top of his head before taking a seat at the stool beside him.

"Good," he continued shoveling food into his mouth. "Nana is going to help me with my Halloween costume."

"And what are you going to be this year?" I looked up at Emily and Phoebe.

"Captain America," Phoebe playfully rolled her eyes over the top of her son's head.

"That sounds perfect." I chuckled.

"Yeah, but his momma cannot sew nearly as well as his nana." Phoebe smiled.

"And his costume is almost done. I just wanted to make sure it fits, and I can adjust the length of the cape so it's not too long." Emily started scrambling some more eggs. "Would you like some eggs and bacon?" She looked at me.

"Please," I sipped my coffee. "What can I do to help?"

"You can fix the toast. I imagine Landon and Robert will be down shortly. So, maybe four more pieces." Emily handed me a loaf of sourdough bread. "And you can slice up some more strawberries. There are also some blackberries in the crisper."

"Morning," The front door opened, and Jocelyn voice rang out.

"In the kitchen," Emily hollered back. "You hungry?"

"Always," her son Jackson entered the kitchen, put his arm around his mother's waist and kissed her on the cheek.

"Of course, you are. Aren't you always." Emily laughed.

"Look who I found on the doorstep." Jocelyn walked in beside Uncle Nicholas.

"Good morning," his hearty voice filled the room. "I hope I am not intruding."

"Nonsense. Are you hungry?" Emily greeted him.

"That would be wonderful." He crossed over and hugged me. "How are you feeling? Jocelyn told me about your visitors yesterday."

"They were delightful." I rolled my eyes.

"Would you like some help?" Uncle Nicholas offered.

"No, thank you. Grab some coffee and have a seat."

Over the next thirty minutes, Emily, Phoebe, and I whipped up a hearty healthy breakfast for everyone. Robert and Landon slowly emerged from their slumber and found their way to the breakfast table. By the time they made it down, Emily was starting the third pot of coffee this morning.

We gathered around the dining table chatting at once and passing platters full of scrambled eggs, toast, bacon, and fresh fruit. All the little stresses floated away as my extended family — these incredible people whom I shared such a unique bond with, filled my life with the kind of love and support that I could no longer imagine living without.

We made it about halfway through breakfast when the doorbell rang. Robert excused himself, but immediately a knot formed in my gut thinking the officer and detective had returned to get my statement. Then the voice that drifted into the dining room turned my little sister and me white.

"Hello Robert, I'm sorry for dropping by unannounced, but Jocelyn said Sidney is staying here. I wanted to give her a bit of time after the accident, I have been worried." Shane's voice reached our ears.

"I understand, Shane. Please come on in." With Robert's reply, Jocelyn and I looked over at Uncle Nicholas.

This was not going to be good.

I closed my eyes and took a deep breath as a silence fell over the room as we heard the front door close.

"Good morning," Shane stood in the doorway to the dining room — his smile quickly faded, and he looked like someone had slapped him unexpectedly. "What in the hell are you doing here?" His eyes narrowed immediately to his little brother, Nicholas.

"Shane, I can explain." Robert put his hand on my dad's shoulder, but he shrugged his off with a hateful glare.

"No. This is on me." Nicholas rose from his seat.

"Uncle Nicholas, wait." I rose from my seat.

"Dad, it was me." Jocelyn pushed her chair back and stood.

"Someone had better tell me what is going on?" Shane took a deep breath as some of the color returned to his face.

Phoebe cleared her throat loudly drawing everyone's attention to her. "Landon, will you please take Wally back to our home." Her voice was firm but polite.

"Um," Landon looked around uncomfortably before his eyes landed on me. I nodded. "Sure," he pushed his chair back and took Wally's hand. "Come on, buddy. Let's go see what Daddy is up to while things get sorted out."

Wally didn't say anything but eyed us all carefully before following Landon out to our car. The room remained silent until we heard them drive away. Jocelyn and I exchanged unspoken words trying to figure out how we could possibly explain the presence of our father's estranged brother at our dining room table.

"Shall we move this to the parlor where we will all be more comfortable?" Emily said lightly. She, Jackson, Uncle Nicholas, and Phoebe rose from the table. "And I will put on a fresh pot of coffee."

Silence followed the empty sound of footsteps on the hardwood floors. I hurried over to my dad and wrapped my arms around his neck. "Thank you for coming. I've missed you." I kissed him on the cheek. "Let me take your jacket." He slipped it off and I hung it in the hall closet.

"Daddy," my sister snuck up beside him and hugged him tightly. "Please don't be angry. I promise, I can explain." She smiled hopefully up at him. "We can explain. Just try to stay calm."

"What is going on?" Shane appeared less than amused, following us into the parlor.

Jocelyn and I took a seat on the couch on either side of our father. The other four sat down on the loveseat and chairs. Everyone was uncomfortable except for Robert I imagine, due to his years of mediation and litigation experience. Minutes passed and an uncomfortable silence rested over us.

Emily finally reemerged with a tray full of mugs, a coffee pot, sugar, cream, and scones. She was always an elegant hostess regardless of the situation and I couldn't help but smile to myself. She set the tray down on the coffee table between everyone and joined her husband on the loveseat.

"Is someone going to explain to me what is going on?" Shane reached over and fixed himself a mug and grabbed a scone.

"Shane," Robert leaned forward on the edge of his seat angled towards my dad. "This is going to be almost impossible for you to understand or comprehend, but you must try to keep an open mind."

"Look," My dad sighed heavily. "I only came out to check on my daughter. I could tell how upset she was the last time I spoke with her, and Jocelyn told me she was staying here. I do appreciate you both looking after my girls and taking such good care of them, but if you knew the crazy ass BS my brother spouted off about at our brother's funeral, you wouldn't want him anywhere near your family or your grandchildren."

"I do understand, Shane. More than you know." Robert looked around at all of us. "We all do."

"I doubt that." My dad muttered before taking a bite of his scone.

"Shane," Uncle Nicholas faced his older brother. "There is so much more to this than you realize. Please hear us out."

"You," my father shook his head. "You have no right to be here. I told you to stay away from my family." Shane said angrily.

"Daddy, please." Jocelyn reached for his hand. "Do not be upset with Uncle Nicholas. This is my fault. I reached out to him."

"What?" Shane looked thoroughly confused.

"I sought him out several years ago when he was teaching at IU in Bloomington. I thought I was losing my mind and he and they," Jocelyn waved her other hand gesturing everyone else in the room except me, "helped me get through it. I would not be where I am now without any of them."

"Why didn't you come to me?" Shane questioned. "You and I have always been so close." I hated the hurt I saw in his eyes, and I knew it was killing my sister to put it there.

"Because I couldn't. You wouldn't have understood." Jocelyn looked sadly at him.

"You can tell me anything. You know I would believe you, even if I didn't fully understand." Shane defended himself.

"Why? You didn't believe me." Uncle Nicholas spoke up.

"You were spatting some crazy BS about living on parallel planes, saying you and Monte had inherited this ability and that others in our family had it too." Shane scoffed. "You realize how insane that sounds? You're lucky I didn't have you committed."

"He was not lying, Daddy." I reached over and placed my hand on his arm. "That was why Jocelyn reached out to him. She inherited it too. So did I."

"What?" he huffed. "That's crazy." Shane continued to shake his head.

"It's true, Shane." Robert spoke up as Emily took a hold of his arm looking directly over at Shane.

"This is unbelievable." Shane shook his head in disbelief. "It's one thing to ramble this crap off to me, Nicki, but to spew these lies to everyone to the point that they believe it to be real. I never would have thought you would have gone this far." Shane shifted his attention to Robert. "Robert, you are an educated man, how can you believe this nonsense?"

"Jocelyn, where's our photo albums and family trees?" Jackson spoke up for the first time.

"At our place," she said back quietly.

"I'll be right back. Excuse me, please." Jackson left without grabbing his coat.

"Shane, allow me to start from the beginning." Robert fixed himself another mug of coffee and settled in for a long conversation.

Robert, Emily, and Jocelyn started at the very beginning when Monte told Robert and Emily about Jocelyn inheriting *EVE* in 1878, their move to Chicago to moving back into their old home. It was an amazing and unbelievable tale. And Shane was silent throughout the entirety. He seemed to be absorbing their words and utterly lost at the same time.

"Daddy?" Shane sat there with Jocelyn and Jackson's album spread out across his lap. He was silent but had tears rolling down his cheeks. "Are you okay?"

"No." The extensive family tree was laid out across the coffee table and Shane had studied it extensively as Robert and Nicholas pointed out all the overlap caused by *EVE*. "This simply isn't possible." He muttered more to himself than the rest of the room.

"I know. I felt the same way when I first found out." I told him.

"All of us did." Jocelyn concurred.

Once Shane got his bearings, Nicholas and Robert further elaborated about other prophets and psychological ties to schizophrenia surrounding *EVE*. Shane grilled them both extensively wanting to know everything we had discovered or speculated about.

"Okay, what I don't understand is that if Nicholas and Monte both inherited this ability, why didn't I?" He looked to Robert for answers.

"We have been trying to figure that out as well." Robert rubbed his chin. "Because your supposed counterpart – Patrick also does not have it. However," he glanced at Nicholas for assistance.

"For a long time, I believed EVE was inherited through the mother, but Bethany nor Irene had it, but your and well, my father – Walter in the nineteenth century and Ralph in the twentieth century did." Nicholas shrugged his shoulders. "So, honestly, I am at a loss. Sidney has been learning more from our grandmother, Marissa in the nineteenth century, but it has been difficult to decipher.

"Let me get this straight," Shane shook his head a bit as if to uncloud his mind. "In the twenty-first century my girls are sisters, but in the nineteenth century she's your niece, and" he looked from me to Nicholas. "Sidney is your older sister in the nineteenth century, but your niece in the twenty-first. That is so bizarre."

"If you think speculating about it is difficult, you should try living it." I laughed.

"So, if it's now October 1882 for all of you," Shane motioned towards my companions. "What is it for you?" His eyes rested on me.

"When I wake up it will be October of 1859. I am married to a physician named Keifer Marshall who is from Savannah, Georgia, but came north for medical school and stayed because of me. We live with my grandmother, Marissa, at our family estate called Terrace Falls. My husband's family owns a large plantation and has more than a hundred slaves."

"And you're walking into the American Civil War." He shifted back towards Robert and Nicholas. "That would mean you two already lived through it." He chuckled with stunned amazement.

"Well, actually all of us here did. My oldest two remember more of it than Jackson, but Jocelyn was alive as well only too young to remember it. Nicholas, Monte, and I all fought for the Union Army. Nicholas was captured and spent more than a year in Andersonville Prison Camp."

"Were you in any notable battles?" Shane quietly inquired.

"Yes, and we were both wounded — multiple times." Robert cleared his throat indicating he did not want to elaborate. "But we survived. That is what is important. Many were not so lucky."

"I'm so sorry, Nicholas." My dad stood up and crossed over to his brother. "I am so sorry I did not believe you."

"It's okay. I can only imagine what you must have thought." Nicholas graciously hugged his brother back.

"Can you please forgive me, little brother?" There were tears in my dad's eyes.

"Already done, brother. I have missed you and your family so much." Uncle Nicholas confessed. "You can imagine how thrilled I was to find this bunch on my doorstep." He smiled. "They were a welcomed sight."

"What about Ethan?" Shane took a step back and posed the question to all of us. "Did he inherit this too?"

"We don't know," Emily was the first to respond. "Thus far, none of us have come across him in our *other* lives." We all shook our heads. "But he is at the age that if he did, we will know soon."

"How? He's alone at Notre Dame. There's no one to help him if he starts hearing voices or seeing things from his other life." Shane looked distressed at the thought of his son thinking he was losing his mind.

"Jocelyn and I have been keeping close tabs on him. We talk to him several times a week." I assured him.

"Plus, I also talk to Liang a few times a week just to make sure Ethan isn't struggling with anything or acting out of character. I casually inquired about his behavior every time I talk to her." Jocelyn clarified. "Unfortunately, that is all we can do right now. We just have to wait and see. But I really do not believe he inherited it, because he has not appeared anywhere in our other families."

"Could he have a different time, like say if he was born into Nicholas's family." Shane turned towards his brother. "You said you have several sons there and so does Monte. Could he be one of them? I mean, the timeline does jump — look what happened to Sidney."

"I suppose it is possible," Nicholas thought for a moment. "I guess anything is possible. What do you think, Robert?"

"You have studied this a great deal more than I, Nicholas. But yes, I suppose it is possible." Robert sat back in his seat and looked over at his wife. "I had not thought of that, but it could happen since you all share the same bloodline.

"Okay, so wait a minute. I have to ask a silly question. I know you told Jocelyn that she was named Jocelyn Alyssa who was the daughter of your great whatever grandfather 's the daughter who was born right before our house in Chicago was complete." My father's eyes widened.

"Oh, my goodness." He interrupted laughing at the realization.

"Yes, laugh it up. We made that connection several years ago and I still find little humor in it." Jocelyn smirked.

"I guess we named you after — well, you." Shane laughed even harder at the absurdity of it all.

"Yes, it is very humorous, I know." My sister playfully rolled her eyes.

"But where in the world did you find my name?" I asked our father.

"When we moved to Chicago, I started doing research on my family since I had always heard stories about the grand house and such. In doing so, we came across two Sidney Harper's in our family tree. One was obviously male, and the other female. Your mother and I thought it was such a unique name that would work for either a boy or a girl." He shrugged with a chuckle. "So, I guess you are named after yourself also."

"Welcome to my absurdity club, sis." Jocelyn playfully rolled her eyes.

"Wow," I snorted utterly dumbfounded.

The remainder of the day was filled with questions and speculations. Some serious, and some poking fun about what ifs. Overall, my father took it better than any of us thought he would. It was a welcomed relief to see Nicholas and Shane mending their relationship and spending time together catching up.

Shane decided to stay with my sister and Jackson that night. She had a guest room in their little house and was thrilled to have him stay with her. Uncle Nicholas hung around after they and Phoebe returned home. He helped the rest of us clean up after everyone departed.

"How do you feel?" I asked him as we cleared the dining room table.

"Wonderful, actually. I never thought I would ever be able to reconcile with Shane." He smiled over at me. "I realized how much I truly missed having him in my life."

"I am happy for you." I patted his arm. "For both of you."

20

SUNDAY, OCTOBER 23, 1859

THE RAIN POUNDED DOWN upon our carriage on our way home from church. Preston led our horse team through the muddy outlying roads back to our estate. I sat beside Keifer with a light blanket across my lap. My grandmother sat across from us with the heavier one keeping her warm.

The temperatures were steadily dropping. It wouldn't be long before the first frost of the season. Hopefully, it will hold off long enough for us to get the last of the fields harvested. Our estate could not afford to take the financial loss if we were not able too.

"I invited Mr. Bennett over for supper today." My grandmother stated casually.

"Really?" I raised an eyebrow at her.

"I think that would be nice." Keifer smiled.

"Do not make a big issue about it. I simply thought it would liven up the conversation is all." She said as a matter of fact.

"As you wish," I smiled over at my husband and squeezed his hand.

Preston pulled up in front of the house and opened the carriage door for us. He helped my grandmother and me out, holding the umbrella for us up to the front porch, followed by Keifer before taking the team around to the stables.

My grandmother hung up her shawl and went off to the kitchen to let Naomi know there would be one more for supper. I watched

Keifer fix himself a bourbon and warm himself by the fire with the Sunday newspaper. I put my bonnet and shawl in the hallway and disappeared into the study. I wanted to take advantage of the free moment to return Annabelle's last letter.

Dearest Annabelle,

It was wonderful to hear from you and that you are all doing well. A heartfelt congratulations on the birth of your fourth healthy son. I imagine Patrick is elated with joy. I cannot wait until we have the opportunity to meet him.

I have some glorious news to share. Keifer and I are expecting our first child this spring. Our child should be here before the first thaw. We are so excited and hope to make it to Chicago next Christmas to introduce my family to their new niece or nephew.

Terrace Falls is doing well, and Keifer's practice is thriving. We are seeing a lot of tension from the Southern States, and Keifer is greatly concerned. I am sure you share my fears for Patrick as well. How are the conditions in Chicago?

I hope Monte and Nicholas are both doing well. Please convey my love to my father. I hope he is doing well. I miss you all and look forward to seeing you soon. Give your beautiful boys a hug and kiss for me and my love to you and my brothers.

We are all doing well. Grandmother sends her love, and congratulations on your new angel. My love to you all.

Sincerely,

Sidney

I folded the letter and placed it in an envelope, addressed it, and put it on the corner of my desk to mail the next day.

The aroma from the kitchen wafted down the hallway. Naomi was an amazing cook. The smell of roast, potatoes, carrots, and fresh bread filled the air. My stomach stirred with desire. It seemed I was now entering a phase of pregnancy where I wanted to eat nonstop.

Mr. Bennett arrived shortly thereafter and joined Keifer in the parlor. The two were enjoying brandy and discussing their irritation with the rain and their inability to finish harvesting the remainder of the crops.

By the time we finally sat down at the table, Mr. Bennett had confessed that the stirring's spreading through Boston with rapid speculations of events that had transpired Virginia had chilled him to the core.

"Did they locate the men that escaped capture?" I took my seat opposite my husband. It seemed all anyone wanted to discuss was John Brown and the raid at the federal arsenal at Harper's Ferry.

"From what I understand, they have not. Still, what surprised me most was how much time Brown spent here in Massachusetts." Mr. Bennett sat down across from my grandmother between us.

"Darling, do you recall the man you met at the dinner party for Dr. Howe in Boston? That was John Brown. He was a stoic, rugged, man that had an ill-tempered look about him." Keifer inquired.

"Yes, I recall him. He was rather hard to miss." I stated.

"I read in the paper just yesterday that they discovered he had been hiding up in the mountains in Virginia and spent the last several years contemplating and plotting against slave owners." Mr. Bennett told us, placing his napkin across this lap.

"Then what in the world was he doing at Dr. Howe's celebration?"

"Seeking money from some of Boston's elitists." Mr. Bennett scoffed.

"So, he was one of those abolitionist fanatics?" my grandmother asked.

"Fanatic would be an understatement." Keifer chimed in. "The Boston *Post* reported that on Wednesday evening, this man, and his band of twenty-two men came out of their retreat in the mountains, murdered the man who was standing guard on the bridge and took control of the federal arsenal at Harper's Ferry with no other resistance. They also took the remainder of the guards as prisoners."

"I read they cut the telegraph wires as well." Mr. Bennett added.

"Oh my, what did he think he was going to accomplish?" My grandmother forged her surprise.

"Apparently, he sent two of his sheep to a couple nearby plantations; one of which was the home of Colonel Lewis Washington, the great grandnephew of George Washington. And to add insult to injury, they stole a family heirloom; I believe it was the sword presented to George Washington by Frederick the Great." Mr. Bennett recalled with disdain.

"How dreadful." I admitted. I had never heard that before.

"Did you hear about the train?" Keifer gestured towards our guest.

"I did. Wasn't it the Baltimore and Ohio train?" He tried to recall.

"I believe it was. Brown and his posse killed a black man working as a baggage master." Keifer recounted.

"Yes, it was horrible. Thankfully, they eventually let the train continue its way." Mr. Bennett stated. "But then when the men who worked at the arsenal came in for their morning shift, most were taken hostage as well. Afterwards, Brown spent the day just sitting there in the arsenal." He shook his head.

"The local militia from the surrounding towns in Maryland and Virginia arrived and took back control of both bridges. Then Lieutenant Colonel Robert E. Lee of the U.S. Calvary and Lieutenant J.E.B. Stuart arrived at nightfall with federal forces. It seems Lieutenant Stuart attempted to negotiate with Brown, but to no avail." Keifer added.

"How horrific. I cannot imagine what his goal was." I tried to create disbelief as I listened to the tale I'd learned about years before and had been discussed in every possible manner over the last few days.

"Brown's eventual goal was to liberate the slaves and incite an insurrection. He planned on arming the slaves with the weaponry seized from the arsenal. He believed the slaves would turn on their masters and murder all white people in the South who held them in bondage." Mr. Bennett concluded.

"And not just the slave masters — Brown wanted the slaves to revolt against all whites; men, women, and children." Keifer pointed out with disgust.

"How could anyone be foolish enough to believe such an absurd act of violence could be productive?" My grandmother sat there sipping her tea and trying to eat dinner.

"The ramifications from this will only enhance the division between the Northern and Southern states." I declared.

"I agree." Keifer shook his head. "As if tensions could get any worse."

"Did they capture him alive?" my grandmother asked.

"Yes. The funny thing is they almost didn't. I read that Lieutenant Israel Green, who was in command of the detachment, was wearing his decorative dress sword, instead of his real one. Therefore, when he attempted to slay Brown, Green was barely able to inflict any serious injuries to him." Mr. Bennett continued.

"How impressive and gallant." I snorted.

"They arrested seven of the twenty-two, ten were killed, and five had escaped." Mr. Bennett finished off his plate.

"I hope they find the men who got away." My grandmother remarked.

"Me too. They killed four people and wounded nine." Keifer added.

"My goodness. They should hang." I remarked.

"From what I understand, the trial is going to begin by the end of the week in Charlestown, Virginia." Mr. Bennett informed us.

"That is quick." I had not realized.

"I know." Mr. Bennett shrugged.

"By doing so, they are only going to make a martyr of him." I declared.

"I believe they are trying to conduct everything so quickly before news can spread any further." Mr. Bennett explained.

"I believe it is too late for that." I muttered, looked distinctively at my grandmother.

"I fear you may be right." Keifer reached over and took my hand.

Mr. Bennett joined us in the parlor for coffee after dinner. The four of us talked well into the evening. It seemed the topic could not be steered away from speculation about what our representatives in Washington were going to do to settle the issue of slavery in the new territories. It was consuming the nation and at the same time, ripping it apart.

I sat there and listened to my husband, and Mr. Bennett talk about nothing else. It was so difficult to remain silent. I continually looked over at my grandmother knowing she was thinking the same thing as me. We knew what storm brewed on the horizon. We knew every detail of the hell that laid before us. Yet, we were both utterly helpless to stop it.

21

SPENT MOST OF MY TIME off doing research. I downloaded books onto my Kindle about the causes of the American Civil War, the battles, the conditions. I read through John Browns' trail, his final words, and the impact it had on the nation.

I was intrigued by Boston's *Secret Six*; which included Boston's elitist Gerrit Smith, George L. Stearns, Franklin B. Sanborn, Thomas Wentworth Higginson, Theodore Parker, and Samuel Gridley Howe. These prominent supporters of John Brown did not back his venture financially on Harpers Ferry, but they adamantly shared Brown's beliefs.

When Brown was arrested, and more than 400 letters were found in his Virginia mountain hideaway, Brown's supporters were named. The *Secret Six*'s involvement became known to all, and there was much speculation as to the depth of their knowledge of Brown's plans.

The research I found told me that Smith had a nervous breakdown after Brown's arrest over the fear of exposure. Sanborn and Dr. Howe, consumed by guilt and fear, disappeared from Boston, and escaped to Canada so they would not have to face interrogation for their actions. Higginson is said to have refused to testify before the congressional committee for his involvement with Brown and knowledge of Harper's Ferry.

Studying it on one plane — living it on another was the most bizarre experience I could imagine. Daily, I watched the events unfold, knowing what the consequences of seemingly minor decisions would have on the nation.

Living on a small estate outside of Boston, being a woman, living in a time when women had no voice, left me feeling frustrated, angry, and helpless. Still, I was determined to do everything I could to prepare for the storm. I may not have a voice, but I could do everything within my limited power to protect those I love.

I was sitting on the chaise lounge reading through the details of Harper's Ferry when there was a soft knock on my bedroom door.

"Come in." I called out without looking up.

"Hello, darling. How are you?" My Uncle Nicholas entered our room.

"Hello." I set my tablet aside and stood up, embracing him. "What has you up this early?"

"I figured Shane would be coming by to see you and visit with everyone. I wanted to see him before he heads back to Chicago."

"Did he say when he was leaving? With everything that happened yesterday, I completely forgot to ask." I chuckled.

"I have no idea." He sat down at the foot of our bed. "But just in case I wanted to make sure I saw him before he leaves."

"I am so happy you two have reconciled. I know it means a great deal to you both and it truly makes things so much easier for Jocelyn and I." I smiled.

"Me too. I missed him." He paused for a moment gathering his thoughts. "Still, it could not have been easy for him — learning about

EVE and finding out his mad little brother isn't so mad after all." His smile was betrayed by the sadness in his eyes.

"True, but it must be a great comfort knowing that we can share our other lives with him. We no longer have to keep half of our lives from him." I reasoned.

"Was it me, or did he seem almost sad or rather disappointed that he did not inherit *EVE*." Uncle Nicholas tilted his head as if he was contemplating all that transpired yesterday.

"If given the choice, would you rather your brother has this gift or not? I know you have a somewhat different view of *EVE* than me but, I suppose perhaps it is because you have had longer to adjust. But I am not sure I would wish this on anyone I love." I confessed.

"I hope someday you do come to awe in the wonderment of *EVE* and view it as the truly unique blessing it is." He reached for my hand.

"Perhaps but given the current climate in my other life and knowing what I am facing," I snorted accidentally. "I am not so inclined at the moment."

"I did my duty honorably and I am proud of it." He assured me. "You look like you could use a bit of fresh air. Why don't you join me for a walk before everyone arrives? It is a beautiful morning." He pulled me to my feet.

"How can I possibly say no to such an offer?" I shook my head slightly and smiled, stepping into my sneakers.

This intervention had Emily written all over it. She had been on me for days to get out of this room and breathe some fresh air. She was worried that I was trading the grief over my baby with an obsession of current events and things to come on my other plane.

Perhaps she was right.

It was a lovely fall morning. There was a slight nip in the air, perfect for a hoodie. The sun was just starting its accent filling the sky with an array of gold, pinks, and pale blues. The trees were almost bare, their leaves scattered about our feet.

The yards were still a vibrant green and most were decorated with various Halloween decorations. Pumpkins and gourds aligned walkways; haystacks sat upon porches with silly-looking scarecrows resting on them. Others covered their bushes with fake cobwebs and hairy spiders. Witches and skeletons hung from tree branches. Some even created fake graveyards in front of their homes.

We strolled down the sidewalk in silence for a couple blocks. I could tell he had something on his mind. I didn't want to push him before he was ready. I figured he was most likely searching for the right words to begin with.

"How are your classes going this term?" I couldn't stand the quiet any longer.

"Good. I only have three on Mondays and Wednesdays this semester."

"Which periods are you teaching?" I asked.

"Two classes are American History, and the other is American Revolution."

"That sounds interesting." I glanced up at his face trying to read him but obtained nothing. He had an excellent poker face. "Do you ever teach a class just on the Civil War?" I was curious.

"I have in the past, and I have one scheduled for the spring semester." He looked over at me with a mournful look. "It is not my favorite class to teach. It's difficult."

"Can I ask you a silly question?"

"There are no silly questions," he smiled over at me.

"How come nothing is taught about the Natick Resolution, or the caning of Senator Sumner on the Senate floor by Congressman

Preston Brooks, or Helper's book? They all seem to have a significant impact on leading up to the war." I wondered.

"Honestly, I do not know. None have ever showed up in the curriculum and I barely remember those events in my *other* life. You must remember I was very young when most of those occurred, and I was at West Point in the years leading up to the war. The school monitored a lot of the news that we received so unless someone's family wrote to them about it, we rarely heard of such things."

"I have been thinking about it a lot *here* and have realized how grossly inadequate most of the teachings are about how things truly were." He nodded in agreement. "I am amazed at how little people today understand what it was like. And I am only at the far edge of the beginning. Truthfully, I am terrified." I confessed.

"Sometimes knowing is worse than not knowing."

"So, was it Emily or Robert that called you?" I asked softly.

"Robert." My uncle confessed. "He was afraid he upset you the other night at dinner."

"No," I shook my head. "I upset him. And I did not mean too."

"I know. And so does he."

"This is all so difficult to decipher." I told him.

"How do you mean?"

We sat down on a bench beside the small creek bed. I watched the water tumbling over the rocks and listened for a moment to the sound of the frogs and birds chirping near us. It was so peaceful.

"For all of us." I looked down and fidgeted with my hands. "It's hard to explain."

"What do you mean?" He gently placed his hands over mine.

"When our souls travel nightly, our bodies are the same age on each plane." I began.

"Yes," my uncle looked a bit confused.

"Okay, well." I wasn't sure how to explain it right without sounding ridiculous. "On *this* plane, you are my uncle — my dad's little brother. But in the 19th century, you are my little brother." I shook my head slightly at the stupidity of it.

"It is strange, I agree. But *there* you really do not know us. In your world *there,* I am in my late teens and at West Point. I was part of the infamous class of 61." He huffed. "Did you know that Custer was in my graduating class?"

"Are you serious? That is amazing." I exclaimed. "Did you know him?"

"Oh, yes. I knew him; very well in fact." He laughed.

"Should I even ask?" I looked at him coyly.

"I can tell you he graduated last in our class." He raised his eyebrows at me.

"I thought he was supposed to be a famous war hero."

"He was. He was a great equestrian and swordsman; just not so bright with the book learning." He perched his lips together in a smirk. "But he was quite the lady's man."

"Oh, I see." I tried not to laugh.

My uncle looked off into the distance beyond the trees. His face looked troubled. I could tell he was remembering his friends that were long gone from this world — in both his lives.

"Things got toxic on campus before graduation. Cadets from the South were fleeing home. Cadets from the North were ridiculing Southerners starting arguments every chance they could." He sighed heavily. "One morning when we were lined up outside hanging our country's flag, we started singing the *Star-Spangled Banner* when the cadets from the South began singing *Dixie*."

"I bet that went over well." I muttered.

"A brawl broke out amongst the cadets. One of the officers fired a cannon to get our attention." His voice sounded shameful. "It was like the war had already broken out on a much smaller scale. When we finally had to take our *Oath of Allegiance* to the Union, the remaining Southern cadets walked out of the auditorium."

"I am sorry," I didn't know what else to say.

"This war," he turned his head away from me as he spoke. I felt for sure it was so I wouldn't see the tears in his eyes. "People now cannot even fathom what it was like." His head shook slightly. "I am not meaning just us at the academy. We were not simply classmates — we were brothers. There was a bond amongst those who went to West Point. The only other time I experienced anything like it was my time in the military."

"I have heard that before." I said softly.

"I witnessed brothers at the academy get into fist fights over allegiances. Long-term friendships were shattered overnight. Some cadets had difficultly trying to get home because of the rioting in Baltimore." He finally looked over at me.

"The Baltimore riots. I had forgotten about those."

Something else to look forward to.

"But I do recall visiting you a couple times when I was young. It must have been before we moved to Chicago. And I remember you coming to Chicago to see us the Christmas before the war began. I came home from the academy to see my family. Annabelle had just given birth to Jocelyn, and everyone was so excited." He chuckled. "She was the first and only girl in our family line — in that generation at least. You were the only one in ours." He smiled over at me.

"So, you saw my baby next Christmas?" I turned towards him.

"Sidney, I have met all your children." He smiled.

"Can you tell me," my hand rested longingly on my abdomen. "Is my baby all right? Are they healthy?"

"Yes. Yes. Your baby was healthy and thriving. And if my memory serves, trying to walk at Christmas." He smiled broadly.

"Do I have a son or a daughter?" I quipped.

"Sidney, we have discussed this. Besides, wouldn't you rather be surprised?" He patted my knee lightly.

"Normally, yes. However, considering all the things that have happened lately, I would like to know."

"Very well. You have a healthy son." He smiled lovingly at me.

"A son." I beamed but instantly felt despair. "Landon wanted a son so badly." I whispered.

"He will have one. You will have more children. I promise you." He assured me.

"His name?" I swallowed hard on the knowledge he had already shared with me.

"You graced him with his father's name." There was a twinkle in my uncle's eye.

"Keifer Lee, Jr." I grinned. "Seems very fitting."

"Yes, I believe so." He looked off into the trees in the distance. "But that is not what is troubling you."

"No." I muttered. "I know you are aware, on my *other* plane, it is October 1859. I am a grown woman, married to a prominent physician, and running a grand estate. I have a stellar reputation amongst my peers. I am a savvy businesswoman — which I mind you is quite a feat in that time."

"Yes, I agree." He nodded.

"You — my younger brothers, Robert, Emily, Alex, Phoebe, and Jackson are all *there*. But you are also *there* thirty years later in the 1880s with Jocelyn."

"Yes," he nodded in agreement.

"Do you see my paradox. How can your soul be with me and as well with Jocelyn?" I implored.

"I understand and share your confusion. I wish I had an answer for you, but I am afraid I do not. It is a riddle I have spent my entire adult life trying to figure out. All I know is that time is fluid. It bends easily and at times, such as with us, it blends." He looked down at his hands for a moment. "Look at your grandmother, Marissa. She is with you in the mid-nineteenth century, but also travels to the mid-twentieth century. Your father *there* — Walter is alive and well in Chicago mid-nineteenth century, but also fought in the King Williams War in the early seventeenth century."

"It's baffling." I pondered. "Who was Walter's mother in the seventeenth century?"

"I am afraid I do not know."

"And you cannot ask him?"

"Walter is a difficult man. He is not a very affectionate man, nor does he open up to his children." My uncle admitted.

"And Bethany?" I did not know much about the woman who was so cold towards me.

"My mother was loving towards her sons, but I know she felt as if she lived in the shadow of your mother. I believe she had hoped by moving our father to Chicago to foreign surroundings that your mother never graced, he would be able to open his heart fully to her." He winked. "But alas, he never could. But she loved her sons; and all the love he did not give her, she bestowed on us."

"She resented me." I turned towards him. "And I always blamed her for taking my father away from me."

"From what I was told, you resemble your mother, Julia, a great deal. You have her build, her flaxen hair, her bright blue eyes." He gently touched my hair. "I am told your mother was a great beauty. If she looked anything like you, I am sure they are right."

"Thank you," I blushed. "My grandmother told me it was difficult for my father to look at me as I got older because of my resemblance to her."

"Do you know much about us *there*? I mean, did our father keep in touch with you after we moved to Chicago?" My uncle asked.

"Not much when I was young. He would send me a card with a few sentences each year for my birthday and a small gift for me at Christmas. But that was it." I shifted a bit on the bench as the feelings of being rejected by my *other* father washed over me. "He moved on with his life. He had a new wife and new children. I was part of a world he wished never existed." A tear escaped out of the corner of my eye.

"Father loved you in his own way. I know he did." Uncle Nicholas put his arm around me.

"I would never know much about any of you if it not for Annabelle. When I traveled with my grandmother and Keifer to Chicago for Patrick's wedding, I was so nervous. I had not seen our father or any of you in years. I did not know what you all would think of me."

"I remember meeting you all at the train station. I have very little memories of any of you. Right before we left the house, my mother told us about you and your mother. She was very stoic about it. I knew then that she had no love for you." Uncle Nicholas admitted.

"I knew it before our father married her. She looked at me like I was an insect that needed to be squashed. Thankfully, our grandparents loved me and wanted to give me a home. I shudder to think of what my life would have been like had our father insisted on taking me with him."

"Cinderella," he laughed. "But with annoying, smelly half-brothers instead of stepsisters."

"You do know I never perceived any of you as my half-brothers." I reached over and took his hand. "In my eyes, all three of you are my brothers — half blood or not."

"I know the three of us feel the same. You are our sister." He squeezed my hand gently.

"Thankfully, Annabelle reached out to me. She started writing me letters every month. She is a remarkable lady; very kind and loving. She let me know about the births of my nephews," I laughed just a bit. "She notified me recently of the birth of William. I know she wanted a daughter desperately." I sighed heavily. "I wish I could tell her that at this time next year, her wish would be granted."

"But you cannot." He grinned with his lips pressed together.

"Nor would I." I assured him. "May I ask you something else?"

"You may ask me anything." His eyes were warm and welcoming.

"You said you were at West Point when the Civil War began." He nodded. "And I know you are aware that Jocelyn found and read Uncle Monte's journals." Again, he nodded. "She gave them to me afterwards and let me read them too. Uncle Monte wrote extensively about you being missing in action and how he and your family longed to hear news of you. Later, they found out that you were taken prisoner and put in Andersonville prison camp in Georgia." My voice dropped almost to a whisper.

"Yes. I was." His back stiffened a bit.

"I do not say this to upset you or to be disrespectful in any way. What I am saying is, well," I took a deep nervous breath. "Is there not some way I could warn you at Christmas before the war starts? I cannot fathom what you and Monte and Robert all went through with the battles or the things you saw. Even the things that Keifer and Patrick must do, taking care of the wounded soldiers." My voice trailed off.

"As you mentioned, we are there with Jocelyn thirty years later in Chicago." He patted my hand. "All that I had to endure, and I will not share the details with you, have made me the man that sits beside you. I survived. Yes, I have scars," he grinned. "But having scars means you have had a life."

"Yes, I agree. I suppose I am fearful of what is to come, for all of us."

"We are blessed with an incredible life; one that most individuals cannot fathom. We get to witness history and the future. We see the world through a unique perspective that allows us to appreciate things differently than others. It is also a heavy burden to carry." He told me.

"It seems to be at a time such as this. The weight of the upcoming war weighs heavily on me. I know what is to come and feel utterly helpless in its path." I confessed, staring unseeingly at the trees across the creek bed.

"You are only as helpless as you chose to be." My uncle noted. "You are a strong young woman, and you will find strength you never knew you had."

"I appreciate that. I truly do." I took a deep breath and stood up. "We should probably head back to the house. I am sure Emily is holding brunch for us, and my dad should be there shortly."

"May I ask you something, Sidney?" He got to his feet.

"Yes."

"When do you plan on returning to your apartment? Sooner or later, you know you must face it." He reached out and touched my arm.

"I know. I have given it a great deal of thought these last few days. But of course, it is not just me. Landon has taken to hiding himself at the hospital or on campus studying. I feel like he is avoiding me. I know he is struggling with the loss, but he will not confide in me." I hated to say.

We started back down the sidewalk. The sun was almost directly above us but held little warmth. There was a chill in the breeze that seemed to seep through my clothes making me feel overly exposed. I took ahold of my uncle's arm trying to draw some of his warmth.

"I am sure he will. He simply needs time to mourn in his own way." He patted my hand on his arm. "Just be patient with him."

"I am trying. I hate that he," I stopped myself, but he caught me.

"You hate that he what?" He encouraged me to continue.

"I hate that he spends most of his nights at the hospital or at the campus library. He has only been home or, well, come back to the Chandler's twice since I was released from the hospital. I know Landon does not blame me for the loss of our child, but it is almost as if he has difficulty being around me now."

"Landon loves you very much, Sidney. He will come back to you." He smiled down at me. "We both know this."

"Yes, we do."

I took comfort in his words although I did know from my sister that Landon and I would eventually be married although I had no idea of when and she refused to tell me. I knew we would be blessed with more children, and they would grow up happy and healthy. But in this moment, I still felt disheartened by his behavior.

Shane, Jocelyn, and Jackson were already there when we returned. Everyone was gathered in the kitchen putting the finishing touches on brunch. There was a platter full of waffles, another with scrambled eggs, and one overflowing with bacon. She topped it off with a bowl of mixed fruit, and pitchers of orange juice and coffee. My stomach grumbled as soon as we entered the house, and the aroma reached us.

"Good morning, darling." My father hugged me as soon as I entered the kitchen. "How are you feeling?"

"Good." I smiled. "How long you staying? I didn't get the chance to ask you yesterday."

"I'm flying home Wednesday afternoon." He kept his arm around my waist. "I wish I could stay longer. I miss my girls."

"We miss you too." I rested my head upon his shoulder.

"Good morning, brother." Uncle Nicholas greeted Shane. "It is good to see you again."

"And you," my dad's smile widened, and it warmed my heart to see them together.

22

THE MORNING DAWNED BRIGHT and beautiful. I climbed out of bed and grabbed my robe. I pulled open the shutters to a vast array of sunshine gleaming down over the fields of emerald sitting in the foreground of dense woods. I pulled open the window and let the cool air flood into the room.

I sat down at my vanity and brushed out my hair with long strokes. I was elated it had finally stopped raining. The wind rustled my hair sending goosebumps down my arms and reminding me that we were well under the grasp of fall.

I slipped into my dark green gown with ivory lace. I pinned my hair up in loose curls instead of a loose bun. I ran my hands lightly over the small bump in my midsection and thought about the words Uncle Nicholas had said.

My son — my little Keifer Lee, Jr.

I still had four months before my son was going to make his appearance. It felt like forever.

I tried to pull myself together and rid myself of all anxiety. Like all expectant mothers, I was filled with the wonderment of pregnancy, and the fear of childbirth overwhelmed me. Not to mention, I was going to have to do this without any modern medicine. I had a feeling I was going to be screaming for an epidural before all was said and done.

~

After supper, Mr. Bennett dropped by with our other neighbors down the way a bit. The McKendrick's estate was about a hundred acres on the other side of the Bennett's along our way into the heart of the town square. They were pleasant, but a little rough around the edges. They always brought along a jug of whiskey with them, and once they arrived, it was difficult to get them to leave.

The library was filled with cigars and pipe tobacco smoke. The stench was drifting out into the other rooms, and I was none too happy in it. The smell was making me nauseas, but I knew I couldn't say anything about it.

My grandmother and I sat in the parlor, doing our best to keep quiet. But the men had left the French doors open to the library. We rocked by the roaring hearth, working on our needlepoint listening to the boisterous noise following the smoke down the hallway.

My ears perked up when I heard them discussing John Brown's trial. It had been mere days since he was captured, and the judicial system was moving at lightning speed. The government was hoping to sweep it under the rug and hoped it would cause as little disruption as possible. Thus far, they had largely underestimated the American people. From the evening paper I had learned that he had been indicted this morning and the trial began this afternoon.

To pass the time, I recounted my conversation with Nicholas to my grandmother. She was intrigued by the same bizarre nuances as I. We were enjoying a lively discussion that was drowned out by the growing intoxicated scoundrels down the hall.

This happened every time the McKendrick's stopped by. Mr. McKendrick was a spirited man with strong convictions. His two sons that had accompanied him this evening were in their mid-twenties, and I had grown up with them. They were university graduates, and when they were not under the influence of alcohol, they were pleasant gentlemen. But when alcohol was added, their rascal side took over.

They each had dark auburn hair with waves through it. Their eyes were a brilliant green that went well with their broad shoulders and masculine build. Although their father presently had white hair, it once was the same brilliant auburn mane his sons portrayed.

"I saw in the newspaper that prominent South Carolina leaders are still pushing for segregation." The eldest McKendrick son, George remarked. "I say let em' go. It's not like we need em'." His words began to slur a bit.

"I do not want to see this country torn apart. My fear is if the Southern states do secede, it will lead to war." His father, Stephen, told him.

"You're from the South, right, Doc?" George asked my husband.

"Savannah." I heard Keifer reply.

"And what are their feelings in Savannah?" Brian, the younger of the McKendrick's, asked.

"I have not been back to my family's plantation in years." Keifer answered honestly.

"Plantation, huh?" I heard George clear his throat loudly. "How many slaves does your family own?"

"My family background is of no consequence here." Keifer stated.

"I believe it is." George stated loudly. "You are a Southerner, are you not?"

"I have spent the last decade of my life in Massachusetts. I came here for medical school and met Sidney." My husband declared.

"That does not make you a Northerner." George stated.

"But it does not necessarily not make him one either." Stephen reminded his son. "I have known the Doc since before he married Sidney."

"Do you believe people should be held in bondage?" Brian asked directly.

"I cannot help what my family does. I have never purchased another human being in my life." I could hear the anger and defensiveness in my husband's voice.

"Now gentleman," Mr. Bennett spoke up. "Please. Remember, we are neighbors and have been so for many years. Stephan, you yourself came to this country as a teenager and built a new life for yourself. You bought some land, got married, raised a family, and become a respectable member of this community." He pointed out. "I know nothing of your youth in Ireland or why you came to America. Would you want your neighbors questioning your morals?"

"I have never owned another person." Stephan stated loudly.

"Neither have I" Keifer reminded them.

"But you were raised as a master." George stated. "You gave orders. You held power over the people your father owned."

I looked over at my grandmother and bit my bottom lip. I could tell by the look on her face she was sharing my struggles. In my distraction, I accidentally pricked my finger with the needle.

"Ouch," I immediately stuck my finger in my mouth. "That hurt."

"Try not to listen to their foolishness." She reminded me.

"Oh, what I would love to say to George if I was not a lady." I jabbed my needle back through the fabric missing my intended mark. "Dang it," I muttered.

"But you are, so you will sit still and be quiet." My grandmother told me.

"Yes. I know." I grumbled. "Sometimes I really hate my station *here*." I lowered my voice. "Just because I'm a woman, I apparently am too weak or ignorant to have an opinion of my own."

"That is not true." She stopped her needlepoint for a moment and looked at me. "You are highly respected in this community and known for your business prowess. However, you also have a reputation as being a graceful and kind lady, and that is something that you must always maintain and protect."

"I know." I leaned a bit closer to her. "It is ridiculous, isn't it?"

"Do you have any idea how many thousands of women have shared your point of view? Unfortunately, it will be another Millenia before anything is changed." My grandmother reminded me.

"How wonderful," I rolled my eyes. "At least *there* I have a voice."

"And how has that worked out for you?" She smirked.

"Pretty well, actually," I laughed.

"You enjoy being impossible."

"I wonder who I got that from?" I chuckled.

"Do you believe in states' rights above the Federal Government?" Brian's voice rang down the hall.

"I stand with our Federal Government." I could tell by Keifer's tone his patience was wearing thin.

"But do you agree that the South would not stand a chance against the North should they decide to secede?" George pushed.

"The North is better equipped with industry than the South. Most of the nation's factories, railroads, and textiles are in the Northern states. The Southern states are largely agriculture with a few modest factories." I heard my husband state the same argument I had previously said to his sister.

"So, Doc. Which side would you fight for?" George asked the question they all wanted to know.

"I am a Northern man, and my honor is to my country, my state, my wife, and my home. I would enlist as a physician with the Union Army and save as many soldiers as is within my power." Keifer informed them.

"You would fight against your kin?" Stephan inquired.

"As I said, I am a physician. My role would be in saving lives." Keifer said again.

"How long do you think it will be before Keifer makes sure one of the McKendrick's needs a physician?" My grandmother leaned forward and whispered, making me giggle.

"This is not going to end well." I tried to restrain myself.

"Does that mean you would give aid to Southern soldiers?" Brian asked.

"I swore an oath to do no harm." I recognized Keifer's voice spoken through gritted teeth.

"Your oath does not state you have to offer aid to the enemy." Brian concluded.

"Then, you would try to save Southern soldiers?" I could hear the anger in George's slurred words.

"I believe the Doc here is a good and honorable man. I have zero doubts about his convictions nor his patriotism." Mr. Bennett stated loudly.

"I could not agree more. I believe you boys have had enough to drink and owe the Doc here an apology." Stephan cleared his throat. "I know I do."

Their voices lowered to a normal tone making it difficult to decipher what was being said. I looked back over at my grandmother and shook my head.

"Sadly, this will not be the end of it." she remarked.

"No. It's only the beginning." I said sadly.

After the McKendrick's and Mr. Bennett finally retreated to their homes and my grandmother retired for the evening, I paced the parlor. Keifer remained in the library consumed with his own thoughts while my mind was spinning over events taking place just south of us in Virginia.

The trial had begun. The city of Charlestown was flooded with people. Every newspaper in the country was covering the story. John Brown had been sensationalized in the Northern states and demonized in the Southern. The thin fabric that was holding our nation together was unraveling at rapid speed.

I held my breath as I read the Boston *Post* and *Liberator*. The news was unsettling. The 400 or so letters had been found in the hideout used by John Brown and his gang of thugs. Prominent members of Boston and New York's elitist were named as supporters of his mission. They spoke openly about starting an insurrection of the slaves.

I crumbled the newspapers up and tossed them into the hearth. My frustration level was high. I knew the Northern papers were going to make a martyr of John Brown, and the papers mentioned how he was brought into the courtroom on a gurney. It would have been better for all if he had been killed instead of captured. That way, he could have gone down in history as a madman.

With the news of Brown's supporters reaching Southern ears, they had their justification for their dislike of Northerners. The papers made it appear that all Northerners shared Brown's outlandish beliefs and would arm their slaves and kill every white man, woman, and child in the South.

Nothing could have been further from the truth, but there would be no convincing them of that now. Too much had been said and done. The sides had been chosen, and the lines had been drawn.

From my *other* life, I knew the course of John Brown's trial. I knew he was going to be sentenced to death within a week. I recalled that on December 2, 1859, John Brown would go to the gallows, leaving behind a long speech in a letter that would go down in history and seal his fate in martyrdom.

I rested my hand upon my abdomen and continued pacing the parlor. My beautiful baby would barely be a year old when this war starts. If Keifer enlists as Robert did, and serves for the duration, our son would be ready for school by the time he returns.

I knew Emily was looking at her children and thinking the same thing as was Annabelle. The three of us shared the same fate as countless mothers across the country.

The idea of being separated from Keifer for such a long time ripped my heart from my chest. I could not fathom it, even though I knew it was coming. He was my life; my everything. We had not spent a day apart since we were married.

I thought about trying to run Terrace Falls by myself. How would we obtain the supplies we needed? Would I be able to hide enough away? The seeds for crops? The money to pay our workers? What would I do if scavengers came to pillage our farm? How could I do this all on my own?

I sat down on the rocker and tried not to think about my brothers. Monte and Nicholas were still teenagers, and yet, they would soon take part in several of the worst battles in American history. The scars it left on them as well as the others, would be apparent not only in *this* life but their *others* as well. I knew that when the gavel fell in Charlestown, with it, it sealed the fate of the country.

23

STUFFED MY TEXT AND NOTEBOOK into my backpack just as Professor Adkins finished up another longwinded lecture on genetic enzymes. I took meticulous notes thanks to the PowerPoint, but barely heard a word she had said. My mind was elsewhere, stressed over the next part of my day.

Phoebe set up a time for us to meet with Officer McCoy and Detective Warner at the Chandler household at noon. I wasn't exactly thrilled about it, nor could I get out of it. Even though she typically sat on the other side of the courtroom, her expertise with criminal cases was invaluable.

Landon was less than thrilled and had been irritable all morning. He wasn't keen on reliving the event, but seeing how the baby was his, he wanted to be there as well. Still, as much as he hated the formalities, he was there, and that meant everything to me.

Phoebe met us at her parents' house shortly before the police were to arrive. She was dressed in her impeccable business attire. Her navy-blue, business suit, flawless makeup, and long, dark, hair twisted up in a French roll made her formidable. She enjoyed a stellar reputation as one of the top up and coming criminal attorneys in Boston.

She sat down with Landon and me in the parlor and went over everything that was about to happen. Robert and Jackson had decided to join us as well even though both were corporate attorneys. They were versed in the basics but were nowhere nearly as skilled as Phoebe in this area. They sat across the room from us and listened attentively.

Phoebe told me to stick to the facts and not to elaborate on anything. She said the officers already knew the setting and the circumstances. All I needed to tell them was what occurred the moment the ambulance doors opened, and I encountered the suspect. I needed to walk them through everything from my point of view.

I rubbed my hands together with nervousness. I had never dealt with the police on anything. I had never even been pulled over for speeding before. I heard the grandfather clock chime in the foyer. They would be here any minute. Landon put his arm around me. I tried to draw upon his strength.

Before the last bell chimed, the doorbell rang out throughout the house. Emily walked to the front door to greet our guests and invited them to join us. All of us stood when Officer McCoy and Detective Warner entered the parlor and shook our hands. They sat down in the same two armchairs as before.

"Mrs. Adler," Detective Warner recognized Phoebe. "Aren't you on the wrong side of the aisle, Counselor?"

"Please, call me Phoebe. Miss. Timmons' is my sister-in-law's older sister and my best friend. She asked me to join her today. I am here in a supportive capacity." She informed him.

"You realize she's the victim here, not the suspect." Detective Warner smiled uneasily.

"Yes. I am aware." From the way Phoebe smiled at him, it was easy to tell there was no love lost between them.

For the next thirty minutes, I gave a detailed account of what I recalled of that horrific night. Detective Warner took notes and recorded our conversation. Officer McCoy jotted down notes but remained silent throughout my interview.

I couldn't have been more relieved when Robert finally walked them to the door. I knew the two were only doing their job, but the interview had left me in tears and reliving the loss of my baby all over again. For that, I did not like them.

Landon sat beside me, holding me, and letting me cry on his shoulder as he wiped away his own tears. I knew this ordeal was just as hard on him as it was on me. During the deposition, Detective Warner had let it slip that our baby was a boy; a fact Landon was not aware of. The information hit him particularly hard, and I could have slapped the Detective for revealing it.

Once the dust settled and Landon and I had pulled ourselves together, Emily came in with a tray of hot coffee. She poured the mugs and handed each of us one before she took a seat beside me.

"How are you feeling?" She inquired.

"I have been better," I smiled weakly. "Is it over now?" I looked towards Phoebe.

"That depends on the suspect; if he accepts a plea or not." She shrugged.

"If he does, then I don't have to testify?" I asked.

"Correct." Phoebe patted my hand reassuringly. "Still, we'll have to wait and see what Detective Warner says. I told him to contact me, not you."

"Thank you. I appreciate it." I looked up at her. "Is there something between you and Detective Warner? A bad history or something?"

"Something like that." Phoebe chuckled. "I may have gotten a half dozen or so of his suspects off on a technicality. He does not have the best opinion of me." She rolled her eyes with a smirk.

"That was obvious." Landon remarked with a grin.

"Detectives have the tendency not to like defense attorney's or prosecuting attorneys or any attorney — period. That is simply the way they are." She shrugged. "Defense attorneys tear apart their cases and prosecuting attorneys interrupt their days, making them sit outside courtrooms for hours just to tell them that the case has been delayed or continued or whatever." She rolled her eyes again. "Detectives don't like anyone."

"I cannot imagine why." I said sarcastically. "Detective Warner is a real charmer."

"I am not defending him, but you must keep in mind the nature of his job. He sees the worst of the worst in this city and lives through some of our worst nightmares." Robert noted. "They put up a wall as a defensive mechanism in order to do their job." He concluded. "It is the only way they can do their job."

"I can understand that." Jackson said as he reentered the room. "I would not want their job. They deal with scum every day and get little to no thanks for it. They must distance themselves."

"Perhaps it wasn't ideal for me to be here. My presence obviously rubbed him the wrong way." Phoebe stated.

"But you know the criminal system better than anyone else I know. Besides, I needed you here." I explained, taking her hands in mine.

"And you know I would do anything for you." She hugged me tightly. "It will get better. The hard part is over."

Shane and Jocelyn arrived after lunch. She did not have classes on Wednesday, so they had been out visiting landmarks and having brunch. I loved how close my sister was with our dad, but I couldn't help but be a little envious of it too. Still, I was thankful that our relationship had grown stronger since my parents got divorced, especially since it had the opposite effect on my relationship with my mother.

We enjoyed a lively afternoon listening to them talk about their jaunt around campus and Boston. It seemed Jocelyn had dragged this poor man everywhere in the last couple days wanting to share with him every aspect of her life. It was difficult to say goodbye when three o'clock rolled around and they needed to head to the airport.

I hugged and kissed my father, thanking him for coming out to check on me. I told him how happy I was that he and Nicholas had resolved their differences. He made me promise to call him more often and admitted that he was curious about the current events taking place in my *other* life.

After they left, Landon followed me upstairs to our room. He'd been quiet throughout lunch while everyone else talked nonstop. I knew what was on his mind, but I didn't want to be the one to bring it up. He sat down on the edge of the bed and fiddled with his hands for a moment.

"I've been thinking, Sidney." He began as I put laundry away.

"What about?" I continued hanging our things in the closet.

"Sid? Will you stop for a moment?" He snapped at me.

"What?" I turned around.

"Sit down." He patted the spot on the bed beside him.

"Okay," I set the clothes on the dresser and sat down. "What's wrong?"

"Nothing is wrong." He took a deep breath. "But I believe it's time we went home — back to our home."

"The apartment?" My voice got a little shaky.

"Yes," he nodded.

"I don't want to go back there." I said firmly.

"Sid. It's time." He put his arm around me. "I know it's going to be hard, but we need to do this. We can't hide over here forever."

"I am not hiding." I said adamantly.

"The Chandler's have been very gracious, but we cannot take advantage of their hospitality. It's time to go home." I nodded slowly.

"I know, you're right." I whispered.

"I'll pack our things." He leaned over and hugged me tightly. "We can do this."

An hour later and after a tearful goodbye, we pulled up in front of our apartment. Landon turned his car off, and we sat there in silence for several minutes. This was something we both had to do, and we knew it. We just didn't know how.

"Are you ready?" Landon reached across the console and took my hand.

"As ready as I will ever be." I squeezed his hand.

I opened the car door and stepped out. *'You can do this,'* I whispered aloud to myself. I inhaled sharply and closed the car door. I held my breath as I unlocked the front door.

I was greeted with the familiarity that had once been such a comfort to me. The small foyer led straight into the family room. It was tastefully decorated with beige furniture, an old trunk that I dearly loved served as our coffee table and accented with an old faded and chipped brick wall. I loved this place.

We had stumbled across it when we first came to Boston. It was a large three-bedroom place with vaulted ceilings and a large kitchen with a breakfast bar. We loved the idea that we each had our own office and own space in which to unwind in.

Last August, we spent a weekend combining our offices and turning what was once my space into a nursery. We painted the walls a light cream color and accented it by painting the built-in bookshelves a rich coffee color. It had turned out elegant and charming.

In the next couple weeks, we purchased a crib, a changing table, and rocking chair. We adorned the nursery with all the necessities for a new baby as well as all the cute little neutral things we could find. Landon and I had had so much fun preparing for our little one and our relationship grew stronger every day.

Landon set our bags beside the old burner stove in the corner of the family room. He paused and looked around as if absorbing everything at once. I knew exactly how he felt. It was a bit overwhelming. I tried not to look at the little bear sitting on the corner of the couch, holding a receiving blanket.

I bit down hard on my lower lip to keep it from quivering. Tears stung my eyes. This place that I loved dearly, my source of refuge, now brought me nothing but pain.

"Are you okay?" Landon walked up behind me and wrapped his arms around my waist.

"No. But I will be." I leaned my head back against his chest. "How are you holding up?"

"I'm breathing." He leaned down and kissed the top of my head. "Should we start clearing things out? We can put everything in our storage unit in the basement for now and put your things back in there and make it your office again. Or, if you're not up to it, I can make it my office. It's up to you." Landon rambled like he always did when he was upset or nervous.

"Honestly," I turned around to face him. "Why don't we wait a bit. I'm not quite ready to put it all in storage. Please." I pleaded; my eyes filled with tears.

"Okay." Landon kissed me softly. "When you're ready."

∾

Curling up beside him in our own bed, in our bedroom, felt strange. The shadows that fell across the walls no longer offered the comfort they once did. The glow of the streetlights outside felt foreign and unfriendly. I closed my eyes and sought the comfort of the strong and steady rhythm of Landon's heartbeat.

I turned my thoughts to going back to work on Monday. Returning to the hospital; looking at Norman again, who I tried desperately not to blame for the loss of my child. But it was almost impossible. If I had my way, I would have him removed from the program. He could go on to become a mortician as far as I was concerned.

I was told right before I was discharged by the head of our program, Dr. Clark, that Norman had moved to another unit. I did not want to sound petty, but I was happy I did not have to deal with him. I wasn't sure I could maintain my professionalism or my objectivity with him.

Perhaps going back to work would do me some good. I needed to get out of the house and return to the life I had on this plane. I had become almost obsessed with research on John Brown, Harpers Ferry, the trial, and the Civil War in general. For me, it was something I could wrap my brain around; something that made sense to me and something I could control in a life I had no control over.

24

KEIFER AND I SAT OUT ON the veranda enjoying a peaceful morning. He was insistent I spend some time outdoors breathing the fresh air and not stay couped up in the house all day exposed to the constant soot from the multiple hearths. The sun was shining brightly upon us and there was a slight chill in the air. I had a shawl draped across my shoulders and an Afghan across my lap. The hot coffee was doing wonders in keeping me warm.

Preston had taken the carriage into town with my grandmother. She wanted to visit the mercantile and pick up some new fabric for a maternity dress she wanted to make me. Since it was to be a surprise, I was not allowed to go with her. They had only been gone a short time when we heard hooves on the pathway out front.

Immediately, I thought something must be wrong. I feared she had fallen ill or gotten hurt. Recognizing my fear, Keifer rose to greet the carriage. Moments later the sound of laughter drifted back around to the veranda. I rose to my feet and made my way around to the front of our home.

"Good morning, Sidney." Charlotte's voice was bright and cheery.

"Good morning," I took her hand. "It is a pleasure to see you. What brings you and your husband our way this good day?"

"Evan insisted on speaking to Doc." She smiled. "So, I agreed to join him to have a visit with you. I hope I am not interrupting your morning."

"No, not at all. You are most welcome. We were enjoying some coffee on the veranda, would you two care to join us?" I offered.

"That sounds wonderful." Evan spoke heartedly, but I noticed the dark circles beneath his eyes.

The four of us gathered in the rocking chairs around the small table on the veranda. Noami came out and brought more mugs and a fresh pot of coffee. She also left us with her cinnamon coffee cake right from the oven. The steam was still hovering over it as I sliced each of us a piece.

"You look exhausted, Evan. Are you feeling alright?" Keifer inquired once everyone was settled.

"Yes, and with good reason. Guess where I have been?" Evan raised an eyebrow at my husband.

"You traveled with your cousin to the trial." Keifer stated rather than asked.

"Indeed," Evan sipped his coffee before continuing. "And what a spectacle it was. I have never in my life seen the justice system move at lightning speed before."

"I read about that. Brown was arrested on the 18th, indicted by the Grand Jury on three counts. One count of treason against the state of Virginia. Two, inciting slaves to rebellion. And three, for murder on the morning on the 26th, and the trial started on the afternoon of the 26th. I have never heard such a thing." Keifer was dumbfounded.

"Oh, it gets worse." Evan took a bite of his coffee cake enjoying the undivided attention of his audience. "First of all, they had the gallery open so there were about six hundred people crammed into this courthouse. And everyone was smoking cigars, chewing tobacco, and spitting it on the floor. They were eating peanuts and walnuts and simply tossing the shells on the floor. So, every time someone moved, there were loud squishing or crunching sounds. It smelled so bad. Plus, the crowd would call out insults to Brown, things I could never imagine saying in front of a lady."

"Unbelievable," my husband muttered while Charlotte and I sat quietly eagerly engrossed in the details.

"After the indictment Brown asked the judge for a continuance, but the judge, a man named Andrew Parker, denied it. Brown pled not guilty to all charges." Evan sipped his coffee before continuing. "They held the trial in Charlestown, nearly eight miles from Harper's Ferry. The people in that town were irate considering a most beloved mayor was shot and killed while he was unarmed." Evan said disgustedly.

"I had not realized the mayor of Harper's Ferry was murdered in the raid." Charlotte said in a low voice, her face appeared mournful.

"There were armed guards and cannons placed around the courthouse. Then they brought Brown in lying on a gurney. And honestly, I do not understand the spectacle of that. Lt. Green had stabbed him with his dress sword, barely injuring Brown. Realizing his mistake Lt. Green beat Brown unconscious with the hilt of the sword. It was obvious that it was a ploy to garner sympathy for Brown." Evan scoffed. "It did not work."

"That does not surprise me," I glanced over at Keifer who was just as engrossed in the tale as us ladies were.

"The first day of the trial was a mockery. The Virginia state prosecutor, Charles Harding sat there with his feet up on the table dozing most of the time. The only time we were sure he was still alive was when he called out that he needed more tobacco." Evan snorted. "When Harding showed up on the second day of the trial, battered and bruised, he insisted to all the reporters and anyone who would listen that he was attacked by a 'blind nigger'. The judge could clearly see how intoxicated he was and immediately dismissed him." Evan chuckled.

"Harding showed up to court intoxicated?" I laughed.

"Very," Evan nodded. "I could not believe it. He is a disgrace to the profession."

"He is," Keifer agreed.

"Judge Parker appointed the more dignified and respectable Andrew Hunter as the lead prosecuting attorney. He called multiple witnesses to the stand including Conductor Phelps, and Colonel Lewis Washington. The most damning testimony came from John Allstadt who said that Brown's men threatened to burn him and his home if he did not get up and go with them. He also said they armed seven of his slaves with pikes and told him they were on a mission to free the county of slavery." Evan raised an eyebrow pointedly.

"My goodness," I whispered in disbelief despite all the research I had done, it seemed unreal to hear it firsthand.

"The defense opened by calling another of Brown's hostages, Joseph Brewer, I believe. He tried to paint a picture of Brown and his men as being principled and considerate of their hostages saying they were treated well by Brown and his men. He claimed that Brown told his followers only to shoot in self-defense." Evan huffed. "That certainly explains all the outright murders, does it not." He stated sarcastically.

"I find it disheartened that a hostage would testify for their murderous captor." Keifer spat.

"Of course, the prosecutor Hunter objected to Brewer's testimony about Brown telling his followers to shoot in self-defense, but the Judge allowed it anyway. I believe the Judge realized that it would make no difference in the end." Evan shrugged. "Finally, they put Henry Hunter on the stand. This was the man responsible for capturing, killing, and the desecration of Brown's closest friend, William Thompson." Evan raised an eyebrow and tipped his coffee mug towards Keifer with a smug smile.

"Really?" Evan nodded. "I am surprised they put him on the stand."

"Hunter admitted that he dragged Thompson out to the railroad bridge and shot Thompson before dumping his body into the gutter to be eaten by hogs. Hunter stated that he did not regret his actions since right before this occurred, he witnessed his uncle being shot point blank by one of Brown's men." Evan shrugged understandably.

"Reasonable enough," Keifer agreed.

"But this was when the supposed invalid Brown — rose to his feet and began shouting at the Judge that he was not getting a fair trial and all those he had wanted to testify as character witness were not there. He claimed he had been robbed of sixty dollars in gold after he was captured and arrested and therefore, could not hire an adequate defense attorney. After his rant, he laid back down, covered himself with his blanket and closed his eyes." Evan chuckled. "It was unbelievable."

"I wish I would have gone with you." Keifer smirked.

"Apparently irritated by Brown's remark about their capabilities, both defense attorneys withdrew from the case." Evan informed us.

"Seriously?" I said thinking this trial was more like a soap opera and better than court tv.

"Yes, ma'am." Evan looked over at my husband. "Have you met George Hoyt?" Keifer nodded.

"Who is he?" Charlotte asked.

"He is this twenty-one-year-old attorney who has barely seen the inside of a courtroom. The poor boy happened to be entering the courtroom right after the two defense attorneys withdrew from the case. The judge recognized him, called him forward and told him he was not representing Brown." Evan chuckled. "Hoyt and I had stepped outside together for moment to relieve ourselves. Upon our return, one of the jailers asked Hoyt to scout about and check to see if there were any possible escape routes that Brown could use — there had been rumors of a possible attempt. Hoyt returned about fifteen minutes after I after reporting back, he saw no possible escape routes and ended up becoming Brown's defense council." Evan snorted. "That could have easily been me. Can you imagine?"

"But Hoyt is not familiar with Virgina law." I pondered aloud. "I know federal law is nationwide, but states do have individual laws, don't they?" I inquired.

"That is precisely what Hoyt told the judge." Evan laughed. "This poor young man stood there in front of the judge, and this packed courthouse practically begging the judge to reconsider because he knows nothing of Virginia law. When that did not appeal to the judge's good humor, Hoyt asked for a continuous stating he had not read the indictment, nor discussed a defense strategy with Brown. Eventually, Judge Parker granted him a day continuation and assigned two other defense attorneys, um — Chilton and Griswold to assist him."

"This trial sounds more like a circus than a criminal trial." I remarked without thinking, drawing peculiar looks from my husband and his friend.

"Griswold gave his closing argument on the 30th. He claimed Brown could not be charged with treason in Virginia because he was listed as a resident of New York." Evan shook his head and scoffed. "Like treason was the biggest issue Brown was facing."

"Did Brown actually murder anyone?" Charlotte asked her husband. "I understand he murdered several people in Kansas, but did he murder anyone in the raid on Harper's Ferry?"

"There is some debate over whether Brown is responsible for killing a Marine. He was firing through a cracked door, but his men were also firing." Evan shrugged. "No one is positive whose bullet took the life of the Marine. But Brown is definitely responsible for his death nonetheless."

"Brown is insane." Charlotte declared.

"Fanatical, but not clinically." I remarked drawing a strange look from my husband. I bit my lower lip realizing I had made an error in speaking out about something I should have no knowledge of.

"Precisely right, Mrs. Marshall." Evan smiled over at me. "Mr. Hunter concluded the trial with the closing argument for the prosecution. He stood firmly on Brown's 'Provisional Constitution' showing not only premeditation to murder, but his grander plans which proved he was guilty of all charges. His closing argument was well spoken and very powerful. It took the jury only forty-five minutes of deliberation before they came back with a guilty verdict on all charges."

"That is a small blessing." Charlotte concluded.

"Brown was sentenced a couple days ago on the second. He will be publicly hanged on December 2nd." Evan concluded.

"Good riddens," Keifer stated before finishing off his coffee and pouring himself another mug. "I am glad it is finally over, and everyone can put this nonsense behind us."

"This is only the beginning," I cut another slice of coffee cake.

"You really believe so?" Charlotte looked uncomfortable.

"Unfortunately, I do." I admitted to her.

"Surely, the South cannot hold the entire North responsible for the actions of a fanatical abolitionist." Charlotte sounded hopeful.

"But they will." Keifer assured her. "I hate to say it, but I do believe my wife is correct. This is only the beginning."

"Do you believe it will come to war?" Charlotte eyes appeared frightened as she looked towards her husband.

"Given the nature of things in the Capital, I believe there is a real chance it could. Of course, a bigger concern for the North is that our Capital is surrounded by slave states. If the South ceases Washington, our federal government will fall." Evan looked over at Keifer who nodded in agreement.

"I have heard talk of it." My husband admitted. "My sister, Margarett, and her husband Thad who have been running our parent's plantation in Savannah, told me that the South Carolina governor has raised more than ten thousand militia ready to take the Capital."

"Ten thousand. My goodness," Charlotte looked astonished. "Could they really capture the Capital with that number?"

"Perhaps," Evan admitted. "If they caught them unawares."

"But the South has been threatening secession for the last twenty or more years. How can we possibly take them seriously?" Charlotte seemed satisfied with her assessment as she refilled her coffee and helped herself to another slice of coffee cake.

"I believe this upcoming Presidential election will decide." Both men turned their eyes towards me.

"How so?" Evan eyed me carefully.

"The Republican party is gaining strength and notoriety. There is a good chance that a Republican could win the Presidency next year.

If that should happen, the South is sure to secede." I chose my words very carefully.

"I cannot think of any Republican currently in office that could gain enough popularity to win." Evan confessed. "Besides, the Democrat party is much stronger and more widespread. That will make the difference."

"No." I shook my head. "The Democratic party is split. They will not be able to mend their differences to champaign behind one person. This split will divide the vote allowing for a Republican to win the popular vote and therefore, win the election." I boasted for half a second before realizing I had said too much. Keifer and Evan stared at me wide-eyed and baffled.

"Doc, I had no idea your wife was so knowledgeable of our electoral process." Evan scratched the scruff on his chin. I could not tell if he was impressed or disgusted.

"My wife enjoys reading and being well informed." Keifer stammered eyeing me curiously before loudly clearing his throat.

Evan and Charlotte joined us for supper. Thankfully, the conversation shifted to more pleasant topics. Charlotte, my grandmother, and I discussed the upcoming holidays and what gifts we were giving to the members of our family.

Keifer and Evan disappeared into the library for cigars and brandy. I tried to focus my attention on the ladies beside me, but I could not help but wonder if Evan would make further remarks or judgement about my earlier statement. I was certain Keifer was going to remark on it later when we were alone. I sat there rocking beside the hearth pondering on how I was going to explain my thorough knowledge of the electoral process.

25

SATURDAY, NOVEMBER 9, 2019

I **LEFT THE HOSPITAL A LITTLE** after six in the evening. The days were growing shorter, and the sun was setting a little after five these days. The temperatures were continuing to decline, and I knew it would not be long before the first snowfall.

I started my car and turned the heat all the way up. I rubbed my hands together trying to get warm. Despite my gloves, my hands were freezing. I despised the winter months. I rested my head back against my seat wishing I could talk to Phoebe or Jocelyn about how I was feeling. The unsettling feeling in my stomach was making me nauseous.

However, Phoebe was only a not even school-age yet in my other life and Jocelyn wasn't even born yet *there*. Neither could possibly understand. I closed my eyes for a moment realizing that even my grandmother, Marissa, would not understand and as much as I hated to acknowledge the dates, I had seen in our family tree *here*, I knew she would not survive the duration of the war.

I hastily brushed a tear off my cheek. I could not allow myself to focus on that now. I still have three more years with her, and I wanted to spend as much time as I could with her. I felt like I wanted to scream. I considered talking to my dad or even Uncle Nicholas. Both have been such a comfort to me. But I knew neither would understand what I was going through.

I felt the heat from my car blowing forcefully across my face and warming my body. I let out a sigh of relief and put my car in reverse. I weaved my way through the parking garage, finally reaching the outside world. I pulled into traffic and made my way to the interstate.

Emily.

The realization hit me like a slap in the face. Emily was only a couple years older than me in my *other* life. She was the mother of three young children and contending with the reality that if this war should start, her husband would be on the front lines. Even though I did not know her *there* yet, I do *here,* and she would have already experienced it *there*. She would understand.

I found myself driving mindlessly towards her home. I quickly hit the button to connect me with Emily and she answered on the second ring bringing her voice through my speakers.

"Hello, Sidney. How are you?" Her voice was warm and pleasant.

"I just got off work. Are you busy this evening?"

"No. I was just doing some research. What can I help you with?"

"Would it be alright if I come by and talk with you?" I hated how desperate I sounded.

"Is everything alright?" she sounded sincerely concerned.

"Yes. I am probably just being overly dramatic." I tried to chuckle, but it did not come off well.

"Are you on your way?"

"Is that okay?" I needed to know as the exit to her place was only a couple of miles away.

"Of course. I will see you soon. Drive safely."

"I will."

The call disconnected and I quickly tapped the little screen on my dash to connect me with Landon. The ring tone blared through my car followed immediately by the sound of Landon's voice.

"Hello darling," he sounded tired.

"Hi sweetheart, how are you?"

"Exhausted. I should be out of here in the next hour or so."

"Are you still at the hospital?"

"Yes. I'm stuck in the lab. I had to rerun some tests because the medium we first tired was contaminated." He sighed heavily. "I may be here a while."

"I understand. I just wanted to let you know I am going to stop by Emily's on my way home."

"Okay. I have to run. I'll text you when I'm about to leave."

"Sounds good. Have fun. I love you."

"Love you too," I heard him say before the line went dead.

I took the next ramp off the interstate and made my way over to Robert and Emily's neighborhood.

Their beautiful Victorian home was in the prestigious part of the outskirts of the city. The homes were all registered with the city's Historical Society and the area was notorious for onlookers driving around gazing at the homes. Thankfully, most stood behind iron fences and gated driveways.

Emily greeted me at the front door before I got the chance to ring the bell. She was dressed casually in jeans and a sweater. Her long blondish brown hair was pulled up in a messy bun and she was wearing only a small amount of makeup that highlighted her features. If someone did not know any better, Emily appeared to be in her late thirties instead of a lady with three grown children and several grandchildren.

"Hello, my dear," She hugged me briefly yet warmly when I entered.

"Thanks for allowing me to ruin your evening. I apologize for dropping by unexpectedly." I handed her my coat after she closed the door.

"Nonsense. I am happy you're here. I have missed you. The house seems so quiet since you and Landon left." She put her arm around me guiding me into the kitchen. "I was going to make me some cocoa. Would you like some?"

"That sounds wonderful." I climbed upon a barstool at the island. "The temperature is starting to drop. I would not be surprised if we get some snow soon."

"I love white Christmas' but would like to have it disappear for the rest of winter the day after." Emily smiled over her shoulder.

"Is Robert home?"

"Yes. He is reading in his study. I told him you were dropping by."

"You said you were doing research," she nodded. "Is it for a new book?"

Emily was a bestselling author who enjoyed a prosperous career. She would occasionally do book signings and interviews, but she was notoriously private about her personal life. Her publisher complained frequently about her lack of interaction with her readers online. Emily hated social media and refused to engage with it. Her publisher finally gave up and allowed their marketing team to run ads and such for her, but she adamantly refused to blog on her author website. So, they controlled that as well.

"Yes." She poured some milk into a pan and stirred in the cocoa. "I am afraid I am still old school when it comes to research. I prefer books to the internet." She smiled over her shoulder.

"I hate reading on the computer too. It always gives me a headache."

"Why do you think we have such an extensive library?" She laughed. "My favorite haunts are used bookstores. I can and have gotten lost in them for hours."

"I love old bookstores." I remarked as Emily stirred the cocoa.

"So, tell me. What has you so upset?" She continued stirring but turned to her side to face me.

"You know John Brown's trial just concluded and he has been sentenced to hang." Emily nodded. "I am six months pregnant *there* and I know what is coming. I am completely helpless." I confessed. "I have started stock piling goods — items I know will be difficult to get in the upcoming years. I have even built hidden shelters to hide our goods from scavengers. But I am terrified, and I cannot shake this feeling of dread that is choking me."

"You are fortunate." She turned off the stove and poured the cocoa into large mugs. She dropped in a handful of marshmallows in each before setting one on the island in front of me. "At least you will be better prepared than most everyone else in the Union. Much better prepared than I was. Although I tried to be, I was not as successful due to where we were. Our home was pillaged for goods by Union soldiers' multiple times." She leaned against the counter and sipped her cocoa. "I got to the point where I really hated them.

"I do not feel prepared." I stared down at mine without really seeing it.

"Sidney," Emily reached over and placed her hand over mine. "I know you are scared. I remember clearly how frightened I was. I was in my late twenties with three young children. I prayed religiously every day that my husband would come home alive." She brushed the tears off her cheek. "I saw my husband twice in four years. There were months that crept by when I did not know if he was alive or dead. It was a hell like you cannot imagine. And our hell is nothing in comparison to what our men will go through." She squeezed my hand before brushing her tears away once more.

"I do not know if I am strong enough for this." I fought back the tear that burned my eyes.

"You realize that every soldier's wife and mother has uttered those words." Emily sipped her cocoa gathering her thoughts. "Alex wanted to join the military *here*. After 9/11 he felt it was his duty, especially since his father served." She brushed away her tears. "I know it sounds so unpatriotic, but I begged and pleaded with him not to join. The memories of what I went through with Robert were still so fresh in my mind. The thought of Alex, Jackson, or even Phoebe being sent to Iraq or Afghanistan sent me into hysterics." She half smiled. "Not that I had to worry about Phoebe enlisting — she would sooner be horsewhipped than wear fatigues." I laughed.

"True."

"But I felt like I had sacrificed enough for our country. I was not about to give them my sons too." She confessed.

"It seems like every generation has a war." I muttered. My eyes dropped to my mug "It is so senseless.

"Every generation, but mine." I looked up at her with curiously. "Gen Xer's had a skirmish, but not a war. Please do not misunderstand me. I am taking nothing away from our brave soldiers who fought in Desert Storm, but that was nothing in comparison to the World War's, Korea, Vietnam or what is going on now."

"True," I agreed.

"Yet, strangely enough, Gen Xer's are by far the smallest generation on record." Emily half smiled. "We are a unique generation."

"The latch-key kids." I grinned. "Some of the stories my dad told us about his childhood were hilarious. I could not imagine having that kind of freedom."

"The world was a different place." Emily sighed, looking dispirited.

"Keifer and I plan on coming to my brother Patrick's home in Chicago for Christmas next year. You and Robert live across the way from them, correct?" She nodded. "Do we meet?" I looked up into her eyes feeling hopeful.

"We do." Emily smiled. "I did not want to say anything to you about it in case your plans changed."

"And we are close to the same age, am I right?" I knew we would have to be.

"Yes, we are."

"You and the children could join me in Boston. We have plenty of space and we are in the process of building hidden cellars by the riverbank for stores against scavengers for the upcoming war." I spoke quickly.

"You are forgetting, Sidney. Your sister-in-law, Annabelle, is my dearest friend and Robert and Patrick are like brothers. Though I appreciate your kind offer, I cannot leave them."

"Then bring them. We have an enormous home and property with hundreds of acres. You all will be safer in Boston, than Chicago." I offered. "And I would feel so much better having all of you there with me."

"I would love to say yes because I believe you are correct. But I cannot answer for Annabelle." She reached across the island taking my hand once more. "Please speak to her and Patrick about it over Christmas. Speak in hypotheticals, of course." She squeezed my hand. "I would feel much better being with you."

"I will." I sighed with an awkward grin. "It will be so bizarre to see you there, but I cannot help but be terribly excited about it."

"Excited about what?" Robert entered the kitchen and turned on the kettle.

"We were just talking about next Christmas when Sidney and Keifer visit her family in Chicago." Emily pulled out a mug from the cabinet and handed it to her husband.

"Oh, I was not sure if you and Keifer had decided to travel yet. We did not want to mention it in case plans changed." Robert leaned against the counter beside his wife.

"Sidney just offered for the children and I along with Annabelle and hers to stay with them on their estate outside Boston." Emily informed Patrick.

"Yes, I was telling Emily that Casper and I have started storing provisions and after the last thaw, we are building hidden cellars along the riverbank to store goods we will need in the upcoming years. I know provisions will be scarce and I need to make sure we do not starve when scavengers pillage small villages and farms." I explained.

"That would be a great comfort to me if she and the children were tucked away at your estate." Robert pondered. "I will encourage Patrick to have Annabelle and the children take refuge with you for the duration."

"I appreciate that." I finished off my cocoa. "I find it so amazing how so much of what is going on is left out of our history books. No one mentions the barbarous behavior and violence that goes on daily in the capital between elected representatives." I smirked.

"True," Robert chuckled. "But do you really believe it is much different now?"

"At least now they are not carrying revolvers and bowie knives." I reasoned.

"No, but they no longer need to. They have social media to do it for them. They use words as their weapons, one political party pitted against the other all vying for the soul and morality of the American populace."

"I can agree with that."

"You are young, so I am sure you have your share of social media accounts — Facebook, Twitter, Instagram, Snap Chat, or Tick Toc."

"I do not have Snap Chat or Tick Toc. The crap posted on those, especially Tick Toc is beyond absurd." I laughed.

"The first amendment is the backbone of our country, correct?" He asked.

"Yes," I agreed.

"But then why is our President banned from Twitter? Why is everything you see on Facebook and Instagram pro-Democrat and anti-Republican?"

"Because big corporations control the narrative." I told him.

"Exactly," he raised his eyebrows. "There may be a few, very few, honest politicians in D.C., but most have made a fortune lobbying the interest of big corporations for whatever incentives, tax credits, breaks they can take advantage of and reaping all kinds of kickbacks. Most do not have a moral compass. Former President Obama and his VP, Biden are prime examples. They have single-handedly corrupted every department and branch of government, made illegal foreign deals that put millions in their pockets, and made a mockery of our country."

"They have attacked President Trump with a vengeance." Emily noted. "These ridiculous impeachment charges." She rolled her eyes.

"The Obama's, the Bidens, the Pelosi's, Maxine Waters, and especially the Clinton's — they are some of the most morally corrupt and ethically void individuals to ever step foot in politics. And that is saying something after the crap Nixon and Carter or even the Bush's pulled."

"I guess I haven't paid much attention to politics — *here* at least." I shrugged.

"I am afraid soon, no one will be able to escape it. There are powerful people working behind the scenes to come up with every conceivable narrative to discredit and destroy President Trump and ensure he will not be reelected — even if they must perform election fraud to do it. I guarantee you; President Trump will not be reelected even if every American citizen votes for him. There are too many powerful people working against him behind the scenes to keep him out of office." Robert shrugged.

"Why do they hate him so much." I asked.

"Because he sees them for who they truly are. And he will not play their games. He cannot be bought, either by those in D.C. or foreign powers. So, they will get rid of him." Robert huffed.

"I am surprised they have not tried to assassinate him." I muttered. "And then frame some inconsequential patsy to take the fall. Our government has done it before."

"President Trump is carefully watched and guarded. Plus, the chaos that would ensue from the populace, the Democrats will not risk it. That is why they are doing everything possible to destroy him personally, publicly, financially, and politically." Robert cocked his head to the side and shrugged his shoulder.

"These people are pure evil. They do not care at all about America. They only care about the number of zeros in their bank accounts." Emily scoffed hatefully.

"It is going to get much worse. Our economy is going to crash in the next couple of years and inflation will destroy the middle class." Robert stated.

～

I tossed and turned fluffing my pillow and kicking the covers. I could not get comfortable regardless of what I tried. The clock on the nightstand glowed in the dark telling me it was almost midnight. Landon was snoring softly beside me completely unaware of my restlessness.

I held onto the hope that Robert would be able to convince my brother to allow his wife and children to join me at Terrace Falls. If they did, I knew Emily and her children would also be there. Their company would lessen my fears and apprehension about the upcoming war. I would sleep so much better having them all with me rather than it simply being my grandmother, baby boy and me. I was not even sure how many of our workers would remain on the estate once the war came.

I knew that Lincoln would enlist black soldiers into service of the Union. I knew there were several regiments of them although I did not know much about it. I had seen the movie, *Glory* with Shane when I was in my teens, but could only remember parts of it and that Ferris Bueller had played the lead alongside the man who played Westley in *The Princess Bride*, Denzel Washington, and Morgan Freeman. I would have to remember to watch it again.

My latter conversation with Robert and Emily continued to play on repeat haunting my thoughts. I feared Robert's words and that things were going to get much worse. The little tad-bits I saw gave me little hope for the direction our country was headed.

26

WHEN CONGRESS RECONVEINED AT the beginning of last week, the investigation into the actions of John Brown and his followers at Harper's Ferry was still being debated. But that paled in comparison to the bombshell that came about due to Hinton Rowan Helper's *The Impending Crisis — How to Meet It.*

Its republication and wider distribution had the South ready to draw arms. Although the book had been banned in the South since 1857, the highly contentious antislavery rant compilation edition was soaring through the North like wildfire. Helper had put into print the thoughts behind the Harper's Ferry raid and widely promoted it.

Helper discussed how slavery was economically harmful, and not beneficial to the South. He stated how detrimental the system was to poor whites and even went as far as encouraging whites to join with the slaves in fighting against their oppressors to abolish slavery. His words were extreme as he promoted class warfare and a slave rebellion.

To add insult to injury, sixty-eight Republican's including two who were up for the Speaker of the House position, signed a letter endorsing the book. Upon learning this, John Clark, a Democrat from Missouri proposed that anyone who supported or endorsed Helper's book should be automatically disqualified and banned from the

Speaker of the House position. After reading off all six-eight Republican names on the list, the House exploded in rage on both sides of the aisle.

I crumbled Boston's evening edition paper and tossed it angrily into the hearth.

"Keifer is not going to be so happy with you for that." My grandmother entered the parlor.

"I imagine not. But I could not read any more of that dribble." I walked over to the window and watched the sun set drift below the tree line across the vast fields.

"But I am sure your husband would have wanted to." She sat down in the rocking chair beside the hearth.

"Why when I am sure that Mr. Morgan will be by before the weekend is out to give him a full account." I smirked.

"At least he brings Charlotte with him. She is such a lovely young lady." My grandmother smiled sweetly. "I worry her husband has greater political aspirations than she anticipates. She is much too nice to be a politician's wife."

"True," I turned away from the window and joined her in the rocking chair opposite her. "I spoke with Robert and Emily last evening after work." I lowered my voice.

"How are they doing?" She rocked quietly looking tired after the long day.

"They are doing well. I asked Emily — seeing as we are close to the same age right now, if she and the children would seek refuge here at Terrace Falls once the war breaks out."

"That would be a blessing." My grandmother smiled.

"Emily said she would love to but cannot unless Patrick gives his blessing that Annabelle and the children come as well."

"I know you would feel more at ease if they were all here."

"Yes. I would. I truly hope Robert can convince Patrick."

"Imagine how strange it will be for you to spend several years with Jocelyn. You will get to see her first steps; hear her first words." My grandmother's face was careworn and content.

"I was there for it in my *other* time," I leaned forward and whispered.

"Yes, but I daresay you do not remember it." She smirked. "But won't it be something to tell her all about her early childhood and tell her details about her life with her brothers during the war."

"That would be something." I muttered, staring into the fire.

"What else is troubling you?"

"Something else Robert mentioned about the political environment taking place *there*. Our current President is a savvy businessman who is extremely wealthy. Therefore, he cannot be bribed, bought, or corrupted by large corporations and politicians who have grown wealthy and accomplished nothing throughout their tenures in government." I tried to explain.

"Do you believe they will assassinate him?" My grandmother raised an eyebrow.

"Robert does not believe so. But he firmly believes they will do anything, including election fraud to keep him from being reelected next year."

"Well, we know that will not be the first time something like that happens. Those who have power will do anything to keep it and those who desperately want it will do anything to get it. Neither care who they harm in the process." She stated.

"Unfortunately, they are willing to take the entire country down with them." I informed her.

"So, politics nor politicians have changed at all in couple hundred years? Somehow that does not surprise me." My grandmother scoffed. "It is difficult to imagine any of them rivaling President Buchanan. "He is the definition of a witless wonder doing nothing to deter the behavior of the representatives. The man is nothing more than fodder for the comics."

"That is proof that some things truly do not change over time, except now we call them memes." I laughed, "and they show up daily on our social media platforms."

"Do you agree with Robert that things are going to get much worse?"

"I fear he may be right, but I hope not."

I stared off into the dancing embers in the hearth. The flames warmed my face and my hands. I rubbed my hands over my growing belly and felt my son kick me back. I patted his foot and continued rubbing it absentmindedly. I hated to think of bringing him into this world at such a time.

Soon, a Civil War would rapture the country and not one family would be left untouched by its wrath. The tears of wives and mothers would saturate the hearths of every home in this great nation as the blood of our sons, brothers, and husbands sow its fields.

The clock on the mantel ticked away.

Author Bio

A. L. Waddington has her master's in military psychology and is currently working on her doctorate. She is an avid reader and researcher, has a slight coffee addiction and when she is not lost in a world of her own creation, she enjoys spending time gardening, hiking, and traveling with her family. Waddington and her husband, Eric, live in East Texas with their daughters and three spoiled puppies.

DISHEARTENED, BOOK 2

THE SPIRIT QUEST SERIES
*Slated for release April 2024

"I do not know which is worse — sitting on the edge of a Civil War you know is coming or watching your country implode from within on the verge of another that could happen at any time."
~ Sidney Timmons-Marshall

Gifted or cursed with the inherited ability of E.V.E., Sidney is forced into the inconceivable — her 1860 self watches on the eve of the American Civil War as the Northerners and Southerners dismantle the fabric of the nation. Whereas her present-day self-witnesses the extreme Progressives and Liberals shred away the decency of the American Culture on a world-wide stage and make the USA the laughingstock of the globe.

Sidney is heartbroken watching everything her loved ones and countrymen from her other life fought to preserve be undone by a minuet mindless minority of entitled fanatics and a political party so hell-bent on spreading hate, they would rather burn the nation to the ground than relinquish power.

But what can she do? Can one small voice change the mind of millions with hate in their heart? Can she find her way back to the solace she once treasured in both her lives?

TRANSCENDENCE

Discover where it all began:

ESSENCE, BOOK 1
THE EVE SERIES

Our minds often wander, but can our souls?

Jocelyn Timmons does not believe she is anything special — just an ordinary high school senior, living an ordinary life full of schoolwork, volleyball, and friends. She's about to find out how wrong she is.

Jackson Chandler moved into the house across the street. His dark wavy hair, green eyes, and charismatic personality draws everyone to him. Everyone, but Jocelyn.

Whenever Jackson gets near Jocelyn, she feels ill and dizzy. When he touches her, she blacks out and has visions of another life, in another time. As the odd hallucinations evolve and become clearer, she feels a strong pull towards the people she sees there. Frightened, she watches her once stable life begin to crumble around her, and she begins to question her own sanity.

Could it be possible that these episodes are actually her own memories of a life she is living somehow, somewhere, some-when? Maybe this is time-travel or some other paranormal mysticism?

ENLIGHTENED, BOOK 2
THE EVE SERIES

Time stands still cause time can't heal.

The barrier between Jocelyn Timmons consciousness continues to dissolve as she better understands the two lives she lives and the enormity of her newly discovered inherited gift of EVE (Essence Voyager Era), which allows her to fall asleep on one plane of existence and awaken on another as her soul travels nightly.

Present-day Jocelyn uncovers the vast wonderment of the Victorian era but soon learns that life during then was not as grand for women as she has read in the classics. Still, she finds comfort in the support of family and friends; a bolstering contrast to her overly hectic, career-oriented family in the twenty-first century. Her love for Jackson Chandler strengthens over time and becomes the light she so desperately needs as the world she has always known no longer makes sense. Yet, the closer she is drawn to Jackson by their mutual ability, the more strain develops amongst those she loves in 2016.

On the other side of Jocelyn's consciousness in 1878, she remains ignorant of *EVE*. Her life is crumbling around her, yet she finds herself anxiously awaiting the images that invade her dreams. Jocelyn longs to be the woman she portrays in that world, yet her jealousy is unbearable. Miscommunication, betrayal, and hidden agendas make trust nearly

impossible. The clearer the visions become, the more she questions the motives of her closest confidants and foregoes revealing the images that plague her perception. As her life seems to unravel, Jocelyn's two worlds collide, and she is enlightened as the pieces start to fall into place. But is she strong enough to survive the truth? Is Jackson really her destiny? And can their love transcend time?

PERCEPTION, BOOK 3
THE EVE SERIES

My hopes, my dreams, and most of all, me…we will finally be, set free.

Questions, questions, and more questions . . . they consume Jocelyn Timmons' life—both of them. Questions that never seem to have an answer. They haunt her, eat at her, and dreams of a normal senior year of high school have finally floated away into nothingness.

Inheriting the gift of EVE (Essence Voyager Era) has become both a gift and a curse. One that Jocelyn doesn't know if she wants or can accept. The world she once knew and thrived in has all but disappeared in the last two months. And now she wonders if she can ever find her way home again.

Her fiancé, Jackson Chandler, and his family seem to be the only ones who understand what she's going through besides her uncles, both of which she's grown very close to. But even they do not fully grasp how turbulent the situation at home has become. Will Jocelyn survive the torments of her mother and brother? Or will she find a hidden key to finally unlock her golden cage?

ILLUMINATION, BOOK 4

Can time predict the future?

In the gripping conclusion of the bestselling EVE series, Jocelyn and Jackson come face to face with the challenges of living combined lives on both planes. While Jackson struggles under the demands of his chosen profession, Jocelyn discovers hidden branches in the family tree. But the more she uncovers, the deeper she finds herself and her family in an uncharted realm that no one considered possible. Can EVE not only skip around with family members but also switch branches?

The happy couple soon learns that a branch, like time, has the tendency to bend in the most unexpected directions and occasionally even break. When that happens, lives are forever changed, the forces of destinies altered, and fates derailed. The fluidity of time begins to take on an obscure meaning as the barrier between the two worlds fades into darkness.

Author's Note

As many can imagine, I am a huge history buff. In researching the historical aspects of this story, I learned a great deal about the American Civil War that I never heard before in school – including during my undergraduate studies and courses I took on the American Civil War. The version I was taught focused on *Uncle Tom's Cabin*, Harper's Ferry, the Kansas – Nebraska Act, the Fugitive Slave Law, and the Dred Scott Case.

I had never learned about the Natick Resolution, the lopsided federal taxes, nor of the epic violence on behalf of state Representatives (Congressmen & Senators) in Washington D. C., especially the caning of Charles Sumner (MA-R) by Preston Brooks (SC-D) in May of 1856. Curiously, I had never heard of the North Carolina abolitionist Hinton Rowan Helper, nor his controversial antislavery piece titled, *The Impending Crisis — How to Meet It* that was first published in 1857 and then republished and widespread in 1859. I was also not aware of the North's struggle for freedom of speech nor the power of the press and the dramatically different stories they published depending on which side of the Mason-Dixon line they were located. It is strange and sad how some things never truly change.

Not to take anything away from the significance of the causes I learned about in school for they were indeed extremely significant events that led to what became the American Civil War, I do believe the other events are equally significant in demonstrating the mindset and behaviors of those who were there.

References

Freeman, J. B. (2018). *The field of blood: Violence in congress and the road to civil war.* Farrar, Straus, and Giroux. New York, NY.

Linder, D. O. (2024). *The trial of John Brown: An account. Famous Trials.* UMKC School of Law.

[1]Wright, H. C. (2024). *The Natick resolution; or, resistance to slaveholders, the right and duty of southern slaves and northern freeman.* Natick Historical Society, MA.

ScarlettInkPublishing.com

ALWaddington.com

www.ingramcontent.com/pod-product-compliance
Lightning Source LLC
Chambersburg PA
CBHW051843180726
48284CB00007BA/2020